ead!'   **Lisa Hall**

...iantly observed, both tender and
...ithout once flinching from harsh
                                    Helen Fields

...ing, consistently compelling thriller with a
...nse of foreboding'   **B.P. Walter**

...*a Mother* is a real rollercoaster of a read, with an
...ionally resonant ending that left me both moved
...d humbled by the strength of a mother's love. I
...dn't put this book down'   **Charlotte Duckworth**

...lly gripping from start to finish. Observational.
...ligent. Beautifully constructed plot'
                                    Amanda Robson

...se, shocking and terrifyingly believable. *Only a*
...*her* turns the psychological thriller on its head. The
...ing is sharp; the characters complex and compel-
...g; the story skilfully plotted. A fantastic read'
                                    Rebecca Tinnelly

...abeth Carpenter skilfully portrays a mother's love
...th unflinching honesty and tenderness'
                                    Caroline England

...eeply moving, compelling story with strong, relat-
able characters that leap from the page in true Carpenter
style'   **Sam Carrington**

Elisabeth Carpenter lives in Preston with her family. She completed a BA in English Literature and Language with the Open University in 2011.

Elisabeth was awarded a Northern Writers' New Fiction Award, and was longlisted for Yeovil Literary Prize (2015 and 2016) and the MsLexia Women's Novel Award (2015). She loves living in the north of England and sets most of her stories in the area. She currently works as a bookkeeper.

Also by Elisabeth Carpenter

11 Missed Calls
99 Red Balloons
Only a Mother

The Woman Downstairs

ELISABETH CARPENTER

ORION

An Orion paperback

First published in Great Britain in 2020
by Orion Fiction,
an imprint of The Orion Publishing Group Ltd.,
Carmelite House, 50 Victoria Embankment
London EC4Y 0DZ

An Hachette UK Company

1 3 5 7 9 10 8 6 4 2

A CIP catalogue record for this book
is available from the British Library.

ISBN (Paperback) 978 1 409 18149 1
ISBN (eBook) 978 1 409 18150 7

Typeset by Deltatype Ltd, Birkenhead, Merseyside

Printed in Great Britain by Clays Ltd, Elcograf S.p.A.

www.orionbooks.co.uk

For Dan and Joe

Prologue

She knocks on the door three times, but there's no reply. That's not unusual; it's just before six in the morning. This is the best time to catch people at home – not yet awake, not at work, not off their faces on drink or drugs (not generally, anyway).

Her colleague taps the window with the knuckle of his index finger. There's a glow from the television in the gap between the curtains, but there's no movement or sound from inside.

'Think we'd better get Doris to work,' she says, picking up the door enforcer.

It takes her two smacks of the battering ram for the door to give way. There's resistance from the other side. He pushes the door harder. It doesn't budge.

'Want some help there?' she says, laughing.

'Fuck off,' he says, as a droplet of sweat runs down his left temple.

She puts both her hands on the door at waist height, standing on tiptoes as she pushes.

Slowly, it opens.

The mountain of mail is almost a third of the height of the door.

'Shit,' he says, treading over the pile. 'It looks like no one's opened this door in years.'

'Or someone's made it look like that,' she says, following him inside.

'How would they have done that? Jumped out of the window afterwards?'

'Just an idea.' She shrugs. 'But we're not paid for our ideas, are we?'

'It's only council tax arrears,' he says. 'It's not like we're searching for drugs.'

She sniffs the air. 'It's a bit musty in here ... a really weird sweet smell ... like a rubbish dump.'

'Weird,' he says, opening the door to one of the bedrooms. 'It's pretty tidy so far.'

There are photos on the hallway wall. Various framed pictures of the same couple. In most of them, they're smiling.

She follows him into the kitchen.

'Jesus Christ,' he says, walking over to the sink.

There's a bowl of unwashed dishes covered in cobwebs – the mould has decayed into dust. A plastic milk bottle stands on the counter. He picks it up, giving it a shake; it sounds as though rocks are inside.

'What's the date on the bottle?' she says, looking around the tiny kitchen.

The clock has stopped on a quarter to twelve; the shelves above the fridge are also draped in thick cobwebs.

2

'Twenty-fourth of March,' he says, leaning towards the window for light. 'Two thousand and seventeen.'

'Bloody hell,' she says. 'How could this place have been empty for so long?'

He shrugs.

'I'm going for a look around.'

She ducks her head around the door to a small bathroom. There are bottles of shampoo and shower gel on the window sill. The first bedroom is neat, tidy. The double bed has a navy throw tucked in with hospital corners. The second bedroom has shoes and women's clothes littered on the floor. A sparkly dress hangs on a metal coat hanger from the curtain rail.

'In here!' he shouts from another room.

She recognises the panic in his voice – they've worked together for three years.

'Though I don't think they're going anywhere,' he says as she reaches the doorway to the living room.

Lying on the sofa, facing the television, is a body. Not much of it is left. The face, arms and hands are little more than skeletal remains. A shroud of black is stained on the sofa around it.

She drops to the floor, her hand covering her nose and her mouth.

'Is it a man or a woman?' she says, almost breathless.

She wants to be at home, shower the death from her skin; breathe in the fresh air and be free from the decay in this flat.

That's what the smell was: decay.

'I don't know,' he says quietly. 'I can't tell from the

clothes.' He takes out his phone. 'Police, please.'

She looks around the living room. On the coffee table are two wine glasses stained red at the bottom. On the floor, near the settee — inches from the corpse's dangling hand — are three wrapped presents.

She glances at the body again.

Its face is lit by the glow of the snow on the soundless television.

A face that couldn't be seen from the gap between the curtains.

A face that nobody has missed for almost two years.

PART ONE

1

Sarah

No amount of concealer will disguise the dark circles under Sarah's eyes. Her shoulder-length brown hair is pulled into an unflattering (but practical) ponytail, leaving her too-pale skin exposed. She wishes she could look amazing with little effort, but she's never been bothered enough.

She dabs some blusher onto her cheeks using her fingers but it's no use; she's always been crap with make-up. Now she looks like a clown that's been brought back from the dead.

Loud crashes came from the flat below at 5.58 this morning, though she'd been clock-watching long before that. The stomping of feet on wooden floors alongside muffled voices followed that. Sarah couldn't hear what they were saying, although she can hear every word from the young couple in the flat above when they yell at each other in the early hours.

It's the first time she's heard anything from the flat downstairs since she and her son Alex moved in two years ago. They'd assumed it was empty as she was vaguely aware of the residents in every other flat in the block.

At least she didn't have to listen to Rob snoring all night. He's been working away for the past three days. Sarah would never admit it to him, but she loves sleeping alone. He doesn't officially live here yet – she's hesitant to make it official. After being married to Alex's dad for nearly twenty years, she doesn't take her independence lightly.

Rob mustn't realise that. He's telephoned every morning and night, which gets a little annoying – suffocating almost. They run out of things to say five minutes in because they always talk about the same things: what he's having for lunch, how tired Sarah is, and exciting plans for the weekend they never stick to.

He thinks Sarah misses him too much. When he first started going away, she reminded him that she was perfectly fine alone with Alex – she'd been a lone parent for over a year before they met. But Rob doesn't like to think of himself as dispensable. She learned just recently that Rob had only one proper relationship before her. He said it was two years ago and only lasted a couple of months. Sarah didn't probe him too much as he seemed uncomfortable talking about it. He's nearly ten years younger than Sarah.

'She was someone I worked with,' he said. 'I was too focused on my career. It didn't end well.' He said that she messaged him constantly for weeks after he ended it. When Sarah asked him her name, he said it didn't matter. Sarah found herself doubting that the woman even existed; his mother didn't seem to know anything about her. Sarah didn't know why she asked – it was curiosity rather than jealousy.

When Sarah first met Rob, he said he'd just come back from backpacking around Europe two years ago (which she thought he exaggerated a bit – he wasn't a camping sort of guy). There was no mention of a relationship. But then, that's normal when you meet someone new, isn't it? Perhaps he had travelled with this mystery woman and wanted to play it down so Sarah wouldn't ask any more questions. Rob has never asked Sarah about her marriage to Andy. She thought it was either that he didn't like to think of her with anyone else or he didn't really care. Probably the latter.

Sarah flings the make-up case onto the bed and sits down to put on the ugly (but practical) flat work shoes. They have a thick sole that gives her a couple of inches in height, but that's the only good thing about them. Thankfully, her feet are hidden behind the counter most of the time.

Why does she work somewhere that opens so early? If she were twenty years younger, she could have been a student who had the opportunity to lie in bed all day. Working in a café seemed the perfect job: flexible hours that fit in with her studies and a decent wage to top up the maintenance loan. But the early mornings are a killer. She never seems to feel anything but tired for the rest of the day.

She stands, walks across the hall and opens Alex's door, peering inside. He doesn't usually wake before seven thirty. His room smells of sweaty socks and Lynx deodorant, but at least he's tidy – his clothes are in the wash basket, albeit overflowing.

'Alex,' she hisses. 'Don't sleep through your alarm. You'll get into trouble if you're late again. It's an important year this year.'

He groans, flops an arm over the covers and pulls them over his head. Sarah tiptoes to the bedside cabinet and grabs his mobile phone. She places it on the floor near the door. It's evil, but it's the only way he'll get out of bed.

'What time is it?' his muffled voice says.

'Quarter past seven.'

He groans again.

'It can't be that time already.'

'Tell me about it,' says Sarah. 'But I told Kim I'd open up the café this morning. I'll ring you later.'

He sticks his hand out of the dark blue quilt and waves.

Sarah puts on her coat, wraps the scarf around her neck, and opens the front door.

It's freezing outside the flat, and the concrete balcony offers no shelter from the bitter wind. She looks over the top of it, which is just above waist height, and still her legs feel like jelly. There's an ambulance parked across the bays, but no lights are flashing. She takes the stairs (the lift is old and it creaks and she's only on the first floor) and finds Mr Bennett from number twelve loitering by the double doors to the ground-floor flats. His first name's Sylvester but she can't bring herself to call him that without thinking of the cartoon cat. He usually wears a scarf, gloves and a tweed cap when it's this cold, but he's wearing a beige cardigan and tartan slippers.

'Morning, Sarah,' he says, without his usual cheer.

He rubs his gloveless hands together, his breath a white cloud that evaporates around his face.

'You're up early,' she says, frowning and stepping closer to him. 'Are you all right?'

'I only went to pop this in the bins,' he lifts up a small carrier bag, the smell of cooked fish wafts in the air, 'but I couldn't get near them.' He moves his head closer to Sarah's, his teeth gently chattering. 'I think they've found a body.'

'What? Who? Where?' A shiver runs through her – from both the cold and the sinister visions running through her mind. 'It's not Mrs Gibson, is it? She's not been too well, has she?'

Mr Bennett shakes his head.

'No, no,' he says. 'It was found in the flat near the bins.' He narrows his eyes. 'Been there a while from what I gather. It certainly explains a few things. Do you remember that smell? Not long after you moved in, I think. Everyone thought it was a dead animal ... and so many flies.'

Sarah's hand goes to her mouth. 'Good grief,' she says. It's only because she's talking to Mr Bennett that she doesn't swear or blaspheme, though she doesn't know if he's religious. 'That was years ago.'

'I know,' he says. 'I feel terrible for not kicking up more of a fuss, but my wife Angela had just passed.

11

That's why I remember the smell and the timing of you moving in.' His eyes are wide and watery. 'Oh, it's just awful. That poor soul inside . . . I must have walked past there hundreds of times.' He takes an envelope from his pocket. 'I found this on the floor – I shouldn't have taken it, really. I just wanted to know who it is . . . was. There must've been hundreds behind the door for them not to notice some escaping. I can't make out the name . . . I'm not wearing my reading glasses.'

He hands it to Sarah, his hands shaking slightly.

'Robin Hartley,' she reads from the envelope, which also states *This is not a circular*. 'Is that a man or a woman?'

'A man,' says Mr Bennett. 'I think my Angela was friends with his wife. I can't remember her name. I haven't seen her for a long time . . . five years, at least.'

'Could it be his wife they found inside?'

'I don't know. They might've moved. That letter could've been sent to the wrong address.'

He's right. There's a small possibility that the random envelope Mr Bennett picked up was addressed to a previous owner. A few of these flats have a high turnover of tenants. Sarah's always getting mail for at least three different people.

Sarah chances one more question – Mr Bennett seems distressed, confused.

'When was the last time you saw Robin Hartley?'

He frowns and looks to the concrete floor, then to the large shared garden behind them.

'I can't remember. A few years ago. Their kiddie

used to play with our grandson.' His gaze returns to the doors, but his mind seems elsewhere. 'Happy days, they were. Always noisy, but a good kind of noise.'

Sarah pushes open the door to the ground-floor flats and looks right.

Police tape flaps in the wind. A woman stands a few feet away from it.

'There's someone outside the flat,' Sarah hisses to Mr Bennett. 'I'm going to have a closer look.'

She tightens the scarf around her neck as she steps over twenty or so envelopes fluttering on the ground that no one seems bothered about. Won't they be evidence? She picks up a few and stuffs them in her pocket.

Sarah stands next to the woman. Her hair is gathered into a bun at the nape of her neck and she's wearing a black padded jacket, jeans and heavy boots that wouldn't look out of place on a building site.

'Do you know who it is?' says Sarah.

It takes the woman a few seconds to register Sarah's presence.

The woman turns to her, frowning. 'Excuse me?'

'Do you know whose body it is?' Sarah says again.

'Who are you?'

'I'm Sarah Hayes. I live on the first floor. I thought this flat was empty. Who have they found?'

In the distance, Sarah spots the woman from the flat next door-but-one, hurrying across the car park. Why isn't she interested in what's going on here?

'I found it with my colleague,' says the woman next to her. 'And I don't know who it was.' She looks pale, as though in shock. She mustn't be a detective. 'We came to ... there were arrears and we had no choice but to break in. And then we found it. The television was still on ... a carton of milk was dated March 2017. There were wrapped presents – they must've been for someone. How ...'

Her voice drifts to silence. No wonder she looks so terrible – Sarah couldn't imagine finding a dead body.

'What did you mean by *it*?' says Sarah.

She has tears in her eyes, though she can't have known the person.

'There was barely any skin left. It was more of a skeleton than a body. How could people not have known before? He must've been there for years and no one noticed.'

He?

The woman picks up one of the envelopes and stares at the name it's addressed to, but Sarah can't make it out from where she's standing without looking as though she has no personal boundaries.

Sarah's mobile phone rings. She reaches into her bag.

Shit, it's Kim. Sarah's over half an hour late opening the café.

'Sorry, sorry,' she says before Kim has time to bollock her. She turns her back on the woman in the padded jacket and walks towards the exit. Mr Bennett must've gone home. 'A body's been found in the flat below mine. It's been there for years, apparently.'

'Are you crying?' says Kim quietly. 'Did you know them?'

'No, I'm just sniffing from the cold. Sorry, I won't be long.'

'It's OK. I couldn't sleep so I've been here since seven.' A strange gagging noise sounds down the line. 'To think that for years there's been a dead body rotting away below you.'

The foyer door slams shut as Sarah walks towards the main road.

'Thanks, Kim,' she says. 'I hadn't thought of it like that.'

'Who is it?'

'One of the envelopes from behind the door is addressed to a man called Robin Hartley.'

'Oh. Never heard of him,' says Kim. She sounds disappointed. 'Well, hurry up, then.' Sarah rolls her eyes. 'We can tune the radio to the news station to find out more.'

Kim seems almost excited. Sarah supposes that she needs something to take her mind off things, but it feels wrong. A person has been dead for years and no one has missed them. Sarah will have to get used to this uncomfortable feeling. Studying for her journalism degree has taught her to distance herself from distressing events, though she hasn't yet mastered total disregard. That's what keeps her interested in a story: the human connection.

She pockets her phone and crosses the road. A woman, who looks to be in her forties, and dressed in a dark grey trouser suit with a black overcoat, stands on the kerb. There's a gap in the traffic but she doesn't move.

Her eyes are on the ground-floor flat. Her gaze suddenly meets Sarah's.

'What's happened over there?' she says, her voice monotone. 'There's an ambulance.'

'They found a body,' Sarah says as the wind makes her ponytail whip across her face.

The stranger nods slowly, narrowing her eyes.

'I knew someone who lived in those flats.'

She pulls a pair of sunglasses from her coat pocket and puts them on, even though the sun is hidden behind thick, grey cloud.

'Did you know the person at number three?' says Sarah. 'That's where they found the body.'

The woman takes out black gloves from her bag and slowly puts her hands inside them. Sarah feels the skin on her arms prickle.

'I suppose you could say that,' she says. 'Thank you for your time.'

Sarah watches as she turns and walks away.

The woman doesn't look back.

2

Laura

There was a lot of noise coming from one of the other flats early this morning, which is typical as it's the first time in months – years even – that I've had to set my alarm clock. I needn't have bothered, but I've an interview for a position in telemarketing. I don't know why I applied – I hate speaking to people on the telephone and I've zero experience in anything. They must be desperate to consider me. I've heard these jobs are brutal, but I've got to show that I'm *actively seeking employment*. Dad's savings are running low; I knew I wouldn't be able to live on them forever.

I stand in front of the only mirror in the flat, which is in the bathroom. It's so old that there are patches of black where the silver has worn off. My hair still looks OK from the cut and blow dry Mandy gave me when she came round yesterday. She said to wear a shower cap or a hat in the night to keep its shape, but that was a ridiculous idea. She's always coming out with nonsense.

Perhaps that makes her sound like a friend, but she

isn't. She's a mobile hairdresser − another thing I inherited from Dad. I don't want her to do my hair any more. She always cuts it the same − two inches below my shoulders, but I can't tell her I want a change in case I offend her and she shaves my head in revenge. When I asked for a fringe a few months ago, she narrowed her eyes − the scissors two inches from my face − and said, 'I style your hair to suit you … your face and your personality. I think it looks better as it is.'

I didn't ask again. I daydream about getting highlights in the salon on the high street − you get a free cup of tea, too (or a glass of Prosecco, which everyone seems to be drinking these days). But instead, Mandy cuts my hair in our − *my* tiny kitchen.

Yesterday, I pretended to read *War and Peace* (opened it in the middle and turned the pages occasionally) so she wouldn't try to talk to me, but it didn't work.

'How long has it been now?' she said, putting a towel around my shoulders and stuffing the edge into my collar.

'Four months,' I said.

'And it'll be the first time you've been outside properly?'

Don't be so ridiculous, I wanted to say, but instead I just said, 'Yes.'

It'd give her something to talk about.

'Oh, Laura,' she said. 'I often think about you here on your own.'

Not often enough for you to pop round in-between appointments, I didn't say, because that would've been my worst nightmare. My eyes were watering as she dragged her comb through my knotted damp hair.

'You should get into online dating,' she said. 'I met my Charlie online.'

From what I gathered from her previous monologues, *her Charlie* sounded a bit of a dick, so she wasn't exactly selling it to me.

'But you're only young,' she said, not waiting for a reply as usual. 'You're only twenty-four, twenty-five?'

'I'm thirty in a few weeks,' I said.

Twelve years she's been coming, and she couldn't remember how old I was.

'No way!' she said. 'I'd have said ten years younger than that.'

She didn't, though, did she?

What she actually meant was that I was a little bit fat and my chubbiness irons out any wrinkles I might have had if I was skinny. My mum used to call me her *little pudding*. Even at seven, I knew it wasn't a positive term of endearment.

'So, when did you last have a boyfriend?' she said.

Why was everything about men with Mobile Mandy?

'When I was about eighteen,' I said.

'Really? I didn't notice!'

'Neither did he,' I said, but she didn't laugh.

She thinks I'm always so serious because of what I've *had to deal with*.

'Has your mum been in contact since—'

'No,' I said.

Uncharacteristically, she finally took the hint and

19

began humming along to the Eighties station on her portable radio. You can see why I've had the same hairstyle for all these years out of politeness. It'd be easier for me if she died, so I wouldn't have to worry about it any more. But, at the end, when Dad was really bad, I used to think that about him. And it's true: you should be very careful what you wish for.

The silence of the flat (which I haven't quite got used to yet) is interrupted by my mobile timer going off – signalling it's time for me to leave for the bus.

As I open my front door, I see an ambulance and a few police cars in the car park. There's knocking on doors from the flats above. Police doing their rounds, probably. I peak out of our— *my* front door, but they're not on this floor yet.

There seems to be no activity inside the ambulance. A couple in one of the flats upstairs are always screaming and throwing things at each other, but I heard nothing like that last night. He must be away again. It's nice and peaceful when it's just her. I don't know their names – nor anyone else's in this block. Most people kept away when Dad was ill – as though he were infectious – and it's still the same now, with me.

I suppose I'll find out if anything serious happened on the news when I get back home.

It's taken me two buses to get here: the middle of nowhere. There was a woman in the seat in front of me, sniffing. A commuter, probably. If I get this job and her cold, I'll be sure to let her know how much I appreciate her spreading it about everywhere.

We had to be careful about germs with Dad. He used to make me sit in my room all day when I had a cold. Admittedly, that wasn't often because we rarely went out. We even had our shopping delivered.

Now, I'm walking down a path alongside a dual carriageway with signs pointing to a nearby Asda. I'll have to learn to drive if I get this job. I'm the only one on this pavement and it looks brand new. A roller-skater's dream, my friend Chloe and I would've said twenty years ago.

I reach the huge grey box of a building called Enterprise House. Its intercom is next to glass double doors that you can't see through. They're for security, I imagine, but I doubt there's much worth stealing.

I press the buzzer and static sounds through the intercom, but nobody speaks.

'It's Laura Aspinall,' I say. 'I'm here for the— '

The doors slide open.

I introduce myself again to the distracted, uninterested receptionist and he tells me where to go.

Luckily, there are also giant arrows – printed on A4 laminated paper – to guide me along corridors and through more double doors.

My destination is a printed *Your Here!* in comic sans.

Jesus. Mum would've walked straight out, citing the bad grammar, irregular capitalisation and unprofessional font as *unacceptable*. She was a bit of a snob, but I have to agree with her on this one.

There are three other candidates sitting on chairs along the wall. Only one of them looks up from his phone. He raises his eyebrows in a feeble acknowledgement, or hello, or whatever it's meant to mean. A woman, younger than I am, dashes out of the interview room in tears. She runs down the corridor as fast as her heels will allow.

What the hell have the interviewers said to her? I've heard that working in sales is merciless. She obviously isn't cut out for it. Neither am I, but it's my first-ever interview – at least I'm showing willing by turning up.

I'm relieved that the crying woman was alone, though. One of the assistants at the job centre said that some companies have introduced group interviews. I imagine them to be like AA meetings, except people try to trump each other with experience and confidence.

After two people have gone in and out and, after what feels like hours (but is probably only forty-five minutes), the interview door opens again. A man sticks his head out.

'Laura Aspinall.'

Finally!

They must have told all of us candidates the same time, which is quite rude, but obviously I don't mention it. Eight thirty is ridiculously early for an interview, though it's one way of skimming off the lazy ones.

I walk into the interview room as the man walks behind a desk. It's very bland in here, as one would expect. The walls and furniture are beige, off-white and grey. The man sits next to a woman; they both look very young. There's a window behind them, offering views of the M6. How depressing. And I thought the sights from the flats were bad.

I think they're introducing themselves, but I can't hear their words. I'm so nervous. They look so self-assured and polished. My hands are clammy; I hope they don't expect me to shake theirs.

I'm standing in front of them, but I haven't said anything yet. They must think I'm an idiot. A very punctual idiot.

I don't know if I can do this. I'm tempted to run out of the room, too.

The woman smiles, flashing unnaturally white teeth, and gestures for me to sit down on the plastic chair. I already know I'm going to leave a sweat patch on it when I stand back up.

There's a few seconds' silence as they peruse my pitiful CV. I have never had a proper job – in fact, I've listed myself as a carer even though it was looking after my own father.

'So,' says the man, tapping a pen on the desk. He's twice the size of the woman sitting next to him. He has a beard and his hair is closely clipped at the sides with a small quiff at the front. He doesn't suit the hipster look – he's trying a little *too* hard. The cufflinks on his shirt sleeves are a pair of dice. I bet he imagines himself as lucky – a bit of a chancer. 'It says here that you were home-schooled from the age of eleven.'

'Yes,' I say. It comes out as a whisper.

I clear my throat and repeat it a little too loudly.

23

I should've lied about the home-schooling. Do they ever check things like that?

'And you gained five GCSEs?' says the woman. (I wish I'd listened when they gave their names.)

She says it as though it's a question, perhaps surprised that I managed to scrape such a number of qualifications.

'That's right,' I say.

I'm clasping my hands on my lap – on the advice of a blogger as the most appropriate of interview poses – and my legs are crossed at the ankle. If you'd just met me, you'd think I was sophistication personified. Until you heard me speak. I've the broadest of Lancashire accents after being socialised from the age of eleven by a man from Burnley (Dad).

'And you were taught by . . .?' she says.

'My dad. He had MS, so I stayed at home with him.'

'Was he a qualified secondary school teacher?' he says.

His eyes are almost black and his gaze is unwavering as though he's trying to read my thoughts.

Dad wasn't a secondary school teacher. But it was what it was. At least I passed English and Maths.

'Yes,' I say, anyway.

These questions are hardly pertinent to talking to people on the phone all day. I've read that Alan Sugar left school with just one 'O' level and look where he is now.

I try not to sigh aloud.

'You stayed at home with your dad?' says the woman. 'Where was your mum?'

24

She leans forward and rests her chin in the cup of her hand.

'Er ...'

The man next to her clears his throat and I want to hug him. I shouldn't have judged him so quickly.

She sits up straight.

I hope she's had a word with herself about her sexist attitude.

'Did you find that you missed out on the social aspect of secondary school?' she says, tilting her head to the side like she feels sorry for me.

'Nah,' I say. 'Dad had his friends round sometimes. I was good at predicting the winners of the horse-racing ... they said I was their lucky charm.'

Her eyebrows rise. I bet she has visions of my home as a crack den; the poor, suffering teenage daughter – a reluctant waitress for her dad's friends. Or perhaps she has more sinister, seedy ideas.

'I see.' She wiggles her bottom in the chair, pulling her skirt further over her knees. I bet she doesn't leave a sweat patch when she stands. 'Well, let's get straight onto the practical element of the interview, shall we?'

As though speaking to them wasn't practical enough. I'm dreading what they have in store for me. It's enough to make a person cry, apparently.

Two laminated sheets are slid towards me on the table.

Hello, my name is _____. Are you the bill payer in the household?

No > Is it possible to speak to the bill payer?

Yes> I'm calling from PeopleServe Northwest. I can guarantee that we can save you at least one hundred pounds on your annual energy bill. Do you have a few minutes to spare?

This is going to be hell.

3

The corpse on the stretcher was encased in a black plastic body bag. There was hardly any substance to it from what I could see, and I couldn't get too close.

I've been looking it up online. Underground, embalmed and sealed in a casket, a body can take over eight years to become a skeleton. But *this* body has been exposed to heat and light. I'm sure the heating was still on when I left. And one of the windows used to always come open. Single glazing, rotten wood.

There must have been insects that contributed to its decay. I read, too, that flies can smell meat from up to seven kilometres away.

Of course, there are teeth and hair that will remain – obvious DNA sources. But I tried to make sure none of my DNA remained in that flat. The old cliché *needle in a haystack* springs to mind. No one knows I was there.

Except you.

A body that hasn't been missed by anyone but me.

It happened so quickly – I thought it was meant to take longer than it did.

If you heard me now, you'd think I was inhuman. I'm not.

I don't know whether to run. Or hide.

I've got too much to stay for.

4

Sarah

The darkness of the morning follows Sarah inside the café. The subtle wall lights Kim had installed have the same effect as birthday candles in a power cut. There's a quietness to the café, but Sarah might be imagining it. Even though she's nearly an hour late, it's still early.

The cold outside and the heat and steam inside have clouded the windows.

'I've heard nothing on the news,' Kim shouts across.

'It hasn't been that long,' says Sarah quietly, to try to counteract Kim's holler.

Sarah takes off her coat and walks into the back room, grabbing her apron and looping it around her neck.

'Shall I prep some more bacon?' she says, walking into the kitchen.

There are several lone diners who look like they want a bit of peace.

'May as well,' says Kim, staring at her mobile phone.

Sarah peels slimy slices of bacon from the plastic packet and lays them on the griddle. The pungent steam blasts her face. She wishes she hadn't offered to do this. She's heard that bacon cooking smells like burning flesh.

'Have you checked Twitter?' says Sarah.

Kim shakes her head.

'I'm on a social media break, remember.'

'Yeah, looks like it,' says Sarah.

'It's just BBC News.' She sighs, putting her mobile into the pocket of her pinny. 'I'm not going to lie to you about something so trivial.'

Kim had tortured herself looking at *he-who-can't-be-named*'s profile with pictures of his new life on Facebook.

'I thought you'd have got over that,' says Sarah, flipping over rows of bacon. 'What with you having a new boyfriend.'

Two police cars race past on the main road. Two of the customers look up; the others must be used to it.

'Think it's a bit late for the blues and twos,' says Kim. 'A few years too late.'

Sarah tightens her apron again, tying it twice around her middle.

'It's not funny, Kim. Imagine people not noticing *you'd* died.'

Kim sighs.

'I often imagine that,' she says. 'Especially after a few wines when Max has stood me up.'

Kim must've had a few wines last night. She's always maudlin when she's hungover.

'Wine won't help,' says Sarah. 'You shouldn't drink alone.'

Sarah feels a bit hypocritical. She was no stranger to a bottle of wine in the evening before she and Andy separated. The only reason she didn't drink as much now was because she couldn't afford it.

She grabs the three outstanding order tickets from the bulldog clips hanging from the bottom of the cake display cabinet. Inside it are freshly made cream scones, custard slices, Manchester tarts and flapjacks. Two years ago, she used to drool over them (not literally – health and safety), but now she's so used to being around and smelling food, it's hard to find her appetite.

Beans on toast; egg on toast; toasted teacake.

There's nothing in the toaster; no eggs in the frying pan; no beans on the hob. From the angry glances and inflated chests, the customers have been waiting a while.

Sarah doesn't say anything. Kim is her boss, even though they've become good friends these past couple of years.

She cracks two eggs into hot oil. Most of the time, the regulars order the same meal every visit so Sarah can prepare the meals without much thought.

Kim's leaning against the counter in front of the toaster. Sarah nudges her gently aside as she pops in a teacake and four slices of bread.

Sarah knows that Kim's waiting for her to ask more about Max standing her up last night, but Sarah hasn't the energy for it. It happens a lot – Max treating Kim like shit. Sarah hasn't met him to make a judgement, but so far, Kim has found pictures of topless women on his phone; saw him in town with one of his daughter's

31

friends (just turned twenty); and has let her down at the last minute countless times. His name might not even be Max, and Sarah seriously doubts that he used to be a fighter pilot.

'So,' says Sarah. 'Who do you think it is? Mr Bennett says Robin Hartley used to live in the flat below me but can't remember if he left.'

Kim drags her gaze away from the floor.

'Mr Bennett? Is he still alive?'

'Yes,' says Sarah. She takes a deep breath. 'Did Robin Hartley ever come in here?'

'I don't usually ask people their full names,' says Kim. 'And I think I'd remember someone called Robin – we don't get many of them around here.'

'There was a woman standing opposite the flats when I left,' says Sarah. 'She acted a bit strange when I asked her if she knew who lived there ... said that she knew someone. Don't you think that's a bit odd?'

'Yeah, it's a bit odd.'

She's not even bloody listening properly.

The toast pops up, but Kim doesn't notice. She's now staring at the blue light of the insect killer. Sarah grabs the slices and plates the orders.

'Didn't anyone notice the smell?' says Kim, raising her voice across the room as Sarah delivers the food to the tables. 'It must've stunk of rotten flesh.'

'Kim!' Sarah hisses as she walks back to the kitchen. 'You can't say things like that around food.'

Kim grimaces.

'Half of this lot are deaf, anyway.'

'I heard that,' shouts Mr Lovelady (a surname *everyone* remembers).

Sarah presses her lips together and covers her mouth. She stands with her back to the customers.

'It's weird, isn't it?' says Kim. 'Finding a body after so long in a place they lived.'

Sarah uncovers her mouth – her urge to laugh out loud has vanished.

'It is,' she says. 'I'd understand if a body was found at the bottom of the river, or buried in the woods, but this person was in a flat ... the television was left on ... letters were posted through the door. How is it possible that no one noticed him gone?'

Kim tilts her head to the side.

'It's really sad, isn't it?' she says, stepping towards the counter. She almost shoves Sarah out of the way. 'Yes, love. What can I get for you?'

Sarah turns around to see a woman is waiting. Her cheeks are rosy from the cold.

'Oh, hello again,' says Sarah.

The woman is still wearing the black hat. She takes it off and light brown curls ping back into shape, resting on her shoulders and around her face.

'This is the first time I've been in here,' she says.

She gives a light, nervous laugh. She looks to Kim, then back at Sarah.

'I saw you opposite the flats, didn't I,' says Sarah. 'You asked about the body that was found.'

'I ... oh yes ... sorry, I didn't recognise you.'

People always say that to Sarah. She thinks it's

33

because she has such an unremarkable, forgettable face.

'Are you a journalist?' says Kim. 'Is that why you were asking?'

'God, no.' The woman laughs, glancing behind her.

Kim narrows her eyes.

'Sarah here is studying to be a journalist.'

'Sorry. No offence.'

The woman's face flushes slightly.

'Did you know Robin Hartley?' says Sarah.

'Not when—' She bites her bottom lip. 'No, I didn't know him. I knew someone who did know him, though.'

'Have you spoken to the police?' says Sarah. 'If you have information, you should tell them.'

The woman opens her mouth and closes it again.

'How did you find out about it?' says Sarah. 'It was only a couple of hours ago. It's not been on the radio yet.'

'I've got to go. Thanks for the ...'

She darts her eyes around and dashes out of the café, slamming the door so hard that the lights on the wall flicker.

'See,' says Sarah, placing her hands on the counter. 'I told you she was a bit odd.'

Kim's staring out of the window as the stranger crosses the road. She folds her arms.

'I know that woman from somewhere.'

5

Laura

The interview *was* hell. They were frustrated with me because I kept 'hanging up' when *potential clients* said they weren't interested in loft insulation (or a replacement boiler or a smart energy meter).

The man with the beard sighed and said, 'Not to worry. I guess this job isn't as easy as some people think.'

I've come to the café up the road from home. I've no decent food in the flat as it's Thursday. We used to get a Morrisons delivery on Thursdays. The habit of eating everything before then has stayed with me even though the delivery's long been cancelled.

The bottom half of the window was steamed up, so I had to wipe it with a serviette. This place has been here longer than I have. When we first moved into the flat, it was called *Kath's Kaff*, like the one in *EastEnders* in the Eighties. Now it's *Kim's Kaff*, with the same naff *kaff* spelling.

I was only seven when I came here for the first time. Mum used to buy me a toasted teacake and a cup of tea (three sugars and plenty of milk or I wouldn't drink it) every Saturday morning. I think she struggled to know what to do with me, really. We never had any money for *girlie* shopping days, which didn't matter as we both hated trying on clothes. And she much preferred the company of adults.

The last Saturday we spent together was three years after we moved in. It was 6 September 1997 (the day of Princess Diana's funeral). I'd left primary school by then and was about to start lessons with Dad on the Monday. Mum, who *was* a secondary school teacher, had prepared my syllabus for the whole academic year. She had to *go out and pay the bills because no one else was going to*. She always said what she thought.

Rather than being her usual distracted self, she was particularly philosophical that day. Everyone was after Princess Diana died. Everyone felt it. Even those who didn't think they cared.

That September day, it was sunny outside. Mum had taken me out because Dad was watching the funeral on the telly and she didn't think it was appropriate for me to watch it, too. Though that was probably a lie – she obviously had other things on her mind.

Mum was sitting opposite me, concentrating on the spoon that she stirred her hot chocolate with. The fluffy, sugary cream had become one with the brown liquid. She'd never done that before. She used to love spooning the whipped cream into her mouth. 'The best bit,' she used to say. 'A dessert and a drink in one.'

Not that day, though.

'You've always liked your own company, haven't you, Laura?'

I shrugged. It wasn't that I preferred it – it's just the way things turned out for me.

I used to have friends. They used to like me. But one day, when I was in the last year of primary, everyone turned against me. I still don't know why.

Mum had let me invite my friend Chloe round for tea after school, about a month before the end of term. Mum made spaghetti bolognese from scratch and presented it with the flourish of Ainsley Harriott on *Ready, Steady, Cook*.

Chloe just pushed the food around the plate as though she was afraid the pasta was worms about to wiggle back into life. It was the best meal my mum ever made. Actually, before that, the only homemade food I'd seen her make was Christmas dinner, and she gave up doing that when I was ten.

'Well that was a whole lot of effort for nothing,' Mum said as she collapsed onto the settee after my friend left. 'When I was a girl, you ate what you got out of politeness ... the amount of vile creations I had to put in *my* mouth. My mother was a worse cook than I am.'

I couldn't imagine that, but I felt bad for Mum after the work she'd put in. Perhaps Chloe expected fish fingers and chips, not pasta with a piping hot homemade garlic baguette that had to be torn apart. People don't blink an eye at food like that now.

When everyone fell out with me at school, I blamed Mum for being weird as the reason for the change in

37

my friends. Especially after the note someone wrote me. Had Chloe gossiped about her? Did everyone think less of us because we had moved into a flat on the other side of Preston?

Thinking about it now, though, the latter reason seems unlikely.

'You're very mature for your age,' Mum had said that day, not looking at me, still stirring the hot chocolate. 'And all that trouble you had at school. At least we've had a nice summer holiday ... six weeks of just being together.' Still, she stirred. 'I don't think I would've been strong enough to cope like you are ... having no friends ... it must be terrible.'

'I still have Chloe,' I said. Mum looked up at me, shaking her head.

'Hmm. Chloe's mother's a ... She's not a very nice woman. She's a gossip.'

'But she's my friend, Mum,' I said, pushing my empty mug towards the middle of the table.

'OK.'

She placed her spoon on the table; she hadn't drunk any of her drink.

'I'm sorry,' she said. 'I've been too harsh. To think ... all the things you do for your father.'

She always said *your father*. I don't think I ever heard her call him by his name because they were always within seven feet of each other when we were in the flat.

He wasn't good, the week before Mum left. He had just been recommended for early retirement at the university. Coupled with the tragic news of The People's

Princess, he took to his bed for a week, only getting up to watch the funeral.

At least, I *think* that was what was bothering him. A child's understanding of situations can be skewed with limited knowledge of the world.

'To think,' she repeated, looking up, 'that when I was ten, I was still playing with dolls.'

'I'm eleven, Mum,' I said.

'Yes, sorry. It always takes me a while to catch up after your birthdays.' She glanced out of the window. 'Did I ever tell you that I once worked for Dorothy Winters?'

'Yes,' I said. She told me about it all the time. Dorothy Winters was a famous writer – well, famous in Lancashire. Mum typed her manuscripts for extra money in the school holidays. 'But you can tell me about it again if you like.'

I smiled at her in the hope she wouldn't think I was being sarcastic. I never knew when she was going to take offence at the most harmless of comments.

A McFly song blasts into the café, bringing me back to the present – well, back to 2005, anyway. I've not heard one of their songs for years.

How long does it take to make beans on toast? The women behind the counter are chatting amongst themselves. The one with the ponytail and greasy strands of hair around her face is getting her ear bashed by the other. Problems with men by the sounds of it. They should leave their personal lives at the door, otherwise they'll have no customers left.

39

The door opens and I'm glad of the distraction.

A man lingers in the doorway, shaking water off his umbrella. He drops it into the stand near the entrance.

He's wearing a dark green coat over his suit. He looks around the café before his eyes rest on mine.

I narrow my eyes slightly as he walks towards me. His skin is tanned, glowing. His dark, chocolate brown hair looks as though it's never allowed to grow half an inch longer than it is now.

When he stands next to my table, I recognise him. He was in my class at school.

It's Tom Delaney.

I used to have the biggest crush on him, I'm surprised I didn't know him as soon as he walked through the door. He has the same friendly face, the same kind eyes. I picture him sitting across the room from me when I was an 11-year-old. I used to look at him all the time but he hardly ever returned my gaze. Even though we played together in the big garden at the back of the flats in the holidays when we were little. He was a different person out of school.

'Hello,' he says. 'I thought it was you, Laura. How funny that you came to the interviews today. Long time, no see, hey?'

Oh my God, he remembers my name. We were only about seven or eight when he visited the flats. I don't think he ever spoke to me in school. I began to think I made it up, that the boy at school was different to the boy who used to fire the hosepipe at me on hot sunny days.

Did he just say he was at the interview?

I open my mouth to speak, but nothing comes out.

Oh Jesus, I've regressed.

My face burns. He looks around the café. 'I can't believe this is still here. Mum used to bring me here sometimes. Remember how we used to play together as kids when I used to visit my grandad? I was sorry to hear about your dad,' he says. 'I remember when your mum left. So many years ago now.'

'Thank you,' I say, feeling strangely flattered that he recalls such details about my life. 'Do you ever see anyone from St Xavier's?'

I feel sick in my stomach at the thought of that god-awful place.

'Not really,' he says. 'Sometimes I see someone in town, but I usually pretend not to notice them.'

The classroom used to be stifling, whatever the weather. White shirts and blue ties for the boys, white polo shirts for the girls. Tables with four boys and girls sitting at each.

'You sat across the room from me,' I say.

'That's right,' he says. 'I used to sit next to Tanya Greening.'

'Oh.'

Tanya Greening. A name I haven't heard in such a long time. She made my life hell ... cornered me once in the toilets and ... Oh bloody hell, I think I'm actually going to be sick.

Breathe, breathe.

'Are you OK, Laura?'

'I have to go. I've an appointment in fifteen minutes.'

'Oh,' he says. 'Another interview?'

He laughs.

'No, no. The doctor.'

'Nothing serious, I hope?'

Oh God, why did I say the doctor? I bet he's imagining what disease I might have – perhaps some infectious skin disorder.

'No, no.' I stand and grab my coat. 'It was nice seeing you again.'

I dash out of the café. I haven't paid, but I only had a quick sip of the tea.

I don't look back when I hear the café door open. I think he's calling after me.

I run across the road, not checking for traffic.

I haven't seen anyone from St Xavier's Primary for years.

Seeing him has triggered memories I had long forgotten.

I hope I don't get this job.

6

Laura

When I left the café, even though I ran towards home, I couldn't face going back to silence. Especially after being around other people for most of the morning. And especially after seeing Tom Delaney.

Instead, I went to visit my dad's friend, Eric. I usually see him on Mondays, but he was pleased to see me even though it was a Thursday.

'Every day's the same in here, Loz,' he said. 'And it always smells of cabbage and p— urine.'

He was sitting in the residents' lounge. He's one of the younger ones. He moved here because the stairs in the flats were getting too much and he figured that because his friends had either died or got themselves *lady friends*, then he might as well take his chances in sheltered accommodation.

He leant forward, taking off his glasses.

'It's karaoke tonight,' he said. 'Though, I tell you what — if I stood up and stripped to my undies, no one would bleedin' notice.'

I looked around. Most of the residents were either gazing at the giant television or looking out of the large windows to the garden. One lady was knitting the longest scarf I'd ever seen. It curled at her feet like a sleeping blue sausage dog.

'So, what have you been doing with yourself, Loz?' he said. 'Have you been lonely?'

Straight to the point, as ever.

'Oh, you know. Just mooching about, really. The flat has never been so tidy. But I don't want to move. It'd feel strange if I ever had to leave it.'

'Are your dad's ashes—'

'Yes,' I said. 'Still on his bed.'

I didn't want to talk about that again. I wasn't ready to scatter them – it'd be like the final goodbye that I wasn't ready for.

'Oh.' Eric winked at the health care assistant as the man placed a cup of tea on the table. He winks at everyone. 'You need to get yourself out. You've been hanging around old people far too much.'

'I don't mind old.'

'Anything interesting happened at Nelson Heights? Is that miserable Mrs Gibson still going?'

'Don't know,' I said. 'But there was an ambulance parked outside this morning.'

He sat forward, resting his elbows on his knees.

'Bloody hell, Laura,' he said. 'Why do you always play down events? I'd have mentioned that first.' He folded his arms. 'Were they alive or dead?'

I shrugged. 'No idea,' I said. 'I'm not sure which flat

either, before you ask. Though the bloke who visits the woman in one of the flats above is a bit weird. Maybe he killed her.'

Eric's eyes almost bulged out of their sockets.

'Do you think?' He reached for his cup of tea. 'We shouldn't really be talking like this. Domestic violence isn't a subject to make light of.'

'I wasn't making light of it.'

'So what's her name? This woman who lives upstairs?'

'I don't know,' I said. 'I don't know anyone's name.'

He tutted.

'And to be honest,' I said, 'there are always sirens about. I've got used to them. It wasn't like that when I was a kid.'

'Oh, it was, Loz,' he said. 'You only had your ears tuned to the chime of the ice-cream van.'

'Ah fuck it!'

The woman knitting the scarf appeared to have dropped several stitches.

'You could visit here a bit more if you need a change of scene,' said Eric. 'There are a few blokes who work here, you know. In fact, there are a few health care assistant positions going. You've plenty of experience.'

'Actually, I had a job interview today.'

Eric rolled his eyes.

'Another nugget of information you could've started with,' he said, laughing.

I wrinkled my nose. 'It's for a position in telesales.'

'Ah,' he said, leaning back, cradling his cup. 'No wonder you kept *that* one quiet.'

45

He winked again.

'Exactly,' I said. 'And someone I went to school with works there. Though I don't think he was one of those who ...'

'You'd have remembered if he was. Bunch of nasty little bastards.' He put a finger to his lips. 'Sorry, love. I know they were just kids and all, but they were just awful.' He placed his tea on the table next to him. 'Did he say anything to you at this interview?'

'I didn't see him there. It was at the café. And he said he was sorry to hear about Dad.'

He pursed his lips for a couple of seconds.

'Well, I suppose that's something. He doesn't sound too bad.'

I smiled and rolled *my* eyes.

'Well,' he said. 'As long as it gets you out and about. You're too young to be wallowing in that flat alone. And at least you're not watching re-runs of *Bread* on UK Gold or whatever it's called these days. They're always changing the names of TV channels. It's ridiculous.'

'I don't have Sky any more,' I said. 'Dad had the DVD collection.'

'Ah that's right. Do you remember, you used to answer the telephone, "Hello, yes?" like Ma Boswell? That was so funny – you were so little. And you made your mum buy a ceramic chicken to put housekeeping money in.' He took a sip of what was left of his tea. 'Anything new on the boyfriend front?'

'I don't think having a boyfriend is worth the bother.'

It seemed ridiculous that we were talking about

46

boyfriends when I was nearly thirty and Eric was nearly seventy-five (which was actually quite young compared to the other residents).

He laughed.

'Course it's worth the bother! Why do you think I've all these wrinkles at my young age? It's because I got myself into *too much* bother.'

He laughed at his own joke.

'Get yourself on the internet,' he said. 'Although I'd keep away from Tinder. I've been on there and it's ...' he leant forward, '... it's a bit superficial.' His eyebrows went up and down. 'If you know what I mean.'

'I think even Mary there knows what you mean.'

He glanced at the other woman sitting next to him, reading *That's Life*.

'I bet she does as well.'

I was waiting for him to ask and it took ten whole minutes after I arrived. It usually took only five.

'Heard from your mother?' he said. 'I still can't believe she didn't come to your dad's funeral.'

'No,' I said. 'And that was four months ago. I've not seen her in a long while. It's my birthday coming up, though. She's normally good with cards.'

'She was such a beautiful woman,' he said. 'I suppose I'm not surprised.'

'Not surprised about what?'

He flapped his hand in the air.

'Oh, you know. The way things turned out. You take after her, you know. Looks wise. You look exactly like her, now. You didn't as a child – your hair was too fair,

47

and you were all arms and legs till you were about six, and then you filled out a bit.'

'You mean I got fat?' I gave his knee a play slap. 'I can go elsewhere if I want to be insulted, you know.'

'I didn't mean it like that. And I should know by now not to comment on a woman's weight. It's just I think of you as family, and ...'

'It's OK. You jump in that hole you've dug yourself.'

He tilted his head to the side.

'It's a shame, you know,' he said. 'Your mum and dad loved each other very much.'

'Really?' I said.

He turned his head towards the garden, his eyes glazed over.

'But things happen,' he said. 'Your dad and I had some right laughs, didn't we?'

It was a rhetorical question. His eyes travelled to the brown and turquoise swirly carpet. Sometimes, he lets snippets of information slide out. One day, I'll have the full story about my parents.

Now, it's nearly tea time and I'm home. The phone is ringing but I hate answering the landline. This bodes well with the prospect of a job in telesales. And I know this call will be about the job. I have a sixth sense about these things. Doesn't everyone?

The ringing goes on and on and on, but I can't get up from Dad's chair. It seems he doesn't want to let me go into the world of work. Or perhaps that's just my lazy brain talking to me.

Dad loved this chair. The mustard-coloured velvet is

threadbare on the arms and the patch where he rested his head. The seat sinks right down when I sit on it – it's still moulded to his shape. He was heartbroken when he was coerced to his bed. He could barely move his arms and legs and he was in so much pain.

'Promise me I won't be stuck in bed forever, Lola,' he said.

The nurse couldn't lift Dad back into his chair near the end. She wasn't allowed to do it on her own because of health and safety (and Dad wouldn't have let her if she tried). His friends came round to haul him out of bed. I could tell by his eyes that Dad loved being back in the living room, watching as his friends drank lager and took the piss out of each other (they liked to start drinking early and finish late; they had no jobs to go to). I could tell as I looked at him, looking at them, that he was taking everything in, filing it in his mind, even though he was dosed up on painkillers.

Sometimes, I wonder where his mind has gone to, where his memories and personality and dislikes and loves have gone. I've never been into spiritual stuff, even though it might be a comforting thought that our life, our consciousness, doesn't end when our bodies give up. Wishful thinking, I reckon. It would be a consolation to think there's a better place out there when you see someone you love suffering like he did. But it was cruel. How could there be a god that allows pain like that? Dad, however, once said, 'He doesn't give us more than we can handle'. And he wasn't particularly religious.

49

I flinch when the phone rings again, piercing the silence.

They're going to tell me I have the job because I don't want it. Dad always said I could achieve things if I put my mind to it, so I conclude that my thoughts have been all over the place. He also said that if you want to avoid an obstacle in the road, you shouldn't focus on it. That's where I've gone wrong.

I dangle my arm to my right, knowing that on the side table is his CD Walkman with big headphones. He was never one for things that had been made unnecessarily smaller – he wasn't the most portable of people, even when he was fully mobile.

I look down at the table. It's been four months, but I haven't emptied the last collection of butts in the ashtray – smoked till no white remained. His friends used to hold them up to his mouth. The remains look like a pile of fat maggots that have lost their wiggle.

Ring, ring. Ring, ring.

It's five to five – they'll stop trying in a few minutes.

I get up and stand in the hall, willing the angry shrill of the phone to cease.

The door to Dad's room has been closed ever since I placed his ashes on his bed. I can't bring myself to open it.

He didn't smoke in there after his quilt caught alight and he nearly cooked himself to death. He'd passed out and only woke when I threw a bucket of cold water over him and the flames. He said I saved his life that night.

I turn my back to his door. Hanging on the hall wall is a photograph of the three of us. I'm so used to it; I don't usually offer it more than a glance. We're on holiday – Cornwall or somewhere like that – on a beach. A stranger must've taken it because even before Dad became ill, my parents preferred their own company to others'.

I heard nothing from her in the first few weeks after she left, and if Dad spoke to her, he didn't mention it. She hadn't even left a note. It was Eric who told me she wasn't coming back *for a while* – that she'd gone away to *think about things*. I didn't understand because it seemed as though she was always thinking about things.

After exactly one month, on 8 October, the telephone rang at 4.30 p.m. Dad was sleeping as we'd finished my lessons at three. I picked it up and traffic noises sounded for ages, but I knew it was her. A rage built inside me and I wanted to shout at her and ask her how she could've abandoned me when I was only a kid, but at the same time I didn't want to upset her so much that she'd hang up.

'Mum,' I whispered down the line. 'Is that you?'

There were tears streaming down my face. She sniffed down the line – perhaps she was in tears, too. But she wasn't much of a crier; she wasn't sentimental.

'I know it's been a few weeks,' she said, eventually, 'and you must be wondering where I am, but I couldn't tell you before I left ... you know what your dad's like. I bet he hasn't stopped slagging me off, has he?'

'Actually . . .' I started.

He hasn't mentioned you. He's quieter than he's ever been.

She didn't wait to hear what I might've said.

'I'll forward you my address when I'm settled.' She paused, sniffing again. 'How are your lessons going? Bet you're glad to be away from those horrible children at your old school.'

I opened my mouth to speak.

No, Mum. I get so lonely sometimes. I haven't heard from Chloe in weeks, after she used to ring me every day and tell me what secondary school is like. She said that people are asking why you left me and that you've vanished, and that Dad might've killed you.

But the words never came out.

'Yes,' I said. 'It's going well.'

'You know, Laura,' she said. 'If I stayed, we'd have ended up killing each other.'

I didn't know what to say to that, but I didn't have to say anything because she said she had to be going as she had an appointment.

I look at the same telephone now; it's stopped ringing.

Mum was right, though. In the end, in some way, they did end up killing each other.

After she left, none of us were the same again.

7

Sarah

The walk to the university is only twenty minutes from the café and Sarah's almost there. She takes out her mobile and selects Rob's number again. It's rare that she calls him during the day, even when he's away. There's no answer, and he hasn't responded to the simple text she sent him this morning. For one who professes to be worried about her when he's absent, he doesn't appear to be that bothered now. She types another message.

Rob – a body has been found in the flat below. No one knows who it is yet, but it's been there for years! x

Even the least curious of people would respond to that.

Sarah's still looking at the screen when the messages go from 'delivered' to 'read'. She smiles in anticipation at the moving dots as he composes his reply – she doesn't usually. It seems she feels more affection for him when he's away.

The dots disappear, but no reply comes.

She presses to call him. After two rings it goes straight to voicemail. She tuts and flings the phone into her bag.

Instinctively, she looks behind as she grabs the door handle to the Greenbank building.

There's a man in the distance, standing still and looking in Sarah's direction. He's wearing jeans and a dark jumper with the hood over his head. He lifts his hand. As a reflex, Sarah waves in return. She stands for a moment, looking at him. Is it one of the residents from the flats? He looks familiar, even from this far away.

A gust of leaves circles her feet. By the time she looks back up, the man has gone.

Another student squeezes past her and rushes up the stairs. It's not the same man. He probably wasn't even waving at her. She's more jittery than usual after the events of this morning, coupled with the darkness of the sky and imminent rain.

After climbing two flights of stairs and walking down the long, open corridor, she reaches her tutor's office. The door to Judy Sinclair's office is always open because she thinks it narrows the divide between student and mentor. She glances up as Sarah walks in. Her glasses are perched on the end of her nose and are attached to a beaded chain around her neck.

'Take a pew,' says Judy.

Sarah can't tell if Judy's northern accent is authentic, or if it's another affectation to *lessen the gap*.

Sarah sighs loudly as she flops onto the chair adjacent to Judy. The weight off her feet feels delicious after standing all morning.

Judy finishes what she's writing, leans back in her chair and clasps her hands on her lap.

'How's the research going?' she says. She leans across her desk and grabs Sarah's file: *'CONSENT: THE SHARING OF PHOTOGRAPHS ON SOCIAL MEDIA AND THE RIGHT TO PRIVACY.'*

'Slowly, actually. I've kind of lost momentum. The subject doesn't seem to offer much academic opinion. All I can find are vox pops about the shady area of parents uploading photos of their children on Facebook. And of course, revenge porn, which has been done before.'

Judy sighs, and Sarah regrets her flippant tone about such a serious subject.

'A piece of advice,' says Judy, 'is to work through it. Even with the greatest of ideas, a person can get sick to death of the subject. It's easy coming up with the initial concept; sticking to it is the hard part.'

Sarah flinches at the insinuation that Judy thinks her topic isn't up there with the best. And she knows that it's meant to be hard work – she just wishes that it didn't *feel* like such a chore. She liked this course when she first started, but the workload feels overwhelming at times.

'Actually,' says Sarah. 'Something unusual happened this morning.'

Judy smiles. 'I like unusual.'

'A body ... or what remains of it ... was found in one of the flats in my block.' Words Sarah's been saying all day. 'It had been there for years.'

'Really?' Judy frowns. 'Do you know that for sure?'

'No. One of the people who found it said there was a milk carton dated nearly two years ago ... and the body was almost a skeleton. There was a pile of mail behind the door.'

'Don't assume anything,' says Judy.

Sarah gets the urge to push Judy off her chair but supposes she's right. Fabricating events with what information she has can't replace knowing all the facts.

'How is it possible that no one has missed them?' says Sarah.

'That's a good point. It would make a terrific subject, especially in a world in which people share everything about their lives.' She scribbles something on Sarah's file. 'Any foul play suspected?'

Blood rushes to Sarah's cheeks.

'I'm not sure yet.'

'ID?'

'There's been nothing on the radio.'

Judy tilts her head to the side.

'If it's already been on the radio, then I imagine loads of people are asking the same questions you are.' Judy doesn't roll her eyes – maybe she actually likes the sound of this story. 'You might have a unique angle, seeing as you live in the same block of flats. Are you close with the other residents?'

Sarah thinks of the several letters that she picked up from the floor in the name of Robin Hartley. She can't mention this to Judy – taking the letters, let alone opening them, is illegal. She makes a mental note to research if anyone's ever been convicted of reading someone else's mail.

'I only know Mr Bennett to talk to. He's lived there

the longest.' Sarah pauses. She doesn't want her tutor to show her exasperation at how little Sarah knows about the people who live around her. But it's not the 1950s – nowadays hardly anyone is super-friendly with their neighbours. 'The television was left on,' she says. 'Someone must've been paying the bills for it not to be found earlier.'

Judy slams the file shut, making Sarah jump.

'Now *that* is intriguing.' She puts the file on her desk. 'Maybe continue with your original topic but keep an eye on this one. Don't get your hopes up. Sometimes things end up pretty straightforward in the end. Same time next week?'

It's almost dark outside. A lecture must have just finished as there are fifty or so students walking across the concourse, most with their heads down against the bitter wind.

Sarah scans the campus; there's no one watching her, no one following. Thoughts of the mystery woman opposite the flats this morning and then in the café have put her on edge. The man who waved earlier must've been waving at someone else.

She checks her phone; there are no messages or missed calls from Rob, but there's a text from her son, Alex.

Mum am sorting tea tonight x

Sarah can count on one hand the amount of times he has cooked dinner – he must have bad news. Either way, the kitchen will be a mess. She scolds herself; she shouldn't be ungrateful.

Thanks love, she replies. **I'll be home soon x**

She tries phoning Rob, but again there's no reply. She turns onto her road. Nelson Heights is one of three blocks of flats within fifty feet of each other, built in the 1960s. Grey, concrete. A blot on the landscape, her mum says, which is ridiculous as this city's hardly picturesque. Still, most of the residents are OK, and not what her father worried would be drug dealers and murderers. He tutted when Sarah countered that dealers could probably afford a nice detached house in the countryside rather than a small flat in town.

There's a figure standing next to the bus stop a few yards ahead. It looks like Mr Bennett. He has his back to the road.

'Hello, Mr Bennett,' says Sarah when she reaches him. 'You're not going to catch the bus if you're not looking out for it.'

She smiles at him, but he's frowning.

'Angela always called me Silver,' he says. 'It's short for Sylvester. Mr Bennett is too formal, don't you think?'

He still doesn't meet Sarah's gaze. The light from the lamppost above reflects in his watery eyes.

'OK, Silver.' The name matches the colour of his hair, which is thick and slicked back. 'Is everything all right? Has something upset you?'

He starts walking towards home; Sarah walks alongside him.

'Nothing more than usual,' he says, looking straight ahead. 'I went to visit Catherine today. I've told you about Catherine, haven't I?'

58

'No, I don't think you—'

'It's hard to see her lying in the hospice like that. And it's been so long. I wish they'd do her hair better for her. Angela was always so good at doing her hair. I try my best, but ... Anyway, what I meant to say was that something happened today – it was like she knew what was going on. She actually reacted to the television.'

'What do you mean? Who's Catherine?'

'She doesn't speak to anyone. She can't, you see. Brain damage after what happened.'

Sarah can barely keep up with what he's saying, and his pace is fast for a man in his eighties. She hates to admit it, but she's out of breath. Luckily they're nearly at the flats.

'She looked peaceful today. She likes to look out of the window at the garden. Well, I think she does.' He shrugs slightly. 'But when the news came on about the body they found this morning, she made a strange noise.' He stops, placing a hand on Sarah's arm. 'She remembers,' he says. 'She remembers what happened to her.' He looks up at the block. 'The connection she had to this place. I knew she was still listening. There's still hope that I'll get her back. Even though they said it wasn't possible.' He turns to look at Sarah, his eyes bright. 'Do you think it's possible?'

'I don't know,' says Sarah. 'What happened to her?'

He points a finger towards the sky.

'I've forgotten the milk,' he says, turning around. 'See you soon, Sarah. Let's have a cup of tea tomorrow or the day after that. I'm sure we'll have some news by then.'

He raises his arm in goodbye.

'Wait!' she says. 'Mr Bennett!'

But he walks briskly in the opposite direction.

He said that Catherine – whoever she is – had a connection to this place. Sarah's sure he's never mentioned a Catherine before, but then, this is one of the longest conversations she has had with him to date. Catherine must be Silver and Angela's daughter. Sarah can't imagine Mr Bennett meeting someone new after losing his wife. He seemed to have adored her, and it's only been a couple of years. Though you never know. Life's short and all of that.

Sarah reaches the foyer to find that one of the bulbs in the stairwell has blown. She glances behind before pushing the heavy door open. The light from a lamppost in the car park lights the upper-floor balcony. She stops at the foot of the stairs.

There's a silhouette of a man standing at the top with his back to her.

'Is that you, Rob?' she says.

Her voice echoes; the man startles.

He turns around.

The man raises his hand as if to say stop. Is it a policeman?

'Is everything OK?' Sarah shouts; her heart is pounding.

He puts his hands in his pockets, turns and walks right.

Sarah waits a few seconds. Her flat is on the left.

There's no sound of footsteps. She slowly climbs the stairs, gripping hold of the freezing cold metal banister.

When she reaches the top, the balcony to the right is clear. So is the left. He must have either gone into one of the flats, or down the fire escape.

She runs to her door, only thirty metres from the stairwell. Her hand shakes as she puts the key into the lock.

She doesn't look back before closing it.

The kitchen at the end of the narrow hall is in darkness. The flat is silent.

She was expecting her son's music to be blaring from his phone as he covered every kitchen surface with pans and ingredients.

'Alex?'

She opens the living-room door, but there's no glow from the television. She moves towards his bedroom. Why the hell is she tiptoeing in her own home?

There's no light under his door. Sarah pushes it open and flicks on the light.

'Jesus, Mum!'

Alex sits up on his bed, taking out his earphones.

'What are you doing, lying in the dark?' Sarah says, her voice almost a shriek.

'Chill out,' he says, getting up. 'I didn't realise the time. It gets dark quickly.'

'What happened to tea?' she says. 'I thought you were cooking.'

'I didn't say I was cooking, I said I would sort it.' He

pulls the headphone jack from his mobile and throws them onto his desk. 'I thought I'd treat us to a take-away.'

Sarah backs out of his room as he heads towards the door. He's at least a foot and a half taller than she is. He still has the same baby face but with fine dark hairs on his upper lip.

'Where did you get the money for a takeaway?'

'Typical,' he says huffily. 'No, *Thanks, Alex, that's a great idea.*'

She looks to the ceiling; it's as though he's been a teenager for at least ten years.

'I thought you were broke,' she says. 'You asked me to lend you a tenner last night.'

He shrugs as he struts to the kitchen, flicking on the light and grabbing the menus from the clutter drawer.

'Dad was round earlier.' He shuffles the menus. 'Gave me the cash for it. Saw you weren't here.'

'What? He knows I have tutorials on Thursday after-noons. It's not as if it's midnight.'

'I didn't say he was moaning about it. He wanted to do something nice.'

'Hmm,' says Sarah. Her ex-husband Andy usually has a motive for anything nice he does these days.

Alex walks past her and goes into the living room. He sits on the sofa and stretches his long legs across the coffee table. Sarah hangs her jacket on the coat stand in the hall before throwing her bag beside her chair next to the fire. She feels the same relief from sitting down now as she did this afternoon.

'No feet on the table,' she says.

Alex rolls his eyes and sighs as he puts his feet back on the floor.

'I don't suppose Rob phoned the landline, did he?'

'Mum, no one rings the landline. Everyone knows it's just there for Wi-Fi ... and ambulance chasers. Chinese food, curry or pizza?'

'When was your dad here? Was it just now? I thought I saw someone at the top of the stairs.'

'I don't know. About twenty minutes ago.' He looks up from the menu. 'And why say that? There are always people coming and going around here. That's why I listen to music with my headphones. It's so bloody noisy – you can hear everything.'

'Hey, less of the language.' Sarah gets up and sits next to him on the sofa, looking at the menus in his hands. 'I don't think I'm that hungry.'

'The Orient Express it is then,' he says. 'Because technically I'm paying, and you're not that hungry.'

'How much did your dad give you?'

'Thirty quid.'

'Bloody hell! He's flashing the cash, isn't he?' She looks at the menu again. 'Vegetable spring rolls, chicken curry, special fried rice, and a side of chips. And a can of Coke.'

He's staring at her.

'Not that hungry, eh, Mum?'

'We can have the leftovers tomorrow. Might as well take advantage of your father's generosity.'

There's a moment's silence.

'He asked again,' says Alex.

Sarah flops her head against the settee.

'But he's seeing that woman from work,' she says. 'He said he was moving on.'

And I'm in a relationship with Rob, she should've added.

She wishes Alex's father wouldn't talk so openly about his life to their son. The contact between her and Andy has lessened now that Alex can make his own arrangements, and they get on far better because of it.

'I don't think he's seeing anyone,' says Alex. 'And he's worried about us living here, especially after they found that rotting corpse this morning.'

'Alex!'

'There's no *nice* way of saying it, Mum,' says Alex. 'And Dad said that he has such a nice big house and asked why we went from that to this.'

She sits back up and looks her son in the eyes.

'*You* understand, don't you, love?'

He shrugs, and grabs his phone.

'I'll phone through the order,' he says. 'Delivery or collection?'

'Get them to deliver,' she says. 'It's freezing out.'

She doesn't want either of them going outside after seeing that man earlier. It's put her on edge.

'Alex,' she says as he's about to leave the room. 'You are happy, aren't you?'

He shrugs.

'I guess,' he says. 'Though Dad seems pretty ...'

His voice trails off.

'Pretty what?' asks Sarah, but she doesn't want to hear the answer.

Alex shrugs again. 'I'm sure he'll be fine.'

Sarah grabs her mobile from inside the bag next to her. There are three missed calls, but they're not from Rob – they're from Andy. From what Alex says, it seems he's got it into his mind that Sarah needs *saving*.

As Alex rings through the food order, Sarah tries Rob again.

No answer and straight to voicemail after three rings. He pressed the red button.

Sarah tries not to read too much into it, although he should've been back by now. She thinks about the last time they were together, and there seemed to be nothing wrong.

Something has happened today; something Rob doesn't want to talk to Sarah about.

8

Laura

I woke early again in a panic that I had no more money – that Dad's funds had dried up and I'd be turfed out onto the street. Dad was so careful with money. He had some savings, but still received his disability allowance every week. I didn't ask about the details but I think it was allowed. Eric helped him with the financial side of things and arranged for accounts to be transferred into my name. There still might be some that haven't been changed – I'm sure he said there were some shares or bonds in both Dad's and Mum's names. She's never mentioned them, which is surprising as she was always asking for money when she came to visit me.

He didn't want to pay for home help when I was younger – he said that I did a good enough job, but we had to get twenty-four-hour care near the end. It was either that or a hospice.

'They might be different to when your gran was in one,' he said, 'but I want to be here to the end. It's my home.'

I wasn't to tell Mum it was *nearly time* if she called,

but he needn't have worried; she didn't ring that often.

PeopleServe Northwest are going to phone just after 9 a.m., I know it. And I want to be prepared. It's a Friday, so they probably won't make me start today.

There isn't a bath in the bathroom – just a walk-in shower that Dad had installed. The water is always too cold as the dial is broken. Dad couldn't tolerate the heat. I've got used to it. It wakes me up and the bathroom feels extra warm when I get out.

I dress and sit on the hallway carpet next to the telephone.

I'm thirty years old in three weeks. Some would call that a landmark birthday, but I've nothing to mark it by. I'm living in the same place as I was when I was nine years old. There have been plenty of significant life moments here, but not many joyful ones. I suppose this is all there is for me, but I don't mind. I've resigned myself to the life that I have. Other people are over-rated, anyway.

I knew at an early age that I'd never lead a *normal* life. As a teenager, I'd watch romantic comedies where the father, or some other close relation, would walk the bride down the aisle (I've never been to a wedding). I knew I'd never have that, so I didn't seek it out. I wouldn't want to be the centre of attention anyway – just the thought of a group of people watching me walk *anywhere* makes my knees shake.

Stories don't always have to end like that, anyway.

Disney endings, my dad called them.

'Life's not a sanitised fairy tale,' he said. 'It's messy

67

and it's cruel, but you're my little ray of sunshine. I'm done with romantic love.'

It was sad, really. He deserved someone to love him as much as he loved my mum.

At ten past nine, the phone rings. My hand hovers over it for five rings – I don't want them to realise I'm sitting next to the phone in anticipation (I must be the only person on this earth who waits for a call centre to ring).

I pick up the handset.

'Hello, this is Laura,' I say, sounding too much like I'd practised.

'Hello, Laura! You answered the landline!' she says, pointlessly. 'We hardly ever get that. This is Nancy, calling from PeopleServe Northwest. How are you today?'

I open my mouth to speak.

Hang on. It's not an *actual* sales call, is it?

I'm blushing, which is silly because Nancy can't see me.

'Er ... I'm fine,' I say. 'How are you?'

'Great!' She sounds so happy for this time of the morning. 'I'm ringing with some fabulous news! Following your interview last Thursday, which went super well – they were impressed with the high standard of nearly *all* the candidates – I'm pleased to offer you one of the positions of junior sales advisor!'

I might have gone off in a bit of a daydream there. Why simply say *You've got the job* when you can surround it with fifty irrelevant words?

'Junior?' I say.

'That's right. Everyone starts off as a junior, so that's nothing to worry about.'

'I wasn't worried, I was just clarifying.'

'Excellent! I'll email you over the details and I look forward to seeing you on Monday.'

I wonder if she's pretending to be so nice because she knows she's being recorded. I think I could say anything to her, and she'd still be as happy as a pig in the proverbial.

We say our overenthusiastic goodbyes and I replace the handset, still sitting cross-legged on the floor. The hallway seems a little quieter without Nancy's voice in my ear.

I can't believe I've actually got the job. I was terrible in the interview.

Perhaps Tom Delaney put in a good word for me. Perhaps he actually hated me in school and this is my penance. If he was one of the ones who was nasty to me, his face would be imprinted on my mind. It was mainly the girls, anyway. All of them except Chloe.

I saw her briefly at Dad's funeral. I was surprised to see her there because we hadn't talked in years. She didn't stay long after the service so I still don't know what I said or did to upset everyone before I left school. Was it so bad that I've blanked out the details or was it simply that they didn't like me?

A bang from Dad's room makes me jump.

I stand and open the door, but don't look at his bed.

It was pristine the last time I came in here, but one of his bottles of aftershave has fallen to the floor. I walk over to the window, lifting up the net curtains. I can see the spire of St Walburge's from here. He must've liked this view. There's no one looking in, but then you'd expect that in a block of flats.

The window is closed; no breeze could have knocked the bottle from the dressing table. A shiver of cold runs over my scalp. I'm not into anything woo-woo or ghostly or anything like that, but sometimes it feels as though someone is watching me in here.

No, no. That's just silly.

It must've been someone banging from the other side of the wall. The bottle must've been teetering on the edge. That'll be it.

I bend to pick it up and pull the lid off. I squirt some into the air – the sun reflects on the spray and highlights the dust shaken from the net curtains.

I sniff. He hardly wore aftershave at the end. Except maybe on Fridays when it was Joyce's turn on the rota, but he always denied it. Said it must have lingered from whatever he was wearing.

I place the bottle back on the shelf, nearer to the wall. My hands are tingling.

I rush to the door, still not looking at the bed.

'Ouch!'

Something sharp.

I lift my foot off the ground. It's a stone, the size of a pebble but with a sharp peak.

What the hell is that doing here?

I glance at the window. It was closed when I walked in. It can't have come from outside.

I place it on the shelf next to the toiletries. Dad used to collect random souvenirs when we went on holiday. It's likely to be one of his beach finds. It's probably been there for months and I've not noticed because I never come in here.

I walk slowly to the hall and close the door behind me.

I must sort out his room. I can't keep it like that forever, with all of his things waiting for him as though he were still alive.

I listen at the door.

No sound.

A breeze glides past my ankles from the bottom of the door.

My hand grips the handle. I can't move. The window was closed. I bend down, putting my fingers in the gap under the door. There's no draught. I must be imagining things.

Perhaps I'm not well.

I look down to my hands; they're shaking.

What if I have the same disease Dad had? Who would look after me?

9

Sarah

It's Friday: Sarah's favourite because the flat is quiet and it's her day off from the café. A research day, which means justifiably spending hours on the internet.

There was only one report on the news about the body found downstairs. In her head, Sarah refers to him as Robin Hartley, even though the report didn't name the person or go into much detail about the circumstances.

She lays the letters she found near the ground-floor flat onto her desk. In the past, she's only ever opened someone else's mail by mistake. When looking online, she couldn't find any cases of prosecution for the crime, but admittedly she didn't look very hard.

One of them looks like a bank statement and has *Private and Confidential* printed on it. Sarah places it aside – she's definitely not going to open that one.

She picks up another with a handwritten address, hesitating for a moment. Its postmark is dated November 2016.

It's fine. No one else was interested enough to have picked it up from the ground.

She doesn't linger on that thought. She tears apart the envelope and opens the paper inside.

Dear Robin,

I can't stop thinking about us since you allowed me to talk to you. Is there anything I can say that will make you reconsider? I know I made a mistake but that was so many years ago now.

I've written my new address on the back.

Please know that I've always loved you and I always will.

M x

Sarah puts the letter to her nose and sniffs. There's no perfume scent that lingers – but would it after two years? It's such a sad letter. Whoever M was will likely have received no reply and would forever think that Robin never cared for her.

Maybe he didn't. Maybe he didn't forgive her for what she had done.

It's such an odd turn of phrase: *since you allowed me to talk to you.*

Was Robin a control freak? Was he abusive towards M? Could M actually be short for *Mother*?

Speculation again. It is so frustrating not having a definite name. Even so, there were hardly any results online for a Robin Hartley from Preston. The guy obviously wasn't interested in sharing his life on the internet.

Sarah picks up her phone, scrolling to find her

ex-husband's name. Having a police officer as a contact is useful, but this one is awkward

When she left him three years ago, he hadn't believed her when she said that there was no one else. He thought she was having an early mid-life crisis because she'd started her degree. He joked that he wouldn't mind if Sarah turned into Educating Rita. '*I* have a degree,' he said. 'It really broadened my mind. I don't mind at all if you want to study.'

He always brought himself into whatever issue she was having. If she had a bad day, it was never as bad as his because he *held the hand of someone who died today*. If she was too tired to cook dinner and suggested take-away, he'd say, 'OK, but I'll choose because I've been on nights and I'm even *more* tired.'

Sarah wasn't allowed to feel less than happy.

It wasn't that he was a bad person, but everything felt like a competition.

She places her phone down and clicks onto his Facebook page. She hasn't looked at it in a while — scared that she'll come up as a friend suggestion to him if she looks too often.

Oh. He's changed his profile photo. He has his arm around a blonde woman. They're both wearing sunglasses and beaming their white teeth at the camera. Typical. Bet he used a filter for that because his teeth aren't that bright in real life.

The woman he's tagged with him has 'loved' the photograph.

There's got to be something going on between those

two. He mustn't be pining for Sarah after all. Not that Sarah minds. No, no. She doesn't care.

Not at all.

A relief, that's what it is.

She drums her fingers on the desk.

Perhaps he put the photo up to make Sarah jealous. He's never been keen on Rob, but then, why would he be? Or does Andy know something about Rob that she doesn't know?

Sarah tuts at herself. Being alone always makes her imagination conjure ridiculous scenarios.

She resists clicking onto Blondie's profile. Knowing her luck, she'd press *Add Friend* by mistake and that would be beyond mortifying.

She clicks onto Twitter and types in *Preston, Nelson Heights, crime* and *body found*.

There are a few older tweets concerning the old woman found in number seven, two years ago, but the more recent ones range in tone from curiosity and concern, to callous and cruel.

Amy Matthews @AmyOne♥andLonely
Anyone know whose dead body was found in those dodgy flats? #preston #crime
Cowboy Dave @davydoesdallas
Replying to @AmyOne♥andLonely Think it might be mine – wondered where it was. Btw nice pic, gorgeous #DMifyourstilllonely

Sarah shudders. What a creep.

Jane Samuels @Janie_Layton81

Replying to @AmyOne♥andLonely My auntie used to live there – it's not as bad as people think, decent folk live there. It's so sad – RIP

Trickie Dickie @RckWllsMthrFkr

Replying to @Janie_Layton81 RIP?? You didn't even know them. Obviously. Or they wouldn't have been rotting in that flat for five years. It was some sad git that no one gave a shit about. Like you, probably.

Katie ⟂;⟂@KbdWarrior

Replying to @RckWllsMthrFkr @Janie_Layton1234 Ignore him, hun. And it wasn't FIVE years 😵

Tech Dude @Anon1mouse

Very sad about the body found at Nelson Heights. I worked with someone who used to live there #preston #NelsonHeightsBody

Sarah's ears tingle with the last tweet. She clicks onto Anon1mouse's profile. He or she is only following thirty people and has only two followers. The profile photo is of a mouse in a shoe. The retweets listed are about conspiracy theories, Brexit and photographs transmitted from Mars and Jupiter. She clicks onto the *likes* tab and whoever this is has liked a page full of tweets about the *#NelsonHeightsBody*.

There is no direct message option, so Sarah clicks on the Tweet button.

@Anon1mouse Hello. I'm a journalist based in Preston and am looking for information on the body found in Nelson

Heights. I would be grateful if you could contact me. Thanks, Sarah.

It won't hurt to stretch the truth a little; Sarah doubts they'd reply if she mentioned she was a student. That's if they're inclined to respond at all. She wishes she'd written the tweet to sound a little less formal. Overthinking, again.

She navigates to the discussion forums she usually lurks on, especially when she can't sleep. Sometimes she can go deep down random rabbit holes, it's ridiculous – from local unsolved crimes to the existence of the Illuminati. At 3 a.m. some of the bizarre theories sound almost convincing. But now, at eleven o'clock in the morning, Sarah hasn't the patience for it.

There's nothing more than speculation on one of the local forums.

City of Preston> News> Crime> *CHAT* topic:
'Remains found in a flat just outside Preston city centre. Any theories?'
PNE4ever (724 posts): How can someone not have been missed for two years? Unless they were a bad 'un and their whole family kept quiet about it.
Squirrel84 (7 posts): It could be a homeless person who snuck in. Or a druggie.
SmokinSam (11425 posts):
Quote: *[It could be a homeless person who snuck in. Or a druggie.]*
*sneaked in.

I assume their bills had been paid – so I think we can rule out this theory. It's obviously someone who had enough money to cover their direct debits until now.

Squirrel84 (8 posts):

Quote *[*sneaked in

I assume their bills had been paid – so I think we can rule out this theory. It's obviously someone who had enough money to cover their direct debits until now.]

Fascist. In all senses of the word.

It's hard to get past petty quarrels to any useful pieces of information in some of these forums – it can easily suck up a few hours. Although sometimes the arguments are more interesting than the topics they're discussing.

Sarah closes the laptop. Just over two years ago, her and Alex weren't living here, but at least three of the other residents were. There's Mr Bennett – Silver – of course, and the woman downstairs who barely glances Sarah's way. Then there's the arguing couple from upstairs.

She grabs her notepad and pen and heads out to Mr Bennett's. Sarah's been thinking about what he said about this woman Catherine and that she recognised the news story. Who and where was Catherine? In some institution? Did she know something about the body – is that why she can't speak any more?

Sarah metaphorically slaps her own wrist at the wild, ridiculous theories she's coming up with. Her tutor's words repeat in her mind, that something intriguing is usually something mundane when the true story is revealed.

As she holds up her hand to knock, the door opens.

Mr Bennett's head jolts back slightly.

'You startled me, Sarah!' He smiles.

'Sorry.'

She blushes. He told her to call him Silver, but she feels a bit silly calling him that.

'Are you all right, love?' he says. 'It's going to be minus one later. You'd better put your coat on.'

She looks down and realises she's just slipped her pumps on and is only wearing a cardigan. She should try harder to be *in the present* – more mindful, as they call it these days.

'I came to ask you a few questions about Robin Hartley, but you're obviously on your way out.' He's wearing his tweed cap, bright red scarf and a charcoal woollen coat. 'You look very smart.'

'I'm off on an important visit.' He fiddles with the peak of his hat. 'I'm going to see my grandson. I'm a little nervous, to tell the truth, but I'm sure it'll be fine once I get there.' Sarah stands back as he comes out of his flat and closes his front door. 'I'm sorry to be rushing out on you, but my bus is due in ten minutes and it could be icy out – I've only given myself a bit of extra time.'

Sarah walks with him along the balcony.

'Will you be around later for a chat? Also ...' Sarah catches her breath – he's walking so fast. 'Do you know that woman's name from downstairs ... she lives on her own?'

'Questions, questions!' He laughs, and grabs hold of

79

the metal rail, lingering at the top of the stairs. 'I'll be back at about five, but that'll be your tea time, I expect. Give us a knock when you're free. I don't turn in till after nine.' He almost jumps down each of the steps. 'I can't remember her name, I'm afraid.' He turns at the bottom of the stairs and tips his cap. 'Until then, young Sarah!'

She walks along the balcony, feeling a little exhilarated from Mr Bennett calling her young.

She peers down to the ground-floor flat. The police ribbon has been taken down, but there's a CSI van parked outside it. A man is standing nearby, taking photos.

She goes down the stairs, hoping she doesn't fall and break her neck in these flimsy shoes. At least there'll be someone to take pictures of her freak accident, should anything happen.

Not the right time for jokes like that.

She puts on her concerned, serious expression as she stands next to the man. He's early thirties perhaps, receding at the front, and thin at the crown. She guesses he's not a police officer because he's capturing the scene with his mobile phone. He's wearing a blue parka lined with orange shiny fabric inside the hood.

'Do they have a name yet?' she asks.

He doesn't look at Sarah; instead he scrolls through the pictures.

'Lease was in the name of Robin Hartley. Not sure of the ID of the victim.'

'Have you looked up his birth certificate? Was he married?'

He glances at Sarah, then raises his eyes to the sky.

'I've got three interviews booked for today. You know that stupidly rich bloke on the Kensington estate? He's giving me an exclusive ... said he's opening a chain of ethical clothing stores. Don't announce it before I do, though.'

He laughs, wiping a drip from his nose.

'Oh.'

'It's big news,' he says, probably trying to convince himself as well.

'Aren't you intrigued about this?' says Sarah, gesturing to the open door of the flat. She leans forward, peering inside. The mail has been put into brown paper bags (she should probably sneak in the letters that she stole), and there are photographs along the hall wall. She's dying to go inside. 'Do you think they'll let us in?'

He wrinkles his nose. '*Us?*' He shakes his head and pockets his phone. 'They're not going to let just anyone in, are they?'

'Yeah, I know. I was only ...'

He shoves his hands in his pockets.

'I'm just getting pictures,' he says. 'Someone else will follow this up.' He looks Sarah up and down, wrinkling his nose. 'Why are *you* so interested? I don't recognise you from this patch.'

Patch. He's talking as though he's the lead in an American cop show, not the incurious hack in Preston city centre that he is.

'I'm studying at the university—'

He turns away, 'Ah, right,' and walks off.

Bloody charming.

A black Volvo pulls up alongside the CSI van. A woman in black trousers and a boxy suit jacket gets out. She glances at Sarah as she walks into the flat.

Sarah turns around as if to leave, but stops as a man − presumably another detective − follows the woman through the door, and shouts, 'Don't we need those plastic foot cover thingies?'

Sarah can't make out what she says in return.

They must be detectives. Sarah doesn't recognise either of them, but why should she these days?

'Do you know who it was?'

Sarah jumps at the sound of another woman behind her. She recognises her voice from the flat above − a voice she would know even better if it were louder and at three o'clock in the morning. From appearance − hair scraped back, baggy pink jumper, jeans and trainers − it's hard to tell her age, but Sarah guesses late twenties, early thirties.

'No,' says Sarah, turning round and taking a step back. The woman is standing far too close. 'I was trying to find out. There must be someone who knows.'

The woman shrugs. 'I guess if someone knew, then this poor sod wouldn't have been there for years.'

'I suppose. Or someone didn't want this person to be found if they *did* know.'

The woman's cheeks flush.

'I doubt it was murder,' she says. 'I'd have heard something about it. I've lived here most of my life.'

'Have you?'

She scrunches up her face.

'Yeah. And?'

'No, I didn't mean anything by it,' says Sarah quickly. 'Mr Bennett didn't mention that he knew you when I've asked him in the past.'

'We've never really got along, him and me. Clash of personalities ...' She glances at the open door to the flat. 'Thought that miserable sod died years ago ... sure there was a funeral for him.'

'What was the miserable sod called?'

She shrugs again. 'Smith or Jones or Hart something.' She walks closer to the door and puts her head right inside the hallway. 'Doesn't smell as bad as I thought it would.'

The woman stands aside as the female detective comes out of the flat.

'And you are?' she says, taking off the plastic foot protectors.

'Kelly Vincent. I live at number eleven.'

'Did you know Mr Hartley?'

Kelly stands straight, taking a step back.

'Nah. I knew his wife, though. Sort of. Only in passing. Our kids were the same age. My Jack is thirty-three now.'

Sarah looks at Kelly afresh. How old *is* she?

'When did you last see his wife?' says the detective, putting her hands in her jacket pockets.

'Oh, God knows. I think she left with their little one about fifteen, twenty years ago. Must have been awful for him living on his own all this time. And then the poor sod dies, and no one thinks to check on him.'

The detective glances at her colleague who's appeared at the door before turning her attention to Sarah.

'And you live here, too? Did you and Kelly here speak to the uniforms yesterday when they were doing house to house?'

Sarah opens her mouth to speak.

'Told them everything I know,' says Kelly.

Bloody teacher's pet. Sarah's tempted to tell the detective that Kelly didn't even know Robin's name a minute ago.

'I left early yesterday morning for work,' says Sarah. Talking to the police always makes her nervous – even though her ex-husband is a policeman. Perhaps that's why. She thinks they all talk, and that Andy's told the *whole force* about the breakdown of their marriage. But Sarah doesn't recognise this detective. 'My son and I moved in nearly two years ago. I thought this flat was empty.'

'Hmm.' The detective takes a few steps backwards and looks up at the block.

'Do you know how the person died?' says Sarah, sounding braver than she feels.

The detective frowns at Sarah.

'It'll be several weeks, months maybe, before an inquest.'

In the distance, Sarah sees a figure walking across the car park. She hears the foyer doors open, slam shut, and footsteps above.

'There's someone at my door,' Sarah says to the detective, who couldn't be less interested.

On the first floor, Sarah walks towards him. He has his back to her, but she knows it's Andy.

'Aren't you with that lot?' she shouts.

Sarah gestures to the flat and the police downstairs.

He shakes his head and rolls his eyes, but she was just making conversation. She realises he's wearing his own clothes.

'Alex isn't in,' she says.

She unlocks and opens the front door, slipping past him to get inside.

'I know,' says Andy. 'I came to see you. Do you have a minute?'

She opens the door wider to let him in. Sarah hasn't seen him in a few months. They separated nearly three years ago, but Alex is old enough to get to and from his dad's on his own now.

Sarah goes into the kitchen and flicks on the kettle.

'You didn't put fresh water in that,' he says.

She turns around slowly.

'No need to glare at me,' he says, raising his palms at her.

She hates it when he does that. Such an overreaction to a harmless dirty look – like she's some sort of screaming banshee that needs calming down. Classic Andy.

'I take my coffee black now,' he says. 'No sugar.'

'On a health kick, are you?' she says, rolling her eyes at the cupboard door.

She stops herself from mentioning the blonde woman in his profile photo.

'Something like that.' He pulls out one of the three dining chairs and sits at the tiny kitchen table that's pushed against the wall. 'I don't know how you can live in a place this size. Our kitchen's at least four times the size of this one.'

'I like it. And it's not ours, it's yours.' Sarah pours boiling water over the coffee granules, gives it a quick stir, and doesn't bother to top it up with cold water. She places the mug in front of him. 'Having limited space makes me realise what useless shit I used to hoard for no reason.'

'Ouch,' he says.

She tuts. 'Not everything is about you, Andy.'

He's almost shivering, still in his coat. He rubs the top of one arm.

'Oh, come on,' she says, smiling. 'You're acting like you're in some freezing hovel. It's not that cold in here.'

He shrugs, picks up the mug, and gasps after his first sip.

'That'll warm you up,' she says.

Sarah sits on the chair opposite. She's been itching to ask him about the body downstairs since she found out about it. Now she's seen his Facebook profile photo, there's no reason for her to hold back.

'Do they know who it is downstairs yet?' she says.

Although if she hadn't seen his profile, she'd still have questioned him about it. She has no willpower — she lasted a whole twenty-four hours.

'I've been waiting for you to ask,' he says, smirking. 'I was expecting a phone call yesterday morning. The curiosity must've been killing you. I knew you'd want to write something about it.'

She lets him have that. They've known each other for over twenty years and he knows her weak points.

'Well?' she says, tapping her fingers on the table.

'You always do that when you're impatient,' he says, looking at her hands, 'or when you're pissed off. Which one is it?'

'Andy!'

He leans back and folds his arms. He's loving this.

'You know that lot wouldn't keep a mere constable like me informed.'

'Yeah, but there'll be talk about it from the house to house. Was it murder?'

'A murder investigation team hasn't been set up yet. Plus, they'll wait to see what the coroner says when they hand over what information they have. You know I shouldn't be talking to you about it.'

'Yeah, yeah, you always say that. I've not betrayed your confidence in all these years, though, have I?'

'I didn't come here to talk about that,' he says, sighing and sitting forward. He lays his palms on the table. 'Well, not as such.' He tilts his head and clasps his hands together like he's a bloody priest about to offer his God-given wisdom. 'You know it's no good having Alex round here. A dead body below you for God knows how long! There are some dodgy characters who live in this area. Come back home, Sarah. We can

87

try again ... you can have the spare room ... get used to each other again.'

Sarah takes a moment to digest his monologue. She hasn't heard these words in a long time – not since she first started seeing Rob.

'Were you practising that speech on your way here?' She mirrors his clasped hands. 'And dodgy characters?' She laughs, trying not to sound bitter. 'You sound like you're from the East End in the Sixties.'

Her smile fades as she remembers the man at the top of the stairs last night.

Andy looks around the kitchen. There's nothing bad he can say about it. The person who owned it before fitted new cupboards and appliances. OK, so they're not top of the range, but they're perfectly acceptable. And Sarah can't afford to replace them until she finds full-time work after her degree.

Andy's only been inside this flat a handful of times. Sarah doesn't know why he hates it so much – she's decorated it really nicely, to her taste. She prefers it to the three-bed semi he lives in – her old home, which was filled with his *hobby* stuff: bike parts, golf clubs, and gadgets he used only a handful of times.

'It's been nearly three years, Andy,' she says. 'I'm seeing someone. Aren't you going out with that woman from work? Alex told me he met her when—'

'It didn't work out.' He looks at the mug, still full. 'About this Rob you're seeing. What's his surname?'

'You're not allowed to do checks on people. I'm not giving you his full name.'

'You can apply for a disclosure – under Clare's Law.'

'That's only if I have concerns, isn't it?' says Sarah. 'And I have no concerns about Rob.'

Not until now, she thinks. She pushes that thought from her mind.

'So you know about Clare's Law?' he says.

'Any single parent would. But that's for domestic violence.'

He's trying to catch her eye, but she can't look at him.

It was only a few times that she tried to contact Rob yesterday. What's a few missed calls, a couple of unanswered texts? It means nothing.

'Look, Sarah. I wouldn't run a check on him.' He sighs loudly, dramatically. 'I'm sure I recognise him . . . I saw him the other day when I was dropping Alex off.' He shifts in the chair. 'And I asked Alex his surname. I'm not even sure Rob is his real name.'

'Jesus, Andy. You asked our son?'

'It was only in casual conversation. It wasn't like I was interrogating him. I care about him . . . and you.'

'How can you possibly *recognise* everyone in a town this big, anyway? You won't know Rob because he's not on the police radar.'

'We'll see.' He zips up his jacket. 'I've been put forward for promotion. I'll be on better money if I get through.'

Sarah still doesn't look at him.

'You have to stop this,' she says. 'Just because your latest relationship failed – and I'm not sure you're being honest about that – it doesn't mean I'm going to be your fall-back.'

'But you left with no good reason ... like you had some kind of epiphany about how you should be living your life. I can be better this time ... I can focus on *us* more. I can stop being so self-involved.'

Sarah stands and pushes the chair back under the table.

'It wasn't about you,' she says. 'Not really. But you have to admit that we'd fallen out of—'

'No,' he says, interrupting again. 'Don't say it. I'll give you more time. You'll see. I don't mind waiting.' He stands quickly and walks towards the front door. 'I think you're worth waiting for.'

Sarah pauses, still standing in the kitchen.

No one has ever said anything like that to her before. It was almost romantic. Why didn't he say things like that when they were together?

She walks into the hall as he's reaching for the latch.

'Is it Robin Hartley's body that was found down there?'

Andy turns, his lips pursed. Slowly, he smiles.

'You're going to be great at this reporter business,' he says. 'Heartless.'

'I'm not heart—'

'I know, I know. I was just kidding.' He opens the door, sending a cold blast of air into the hallway and onto Sarah's legs. 'But you have a name. Try looking him up on Births, Marriages and Deaths. You might find his wife's name ... his date of death.'

'Oh. I was going to do that today.' She goes to the door as he walks onto the balcony. 'So it's not Robin, then?'

He shakes his head.

'So who is it?'

He shrugs and walks away.

'If you find out,' he shouts behind him, 'be sure to let the grown-ups downstairs know.'

10

Laura

It's Saturday morning. I always feel like I should be doing something on a Saturday morning, like we used to. When Dad was alive it was cleaning time (for me), and when Mum was around, we used to go food shopping.

There is only £271.75 in my bank account, but there's still a decent amount in Dad's savings. Enough to last until . . . well, I don't know. I don't plan much in advance, these days. There's no point.

I need to snap out of this.

Sometimes, it was easier to snap out of it when other people were around. I had others to compare myself to. Dad was ill, but at least he could see an end to it all. This is one of my thoughts I'm most ashamed of. He didn't want to see an end – he didn't want to experience his own gradual decline. I would have swapped places with him in an instant. He had so much to live for, whereas I was – am – living an empty shell of a life.

The day before my interview – during a fleeting good mood after hearing about it (and a vision of escape from loneliness) – I went browsing in the charity shops in town for potential work outfits.

When she was last cutting my hair, Mobile Mandy said there are more *chazza shops* than normal clothes shops these days. 'Because most high-street shops are online, now,' she said. 'It's not worth leaving the house to buy clothes. Even when I'm doing my weekly food shop, I can buy an outfit for my Saturday night at Sainsbury's.' I agreed with her, but only to shut her up. I seriously doubted she shopped at Sainsbury's. She told me that Primark is even cheaper than charity shops, so she kind of gave that away. She didn't realise the good quality of the items you can buy second-hand (or *vintage*, if you're that kind of person).

The thought of Mandy's weekly pub outings petrifies me, not that she's ever asked me along. But all those drunk people under one roof. Don't get me wrong – Dad's friends liked a drink, but they only ever bickered if one of them cheated at cards in order to win the whole three quid on the table.

Anyway, Age Concern had a nice dark grey suit, which was a size 14 (I'm a 12), and it looked passable. I asked if they'd keep it behind for me, but they wanted a pound deposit. This might have been a waste of money if I wasn't offered the job, so I declined her ever so kind offer.

The volunteers at that shop weren't interested in me trying the suit on – they were too busy talking about that body that's been found. I wasn't expecting oohs and ahhs at my reveal, but they could have at least lied to me

93

and said I looked good. At most, they could've noticed me taking it into the changing rooms. I could've stolen it for all they cared, and I've seen a few people nicking stuff from charity shops – you'd be surprised. One woman put a handful of second-hand bras into her handbag. *And* she was about seventy. You never can tell.

But no. When I opened the curtains to have a walk around in the suit, they didn't even glance in my direction.

'I wonder if it's Mrs Banks,' one of them said. 'She's been looking a bit peaky.'

'To be honest, Irene,' the other one said, 'most of our customers look a bit peaky.'

I should have walked out there and then.

Whenever I went shopping with my mum, they always kept things back for her, but that was mostly at The British Heart Foundation. We went there because my grandad died of a heart attack and that was Mum's way of contributing to the cause. Mum used to smoke fifteen cigarettes a day, though, so I think she was hoping that donating to charity would cancel that out.

Used to.

Past tense, again. I can't help it.

I suppose I could wear my interview suit (which was also my funeral suit) on Monday, but I've a feeling they'd notice I was wearing the same thing twice. They seemed a superficial bunch at PeopleServe Northwest (except for Tom, of course). I noticed this when I passed the actual call-centre phone stations or whatever they called them on the fifth floor. Nearly all of the women under twenty-five (the age of most of the workforce) had those thick, painted on eyebrows. I, on the other hand, have what they call Nineties brows. This isn't by design as I was only twelve in 1999. It was because I borrowed my mum's tweezers when I was ten and plucked them into a thin line and they've never been the same since. Mum said I looked like an alien child, and she cut me a long wonky fringe to cover them. In my opinion, this was far more embarrassing than looking like an alien. No wonder everyone thought I was weird.

The letterbox rattles, bringing me out of my day-dream. Dad often said I could just sit there with a blank look on my face when I was thinking about all sorts.

I get up out of his chair, leaving the chefs on *Saturday Kitchen* wittering on about crap to a film star of a film I'm never going to watch, while they try to squeeze in actual cooking. It's all very unappetising. Slimy squid they're cutting apart by the looks of it. Wonder if anyone likes that, or if they just pretend to. Like olives. They take some work.

There's a pink envelope on the mat.

My birthday is still a couple of weeks away. I flip it over and recognise the writing as my mother's. It's earlier than usual. Did she send it early in case she forgot, or has she *actually* forgotten when my birthday is? She might have turned to drink, and this was sent in one of her lucid moments. I often wonder if she has developed any more vices since I last saw her – to add to the smoking, the inappropriate shopping, and the abandonment of her only child.

Her writing looks the same as it always does: my name and address is in small capitals. It could be anyone sending it, really.

I smell the card, concentrating on the lick lines. There's no hint of whiskey or the horrible tang of wine. So that can't be it. Perhaps she's going on holiday and she's making sure that I get my card in time. She's never been late with my card. I'll give her that.

I'm usually good at saving my cards until the actual day, but I'm trying to distract myself before I start work on Monday. My imagination always gets the better of me before I open anything. She could have posted it early because she's put tickets for a holiday inside and wants to see me on the day. It is my thirtieth, after all. The last time we spoke, she said she was going travelling.

But she didn't ask if I had a passport, and it's not like her to surprise me with something so indulgent.

'Enough!'

I say it out loud.

I don't often talk aloud when there's no one around as it sounds silly. As silly as my absurd speculation of what will be an ordinary card, with ordinary words, from an ordinary relative. Or should that be extraordinary mother? Who knows? She might be. I always set myself up for disappointment. And I'm not usually wrong.

You're wallowing again, Laura. You're healthy; you have your whole life in front of you. Have a word with yourself.

That's what Dad would've said. And he had enough to wallow about without me adding to the mix.

I take the envelope through to the folks on *Saturday Kitchen*. They're actually doing some cooking now, but I've lost interest. I grab the flicker and turn the sound off. I can't bring myself to be totally alone and without the picture.

I lay the envelope on my lap, still in two minds as to whether to open it or not. But I know if I'm hesitating, it's because I'm going to open it within the next two minutes.

I smell it again. This time, I'm hoping for a hint of her perfume. She always used to wear Chanel No 5. When she left, I couldn't bear the smell of it. The scent of Old Spice reminds me of Dad – his aftershave choice didn't evolve past the Seventies.

It reminded me of him when he was still alive.

I should walk around with a peg on my nose, really. So I'm never taken off guard. Memories are too vivid when triggered by smell.

I'm trying to make it last longer, aren't I? This delicious anticipation.

There's no scent from the envelope. It just smells how stationery smells. Sterile; not even of the wood it was made from.

The postmark on it says Newcastle. Not far at all – only a few hours away. If she's still there.

I tear it open.

On the front is a picture of a woman leaning against a woman-sized bottle of Prosecco.

97

It's Prosecco time! it tells me.

It's one of the lamest, most impersonal cards I've ever received. Another sign that my mother knows very little about me. Does she think I'm living a different kind of life – a life that she hopes I live?

I open it and a ten-pound note flutters down onto my lap.

DEAREST LAURA,
WISHING YOU A HAPPY 30TH BIRTHDAY.
YOU ARE ALWAYS IN MY THOUGHTS.
LOVE, MUM

It's the sort of thing you'd write on a funeral flowers card. Again, it's written in small capitals. Anyone could have written that, too.

I grab my mobile phone from the coffee table and scroll through to see when she last telephoned me.

Twenty-seventh of September, last year.

Dad was still alive.

I still can't believe she didn't come to your dad's funeral. Eric's words are in my mind now.

My mother's 'calls received' entry is obvious in my phone's history because it was an unknown number and to be honest, I don't receive many other calls (local takeaways asking me to buzz them into the foyer rank higher than anyone's now).

I thought the number she called me from was 'unknown' because she was so far away on one of her fancy holidays, and all of this time, she's still been in bloody

Newcastle? I've nothing against Newcastle, but it's such a short distance away! Even if she's as broke as she's made out in the past, she could get here for about a fiver on a National Express coach.

She just never cared enough.

That's my thought and I keep that to myself.

I remember her words during our last phone call. There weren't many.

'Is that you, Laura?' she said, after dialling my very own personal mobile phone that I'd had for years.

Her voice was always muffled, always accompanied by traffic or the ambient noise of a place that wasn't her home. Who did she live with? Did she have another family? Dad said Mum couldn't bear to be satisfied in her own company. She always wanted verbal stimulation.

Maybe I was too stupid for her.

'It is,' I said.

'Have I caught you at a bad moment?' she said. 'I can call back another time?'

I'd learned not to say *yes* because she never called back another time – unless you counted a month later at nearly midnight a more convenient time.

'Now is fine,' I said, lowering the volume of the film I was watching.

Love Actually, probably. There's not a proper happy ending to that.

'Just wanted to let you know that I'm going away for a while,' she said. 'I won't be at the number that I gave you last time. Is everything OK with you?'

'Yes,' I said. 'Though Dad isn't—'

'What was that about your dad?'

There was static or heavy breathing down the line.

'He's not very—' I tried to say.

'You're breaking up, Laura. I'll have to call you back.'

She never did, but I don't really need to tell you that, do I?

I hadn't seen her for nearly two years at this point.

And Dad was still alive, then. There was so much she could've said. It was like she wanted it to be known that she wanted to make contact, but at the same time didn't know what to say to me. She didn't know me, really.

Doesn't know me.

The last time I saw her, she asked to meet me in the café at the top of the street, *for old times' sake*. It was *Kim's Kaff* then. It's still *Kim's Kaff*. At least there's still a constant in my life.

Have a word with yourself, Laura.

Just let me have this one, Dad.

I always have a narrative in my head that's not my own.

It's been months since I've heard her voice, and two years, forty-three days since I've seen her in person.

Mum ordered a latte and a flapjack that last time. She must've gone off hot chocolate.

'Do you still get carers' allowance?' she said as we waited for our order.

I frowned at her, and she leaned forward, looking horrified.

'I've not come begging,' she said. 'I just wanted to make sure you were OK financially. I could only afford to send money to your dad until you were eighteen.'

'I know, Mum. You've said before. I didn't think you were begging – you must've misread my expression.'

She hadn't misread my expression. She asked me for money the last time she came to see me.

'I've got a new job, now,' she said. She reached into a handbag and laid a brown envelope on the table in front of me. 'I told you I'd pay you back for that course I did. I'm teaching adults now – English, mainly. It was too stressful working in the high school – I nearly had a breakdown ... well, I did, really, didn't I?'

'Have you met anyone else yet?' I said. 'Since that Vince or Victor you were seeing?'

She looked out of the window.

'No,' she said. 'I'm much happier alone.'

She quickly turned to face me.

'Though, I didn't mean without you. You know I've always said you can come and live with me.'

'And I've always said that I could never leave Dad,' I said. 'He's getting worse.' I glanced down at the envelope. I didn't want to look vulgar and count the cash inside. 'Have you ever thought about—'

'Seeing your dad again?'

I nodded.

'That's why I came today, actually. Do you think he'd see me? It might be the last ...'

She didn't need to finish the sentence.

'I could go and ask him?'

I sounded too eager at the prospect of them seeing each other again after nearly fifteen years. Perhaps she wanted to come back home. It might have been nice to have her back. We could have forgotten about the past for Dad's sake. And, though I hadn't told her, I *was* finding it hard, especially during the night when silence, loneliness and darkness made everything so much worse.

But what if she had changed? She might have become even more selfish than when she was around. It might have been easier if she lived closer to us without her actually moving back in.

'OK,' I said.

She clasped her hands in front of her; her eyes were wide, glistening.

'You want me to ask him right now?'

She nodded quickly. 'OK.'

I wasn't that hungry anyway.

Dad was pretty good that day. His tremors had been suppressed because his ever-loyal friend, Eric, had brought his *special medicine*, aka marijuana, and it helped a lot.

'You're back quickly, love,' he said. He was sitting in his chair, the remote with the giant buttons on the arm of it. 'Is your mum OK?'

'She wants to see you,' I said.

'Ah.' He narrowed his eyes, but I couldn't tell if that was on purpose or not. 'She thinks I'm on my last legs, then.'

'I think she's probably been reading up on it. She was always in denial before. You know she likes to bury her head in the sand. If she can't see it, then it's not happening.'

'If she sees me now, she'd think there's been a miracle,' he said, his eyes twinkling. 'It's a pity I can't take that medicine twenty-four seven – it's too bloody expensive. It should be available on prescription.'

I knelt at his feet.

'I know, Dad.'

'Tell her, the answer's yes,' he said, patting me on the head. He used to do that all the time when I was little. He seemed to get smaller and smaller every day. 'I'll see her.' He smoothed down his hair – it was wild and grey and curly. 'How do I look?'

'You look great, Dad,' I said. 'You always look great.'

I stood.

'Shall I leave you two alone?' I said. 'Give you a chance to talk in peace?'

'Aye,' he said. 'Thanks, love. Take the spare key for her so she can let herself in.'

The food was on the table when I got back to the café. I had half expected her to have fled the scene.

'Well?' she said as I sat.

'He said yes.'

Her eyes glistened with unshed tears. I hoped they were for him and not herself.

'Are you OK if I ...?' she said, getting up. 'I've settled the bill.' She pushed her plate towards me. 'You can have mine.'

'Of course,' I said. 'I'm fine here.'

'Thanks, love.' She patted my head, too. She bent

down and kissed my cheek. 'I'll see you soon. Wish me luck.'

'Good luck!'

I flick off the television now, and I scroll through the contacts on my phone to find the last number I called her on. It'd be nice to speak to her again, to thank her for the card and the birthday money. Sometimes I'm too harsh with my thoughts about her. She wanted to see him, in the end. And neither she, nor my dad, ever talked about what they spoke of that last time.

I press the call button, and it rings until the voicemail kicks in. I don't leave a message. I search for the landline number she gave me, which was her last address in Longbenton.

It rings and rings and rings. There's no answer machine.

I compose a text in case she still has the same mobile number.

Hi Mum,

Thank you so much for the birthday card and money. I wanted to say thank you over the phone, but you must be busy. I will try calling later. I hope everything is OK with you.

With lots of love,

Laura xxx

I press send and lean back in the chair.

This room is so quiet.

Dad was quiet, too, the day after he saw her. He had taken himself off to bed (he wasn't confined to his bed, then) and had stayed there until midday the next day.

She was wrong about it being her final chance to speak to him; he didn't die until two years later. She had plenty of time, but that was the last time she saw him.

It was the last time I saw her, too.

11

Sarah

Alex is still in bed and will most likely be until after midday. Rob finally returned Sarah's calls at 11 p.m. last night to say that he was staying an extra night in Newcastle because he had to entertain potential clients.

'Do IT geeks even leave the house after dark?' said Sarah. 'And on a Friday night!'

He sighed. 'Yeah, very funny. I want to be here as much as they do, but it's expected of us. And, by the way, we're not computer geeks who sit tapping away in our underwear – we're infrastructure architects.'

Sarah coughed to disguise her laughter. She had never known Rob to be the one tasked with entertaining clients. She imagined their conversations to be dominated by *Game of Thrones* and *Star Wars*, but she shouldn't judge. They're probably just normal people.

'Were you too busy to answer my texts?' she said.

She wasn't going to mention it as a fear of being someone *like that*, but he was rude not to reply. Two years is a long time to have known each other.

'Sorry.' He sighed again. 'Things are a bit tense

around here. There's been talk for ages that they're going to move the whole business to Germany. Like most large companies, they're scared of a future in the UK.'

'I understand,' said Sarah. She was a bit pissed off at his sighing but at the same time, she wondered if he actually wanted to keep talking about the threat of losing potential business. Brexit affected so many things now that she'd become a bit desensitised to it. 'So strange about that body they found, isn't it?'

He was silent for a few moments.

'Have you read anything about it online?' she said.

'What? No, no. I haven't got time for all of that. I've got to go, Sarah. Talk to you later, or maybe tomorrow if I get in late.'

He didn't say goodbye.

He must be stressed, not thinking straight. It was so unlike him to snap like that. If he was pissed off at her for some reason, he would usually tease her about it.

Maybe she *had* been a bit of a cow.

He texted her three hours later last night – well, at two in the morning and no doubt full of Peroni – and arranged to come to hers straight from the train station. Sarah didn't press for a time.

It's now eleven o'clock in the morning on the Saturday, and she can't imagine him being here before midday after a night out in Newcastle.

She still has at least an hour to herself.

Yesterday, after Andy told her that the body found downstairs was not that of Robin Hartley, she found an entry on Births, Marriages and Deaths that stated a man of the same name, who resided in Preston, died in 2016. It seems that Kelly from the flat upstairs was the only one who remembered the man dying. She'd said that his wife had taken his child nearly fifteen years before. Sarah makes a cup of coffee and sits at her desk. She clicks on the latest Northwest news article on the BBC news feed.

The headline makes her stomach flip.

UNIDENTIFIED REMAINS OF WOMAN
FOUND IN PRESTON

A woman!

Had Robin Hartley lived with someone after all? Or had someone else taken over the tenancy?

She continues reading the rest of the article.

Police are appealing for information regarding a body found in a ground-floor flat in Nelson Heights, Preston. Lancashire Police stated in a press release that the tenancy of the property was still held in the name of Robin Hartley. Records show, however, that Mr Hartley died in 2016 following a long illness.

Police believe that the remains belong to a person related to, or who has connections to, Mr Hartley. No foul play is suspected at this time, but due to the decomposition of the body, it has been difficult to determine the cause of death.

An inquest into the death will be held 17th March 2019.

Sarah reads it several times.

The police can't rule out foul play, but there is probably no evidence to suggest it. No blood on the clothes perhaps, no sign of forced entry, no sign of a burglary. Sarah can't help but picture the poor woman.

Why didn't the detective mention that it was a woman, when everyone was talking about a Mr Robin Hartley? She would have had an idea, based on the body that remained. There's no mention or reconstruction of the items the woman was wearing. Maybe the material had disintegrated after being in contact with the decaying corpse.

Sarah looks at her coffee, places the mug on the table and stands. She puts on her sensible shoes, her big coat and heads outside towards Mr Bennett's flat upstairs. She tried knocking on his door last night, but there was no answer.

Sarah knocks three times. She can see through the net curtains that the TV is on, but what kind of sign is that? The television was on in the flat downstairs and everyone knows how that ended.

She peers through the window, trying to see signs of movement, but there are none.

Her heart begins to pound. What if he's dead in there?

She knocks again, louder, and peers through the letterbox.

'Silver! It's Sarah. Are you all right in there?'

Mr Bennett's cat, Jess – that's what she's heard him call her – strolls from the living room, down the hall, and into the kitchen.

'Jess!' says Sarah, almost singing, through the letter-box. 'Is Mr Bennett there? Is Silver there?'

Oh my God, she's talking to a cat now. At least she didn't refer to Mr Bennett as the cat's *daddy* ...

Sarah stands when her back starts to ache.

She goes to look through the living-room window again when the front door opens.

'Sarah!' he says. 'What are you doing loitering around outside?'

'I tried knocking, but you didn't answer.'

He beckons Sarah inside.

'Sorry, dear,' he says, closing the door. 'I had my headphones on. Do you know you can get nearly every book on audio these days? It's a revelation! I've never been so well-read ... well-spoken to ... whatever it is.'

'I tried calling for you last night,' she says, not quite knowing the correct expression without sounding like a child knocking on the door of a friend, 'but there was no answer.'

'I ended up staying for dinner with my grandson and his wife. Their little girl comes out with the funniest things ... though Thomas didn't seem his usual chatty self. I asked him what was wrong, but he said it was work. People always say that, don't they? It's the excuse for anything when they don't want to talk about what's really troubling them.' He flaps his hand in the air. 'Sorry. I'm wittering on, aren't I? It's because the only company I have in this flat is the cat ... and, well, she hasn't much to say for herself. Would you like a brew, love?' He leads Sarah into the kitchen. 'Or I've that instant hot chocolate if you fancy it.'

'Hot chocolate would be great, thanks,' she says. 'I haven't had that for years.'

'My mum used to make me a proper cocoa of an evening, probably added a drop of something to help me go to sleep.' He winks at Sarah as he flicks the kettle on. 'Did you have it as a child?'

'Only if one of my older sisters made one,' says Sarah. 'There are six of us, altogether.'

'Lord!' says Mr Bennett. He turns to her with two mugs in his hand. 'That must've been very busy. Bet your parents were run ragged.'

Sarah shrugs. 'They were pretty chilled, really. Well, Mum was. Dad was a lecturer in Engineering at the university, so he was always researching. They just let us get on with it most of the time.'

'Did they really?' he says, placing the mugs on the counter.

'They liked reading together of an evening. Used to shut the door in Dad's study so they had some peace.'

'Reading, you say?' He turns to Sarah and raises his eyebrows. 'And there were six of you? They must've been able to drown out the sound pretty well.'

'I guess. We had to be unique, intelligent or funny to impress them. Still do, really.'

'That must've been quite tiring.'

'I'm a late bloomer. This is my final year at university.'

'I'm sure they're very proud.'

'Yes,' says Sarah, but she's never heard them say as much. She gives herself an internal shake for reverting back to when she took their snubs so personally.

'It's not you, it's them,' my eldest sister, Jessie, said to me once. 'You'll self-destruct if you constantly keep trying to stand out from the rest of us.'

'Apparently,' Sarah says, quickly, 'Robin Hartley died over two years ago – at the end of 2016. Are you sure you can't remember anyone moving in after him – even for a short time?'

'I'm not sure of anything around that time,' he says, warming his hands around the mug of hot chocolate. 'Angela was in hospital for longer and longer each time, especially when they said the chemo was no longer holding it off. Angela was relieved about that in a way. There was no more sickness. For a couple of weeks, at least – until the end. She was in so much pain.

'We had one last evening, though. She asked me to get her a glass of Chardonnay, so I sneaked one in. I wasn't sure if that was a good idea, but the nurses turned a blind eye. We talked about Catherine, and our grandson, and what we thought his little girl might turn out to be like. We talked about the time we sneaked Catherine into the pictures as a baby in her pram at least seven times so we could watch *The King and I*. She loved that film. I borrowed my grandson Thomas's laptop so we could watch it in hospital, but she was unconscious by the time it ended.

'She didn't come round again. A few days later, she slipped away from me ... so quietly.'

A tear runs down his cheek. Sarah places a hand over his.

'I wish I'd met her,' she says.

Mr Bennett smiles, his eyes glistening. He wipes his eyes with a handkerchief from his shirt pocket.

'I always keep one handy,' he says. 'I never know when it's going to hit me – even after all these years. They never leave us, you know.'

He excuses himself. Sarah hears him blowing his nose in the bathroom.

A few minutes later, he's standing at the kitchen door.

'I've been thinking,' he says. 'Angela used to talk about Robin's wife. She got so angry about it. It was something to do with what happened to Catherine, but the timeline seems off.' He picks up his mug and pours the hot chocolate down the sink. 'What did I do that for?' He frowns at the empty cup in his hand. 'Angela hated waste.' He grips the counter with both hands.

Sarah stands, putting her arm across Mr Bennett's back. She follows his gaze. Through the window, the steeple of the Catholic church is visible over the sea of concrete.

'What happened to Catherine?' she says. 'Is she your daughter?'

He nods quickly and brushes a tear away with the back of his hand.

'Yes, she's our daughter. There was a car accident.

113

No one really knows exactly what happened. Angela kept going on about that woman in the ground-floor flat – Maria I think her name was – causing *nothing but trouble* and blamed her for what happened to Catherine, but I don't know how that could be possible as Catherine was found alone in her car.'

'Who are you talking about? Was the woman downstairs – Maria – Robin's wife? Did she hurt Catherine?'

'She didn't hurt her directly, no. It was all so messy what happened. What if I'm wrong about her leaving Robin? They had a daughter, too, I think. She used to play with Thomas in the paddling pool out the back years ago, but I'm always getting things mixed up these days.'

'So you think Robin didn't live alone?'

He shakes his head.

'I think I do remember seeing a woman coming in and out of number three.' He looks aside at Sarah, meeting her gaze. 'What if Robin's wife never left him at all?'

12

Sarah

Rob arrived at Sarah's at half past twelve but he looked so ill that she guided him straight to the bedroom.

'I am never, ever, drinking again,' he said.

'I don't know how you made it here in this state,' she said as he lay on the bed, groaning.

'I think I was still drunk on the train.'

She closed the curtains and placed a glass of water on the bedside cabinet, trying to make up for her sarcasm on the phone to him last night.

There's been no sound from the bedroom since she closed the door.

She's been searching Births, Marriages and Deaths for over two hours. So far, she has found that Robin Hartley married Maria in 1986 when he was thirty years old, and she was twenty-three. Sarah has looked at records for so many Maria Hartleys but has found no record of her child from two years before their marriage and to up to ten years later.

Kelly from the flat above mentioned that Robin had a child – and Mr Bennett earlier believed they had a daughter. But if they did have a child, where is she? Was Mr Bennett mistaken? There seems to be no trace.

Sarah goes onto Facebook and looks up Maria Hartley, but without knowing where she lives, it's difficult to know if it's the right one. She could message all the ones who are in the right date range, but it's hard to tell just from a photograph.

She sighs and slumps in her chair.

Andy might know. He could give her a clue.

She picks up her mobile phone and scrolls to find his number. Again.

She shouldn't really, but she hasn't got much to go on. Desperate, one might say.

Desperately nosey, Andy might say.

Alex wanders into the living room.

'Have you seen that black T-shirt?' he says.

'Alex, you have hundreds of black T-shirts. Which one do you mean?'

'The Next one that Dad got me.'

'I've no idea,' says Sarah.

He tuts. 'Then why were you pretending to help?'

She opens her mouth to speak, but it's not worth it. She'll never win the battle against a teenager this afternoon – she's too distracted, too jittery from too much caffeine, too frustrated at not magically finding the answers to the mystery of the flat downstairs.

'Hey,' says Sarah. 'Do you want me to call your dad and ask if it's there?'

Alex puts his head around the door.

116

'Why would you do that?' he says. 'I thought you hated Dad.'

'I don't hate your dad,' she says, trying to make her voice sound jaunty. She never sounds jaunty. 'I was just trying to help you.'

Alex leans against the living-room door and folds his arms.

'What are you working on there?' he says, narrowing his eyes.

'The body that was ...' Sarah swivels her seat to face her son. 'Hey, you're not meant to be so perceptive, you're a teenager.'

'And you're not meant to generalise, you're a journalist.'

'Actually,' says Sarah, turning her chair to face the screen again, 'journalists are notorious for generalising, but don't quote me on that.'

'Go on then, Mum,' says Alex. 'I can tell you're dying to ask Dad about it. You can ring about my T-shirt if you like, but he'll see right through it.'

'Thank you, light of my life,' she says.

Andy answers after three rings.

'It's a woman, then,' she says. 'Related to Robin Hartley.'

'Hi there, Sarah,' he says. 'I'm really good today. I really appreciate you asking.'

'I can't find any entries for a child he and Maria might have had,' she says. 'Does that mean it's Maria Hartley's body that was found?'

'You know we haven't released that information yet. You wouldn't be ringing me if they had.'

'It *is* Maria Hartley?'

'I can't say who it is – the family haven't been informed yet.'

'But you know I won't tell anyone.'

He pauses for what feels like minutes.

'Look, OK,' he says, finally. 'I think they're going to announce it later today anyway. I'm not going to give you a name, but I can tell you that it isn't Maria Hartley who they found. In fact, in connection with Robin Hartley, Maria Hartley doesn't exist.'

'You're talking in riddles, now, Andy. Didn't Robin marry a woman called Maria?'

'He married Maria, but she kept her maiden name. Her child was also given her maiden name.'

'Really? That's unusual.'

'Yeah, well. You women, getting all these ideas of liberty.'

'I know. We'll be voting next.' She types the name into the search engine. 'Thanks so much, Andy. I really do appreciate it.'

'I know,' he says. 'I'd say any time, but I'd never get rid of you.' He laughs for a second, then pauses. 'Tell Alex to bring his PlayStation later, will you? I fancy a game night.'

She says goodbye and presses enter on the search database.

'Well?' says Alex.

118

'It's Maria and Robin's daughter they found, which is awful. I don't know how old she was.'

'That *is* very sad,' says Alex, 'but does Dad have my T-shirt?'

'Oh, crap,' says Sarah. 'I forgot to ask.'

'Mum!'

'Sorry, love. But he said to bring your PlayStation. That bit I *did* remember.'

There is just one entry that matches Maria's name for a birth in Preston in 1987 – the year she and Robin were married. Why hadn't Sarah thought of searching under the woman's maiden name?

Maria Aspinall gave birth to Laura on 25 March 1987.

'So that's who you are,' says Sarah to the screen. 'Laura Aspinall.'

PART TWO

PART TWO

13

Laura

Monday, 13 March 2017

Do I introduce myself as Laura Aspinall, or just plain Laura? I suppose it would sound too formal to give my full name, unless everybody does it.

I'm right on time because I worked out from the journey to my interview that it takes one hour and seventeen minutes door to door. A weekly bus pass is £12.00, which is pretty reasonable as it'd cost around £32 a week to maintain a car, and that's not even including the cost of the actual car.

It's time, not money that I'll be losing by taking the bus, but there's nothing I can do about it at present. Driving lessons are so expensive.

I bought that grey suit from Age Concern with the ten pounds Mum gave me. I'll probably have to get a whole new wardrobe of clothes if no one else wears a suit to work at PeopleServe. I always found wearing school uniform much easier than choosing my own clothes before I left aged eleven. Wear-your-own-clothes days were a nightmare as a child.

Oh God. It's the same man at reception. His name is Dane (parents must be the zany/whacky sort – or fans of the band Another Level. I can't believe I remember the name).

I suppose I'll have to try to make friends with Dane, now we're going to be seeing a lot of each other.

'Good morning, Dane,' I say, cheerfully.

Now I'm thinking about Danepak bacon. I could murder a bacon sandwich right now. I was too nervous to eat before I left home.

I smile my best one. *Fake it till you make it*. I read that online last night in an attempt to learn self-confidence.

'Morning,' he says with a smile I'm sure is as fake as mine, but his is tinged with sarcasm. 'Your first day today, then, love?'

I've never been called *love* by someone younger than me before.

I give him my name, and, without warning, he picks up a digital camera. The flash leaves lights in my vision.

'That'll be a terrible picture,' I say. 'Can we take it again?'

He tuts and rolls his eyes. He's clearly in the wrong job. Which, I suspect, makes two of us.

I turn my body to the side, then turn my head to face him, tilting my chin slightly upwards. It's the technique to minimise a double chin.

The security pass is printed out and I clip it to the

edge of my suit jacket. He opens his mouth as if to speak, but just sighs.

'Where do I go from here?' I say.

He points to the A4 print-outs of giant arrows Sellotaped to the wall. Again.

I wrinkle my nose. Does he think I can't read or understand verbal instructions?

It must be a test, so I salute him, and say, 'Thank you very much, Dane.' Fake, with a tinge of sarcasm.

There are several print-outs that guide me to the second room on the right. Hardly the need for orienteering. They must know what Dane's like.

I push heavily to open the door.

It appears that I've walked into a classroom. There are others, sitting at almost all of the twenty individual tables and chairs facing a white screen.

They've chosen everyone who applied for the job, by the looks of it. I spot the woman who ran out in tears sitting near the front. She must be as desperate as I am.

I take one of the two remaining seats, next to a bloke with long hair in a ponytail at the base of his neck. He's wearing black-rimmed glasses, and a white shirt, open at the collar.

He smiles at me.

'Wasn't expecting so many people,' he says.

'Me too,' I say. 'I feel really special now.'

He laughs.

'I'm Jeff,' he says.

'I'm Laura,' I say. 'I've never met a Jeff as young as you before.'

'It's a family name,' he says.

'Oh.'

The door opens and the chatter in the room ceases. A man in his early forties, wearing a grey suit, black shirt and black tie walks in. He looks as though he's going to a funeral. I'm glad it isn't Tom. I wouldn't want him to see me doing whatever they have planned for us here. I can tell it's not going to be dignified. Even if they just ask me to stand and give my name, I'd cock it up.

'Morning, folks,' he hollers. 'I'm Brad, your Team Leader! Welcome to PeopleServe Northwest!'

I look around. Are we meant to clap?

He walks to the front, grabs a remote control and points it to a sound system.

'Eye of the Tiger' booms out of the speakers.

'Come on!' he shouts, pointing a fist to the ceiling. 'Out of those chairs! Let's get some energy into this room!'

A couple of the young ones immediately get up and start dancing.

I look at Jeff. He looks as horrified as I feel.

'I'm more of a Metallica man myself,' he says.

'You two,' bellows Brad over the music. 'Come on! Energy is what we sell! Energy!'

Jeff and I are the only ones sitting. I'm tempted to run out of the room, dragging Jeff in my wake. Jeff stands, shrugs, and starts head banging to the music.

Oh dear God. This is my worst nightmare.

I stand anyway. No one is paying attention to me, except Brad, who now has his hands on his hips, waiting for me to stand.

'Nice one, Laura,' he says, winking at me. He shakes his shoulders and wiggles his arms. 'Let me see you loosen up.'

Thank God he walks back to the front.

I sway a little and hope that this nightmare ends soon.

I'm sitting next to Suzanne (one of the top sellers) and I'm wearing headphones. I'm to listen to her calls in the hope of emulating her *winning style*.

'I've been top of the list for six weeks now,' she says, pointing to the whiteboard on the wall.

Her name has been written in red pen, while the mere craplings are in blue. Poor Billy (Suzanne pointed him out when I first got here) has been bottom for the past four weeks. He's sitting in the corner like he's been banished because of his poor performance. He keeps trying to catch people's eyes, a hopeful smile on his face. I keep trying to catch his, in the hope of giving him an encouraging wave, but I'm new; maybe in his eyes, I'm even lower on the table than he is. I wonder if they supply free counselling here. I think they might need to. Surely it's illegal to bully people in this manner.

Suzanne's make-up is immaculate, though I don't know why she's making such an effort. It's not as though she's facing the customers she's talking to. It's like being on the radio and dressing for the red carpet.

Her desk has three framed photographs on it. One of her mum and dad, I assume; one of her and her boyfriend, Jack. ('He works for a car dealership, but he's not your average salesman wanker.' No irony in her tone whatsoever); the third is a picture of a cat.

She claps her hands (which makes me jump) and rubs them.

'It's show time,' she says, adjusting her headphones. 'Make notes, if you like.'

She wiggles her fingers as the call connects. She appears to actually like this job.

'*Hello?*'

It sounds like an elderly gentleman on the other end.

'Good morning!' Suzanne says excitedly. 'May I speak to Albert Leonard, please.'

It's as though she's about to tell him he's won the lottery.

'*Speaking.*'

I've a feeling poor Albert doesn't know what's about to hit him.

'I have a great offer for you this morning,' says Suzanne. 'I can guarantee you can save one hundred pounds each year on your gas and electric.'

'*I have my son here at the moment, can I call you back?*'

'This will only take a few minutes, and it would be such a shame for you to miss out. We'll send you a free pen, if you sign up today.'

'*I've enough pens,*' he says. '*It's someone trying to sell me something.*'

'*Who's this?*' It's another man. '*Will you people stop ringing my father. You're all a bunch of con artists.*'

'Not at all,' she says, still as chirpy as when she

started the call. 'I'm here to help your father ... to save him money. Surely you can—'

He hangs up the telephone.

Suzanne glances at me.

'We're not allowed to end the conversation. We have to wait for them to do it.' She shrugs. 'Next!'

The same script goes on for ten minutes, until some poor soul takes up Suzanne's offer, complete with a free mug (the pens weren't clinching the deal).

'Do you get paid commission on what you sell?' I ask, when she stops for breath.

'Nah,' says Suzanne. 'Though we do get bonuses every six months if we exceed our target.'

'Ah, right.'

She stares at me as she takes off her headset.

'You're brand new to sales then?'

'Brand new to pretty much anything in an office,' I say.

'Really?' she says. 'How old are you?'

'Twenty-nine. I'm thirty in a few weeks.'

'Oh, I thought you were older than that. Been at home with the kids, then?'

'No,' I say. How very judgemental of her. 'I was a carer for my father.'

'You're not married?'

'No.'

'Boyfriend?'

'No.'

Why are people so obsessed with relationships?

She spins her chair to the side and stands.

'Don't blame you. Men can be bloody hard work, if you ask me.' She grabs her bag. 'Come on. Early lunch. Feel like I've run a bloody marathon.'

'But it's only eleven thirty.'

She glances at the clock.

'We can go any time between now and two. Can't have the whole floor going to lunch at the same time, can we? No. Not when we're meant to sell, sell, sell!'

I look around to see if we're being filmed.

She swipes her mobile from the desk and walks away faster than anyone I've seen in three-inch heels. She stops and rests a hand on her hip.

'Come on, Laura,' she says. 'Time is money.'

I expect everyone around us to laugh at the ridiculous things she's saying, but they don't look up from their monitors.

I think I will only last a week here.

'Here's a tip,' says Suzanne, using tongs to load lettuce onto her plate. 'Don't go for the meat pie. I heard that the butcher who sells the meat to the company that makes the pie was arrested for putting human flesh in with the minced beef.'

'What?' I glance at the tray of pie under the hot spotlights. 'That can't be true.'

She grabs a boiled egg with the same pair of tongs. She shrugs one shoulder.

'Life's stranger than fiction sometimes.'

I grab a pre-made salad sandwich in the hope it's the

safest option, but even that might have creepy crawlies in it. I'm going to bring my own lunch tomorrow.

I follow her to the table by the window and sit opposite. The canteen is huge, with hundreds of plastic tables and chairs, but it's three-quarters full already.

She takes a sip from her black coffee, pushing the salad to the side.

'Don't take this the wrong way,' she says, 'but aren't you a little old to be starting a career like this?'

'You're around the same age as me, aren't you?'

She flinches slightly.

'I'm twenty-seven.'

'Yeah ... so not that much younger.'

Why are some people so competitive about age?

It's the total opposite to the way my dad and his friends used to trump each other with how crap their lives were.

'I've no money for gas this week,' one would say. 'Had to get the telly repaired.'

'At least you have a telly,' said another.

Always a race to the bottom.

'I've been here for five years,' says Suzanne, wrinkling her nose. 'I've seen loads of people come and go. It's not ideal, I know, but they've inflated my job title and they pay me pretty well, considering I'm qualified for nothing except talking.' She laughs. 'But I've almost got a deposit for a flat. I can't leave here until I have a mortgage secured.' She flaps a hand as though swatting a fly. 'Anyway, enough boring talk. How long were you caring for your dad?'

'Officially, since I was sixteen, but my mum left when I was eleven.'

She places her coffee on the table.

'You were a carer from the age of eleven?'

I open the top slice of my sandwich, checking for caterpillars or centipedes. All clear on that front, but the lettuce has specks of dirt on it. I push the plate away.

There's a man five tables along, taking a sandwich from a Tupperware container. His eyes are fixed on mine, a strange smile on his face. He's wearing glasses, and a denim jacket, even though it's boiling in here.

'It's not as unusual as you think,' I say, turning my attention back to Suzanne, my face burning. 'There are a lot of kids who do the cleaning, cooking, dressing if their parents can't. It wasn't so bad. It was mainly cleaning and cooking in the beginning.'

It was also feeding – even in those early years, Dad's hands would shake with a knife and fork, but I don't want to tell Suzanne that. His shaking hands and occasional memory loss were what made the university suggest he take early retirement, but he was still quite mobile, then.

'That must have been hard,' says Suzanne, 'what with going to school.'

She's more perceptive than I had anticipated, but then, I shouldn't have judged her so rashly.

'I didn't go to school. I was taught at home.'

I can still feel that man's eyes on me. I wish I'd faced the wall.

'Jesus.' She picks up her mug and swirls the contents. 'That must've been a nightmare. I'd have gone bonkers.'

'It wasn't so bad,' I say.

'So you didn't mix with kids your own age at all?' she says.

'Mum made me join a few clubs to get me out of the house.'

'Just as well,' Suzanne says, getting up.

Suzanne's actually not *that* perceptive, given that I just told her that Mum left when I was eleven. It's easier to lie when people don't make connections inside the web I weave.

I didn't mix with people my own age after primary school. In some ways I became scared of fellow teenagers. They seemed so loud, so anarchic. Every time I went to the shop at the top of the road, I worried there'd be a gang of them outside. 'All right, babe,' one said once. 'Not seen you around here before.' People I remembered from school became unrecognisable and I forgot who they were. It seemed it was mutual.

I imagined they were that way because they were all high on drugs, or off their faces with alcohol, but they probably weren't. It was what Dad had told me and I was very suggestible.

'Who's that man there?' I ask as Suzanne and I stand. 'Don't make it obvious that you're looking.'

She flicks her hair and has a quick glance. She's done that before.

'Ugh,' she says, rolling her eyes. 'It's Rob Roscoe.

133

He's not as cool as his name sounds, believe me.'

I grab my tray and place my uneaten sandwich on the trolley under Suzanne's.

'He's one of the tech guys,' she continues. 'They rotate them – God knows why. We're probably a bit much for them. We've got Justin at the moment, though you probably won't notice when they change. I can only tell them apart because Justin has a beard ... confused me when he shaved it off one week.' Her eyes widen and she puts her head close to mine. 'They listen to everything we say,' she whispers. 'They know everything about us.'

My hand goes to my mouth.

'Really?'

'Nah,' she says, laughing. 'Though they might do.' She shrugs. 'Who knows?'

She takes hold of the top of my arm.

'Look,' she says, looking across to the entrance of the canteen. 'Fittest bloke on the fifth floor. Unfortunately, he's one of the managers – though I suppose that's what makes him more appealing. He wouldn't be as attractive if he were one of us minions. I love a man with ambition.'

I follow her gaze.

It's Tom Delaney. I should've known it would be.

I shuffle left, so I'm hidden by the tray rack. Suzanne doesn't notice; she's smoothing back her ponytail.

I look through the gaps to see him grabbing a tray. He slides it along the counter. He looks quite handsome in profile. His hair is chocolate brown, shiny. His skin is clean shaven, smooth. I couldn't look at him properly in the café. He looks so much better than he did at school, and he was beautiful, then.

I found his Facebook profile when I was bored at the weekend. It looks as though he was married to someone called Nicole but there haven't been any pictures of them together since before Christmas. The last time she 'liked' one of his photos was October last year. She wasn't on his friends list – it must have ended badly.

No, no. I can't get another one of my crushes.

The last one I had was just under a year ago. He worked in the corner shop at the top of the road. His name was Jakob Jankowski and he came to England from Poland in 2008. He was lovely and would ask about my dad, and we would talk about British Eighties sitcoms because he loved them, too. I started going in every day and I thought about him all the time. Then my dad asked me why I went to that shop so much and what this Jakob was like, and I realised I knew very little about him and what I didn't know, I made up. The Jakob I liked didn't even exist.

I never went in that shop again. If Dad had noticed that I liked him, Jakob must have guessed, too, and I felt so humiliated. Eric told me that a few months later, his girlfriend disappeared and Jakob was under suspicion of *doing away with her*. It was probably just gossip and rumour based on lies, but I like to think I had a lucky escape.

'I know him,' I say, still staring at Tom Delaney in the canteen as he waits in line to pay.

135

Suzanne looks at me. I flush as I'm caught in the act of spying on him.

'You know Tom? I thought you'd never been anywhere before.'

'We went to the same primary school.'

'Ah, I see. Small world, eh? Have you spoken to him today?'

'This is the first time I've seen him here.'

He's going to notice us staring at him if we don't move along soon. Suzanne is as subtle as an elephant in a kitchen.

'That makes sense,' she says, smoothing her hair. 'I've never seen him mingling much with the sales team. He's been here for three years, yet he's only looked at me a few times. Was he like that at school?'

'He was a nice boy, as far as I remember,' I say. 'Why don't you talk to him?'

She places her hand on her chest and pulls an expression of mock horror.

'I pride myself on not mixing business with pleasure.' She looks back at him. 'And of course, there's my boyfriend Jack. We've been seeing each other for three months now, although to be honest, I'm not sure we have that much in common.' She leans her head towards mine. 'I'd break my own rule about pleasure and business for Tom. Whenever I've tried to talk to him in the past, my mind's gone completely blank. It's ridiculous. I can usually talk to anyone about anything.' She shakes her head at herself. 'And I'm a feminist.' She shrugs and takes me by the hand. 'Come to the lav with me,' she says. 'I need to reapply my lippie.'

It seems I didn't have to attend high school at all. I'm living it right now.

I am home at last after what feels like the longest day in the world. I've taken my dinner (treated myself to fish, chips, and a pot of gravy) to bed and am already in my pyjamas. I'm not really concentrating on my portable television. I've had too much human interaction for one day. I feel like I need to hibernate for a fortnight to get over it.

I listened to about three hundred telephone calls to people who didn't want to be spoken to, and I regretted not eating the dirty sandwich at lunch. I spent the rest of the day absolutely starving.

There was a man in the corner who kept staring at me. I can't remember his name, but Suzanne said he was the other IT guy. Justin or James or something. He wasn't the one from the canteen as he had a beard.

He was lingering outside the ladies' when I came out. He was the only one wearing jeans. And he wore a fleece, which was quite sensible as the air-conditioning made it feel like minus one.

'Hey, there,' he said, offering his hand for me to shake, the other one swept his too-long fringe out of his eyes. 'Welcome to PeopleServe.'

'Er, thank you,' I said.

'Anything you need, just come to me. I can help with all your technological needs.'

'OK,' I said. 'I haven't got any technological problems at the moment, but I'll be sure to keep you updated.' I don't think he realised I was being sarcastic. Just as well, as I felt a bit mean about it afterwards. 'I'd best get back.'

I felt his eyes on me as I walked back to my desk.

'What did he want?' said Suzanne, sipping a herbal tea.

'He was just being nice,' I said.

'Be careful,' she said. 'There's something a bit weird about him and that Rob. I can't put my finger on it. I bet they have our photographs plastered to the wall of their poky little office and they're going to kill us off one by one.'

'Is their office poky?' I said, looking around the massive room we were in.

I imagined them taking it in turns to sit in a broom cupboard. No wonder they wanted out of it.

She shrugged. 'No idea ... never been down there.'

When I looked over at him, he was sitting back at his desk, staring at his screen. Maybe he wasn't so bad.

I only manage to eat half of my fish supper. I place the plate on the floor near the bottom of the bed in case I wake in the night and stand in it. I should put it in the kitchen as it stinks, but my legs and arms are aching. Is it because I've been out and about all day, or is there something seriously wrong with me?

I flick off the bedside lamp, and my body sinks into the mattress.

I will dream of Dad tonight. I always dream about

him. I was scared of it at first because I thought it might be his ghost visiting me, but it's a comfort now.

'Night, night, Dad,' I say.

And close my eyes.

14

Sarah

Sarah and Kim wait in the car park outside the coroner's court for the inquest into the death of Laura Aspinall. They're sitting in Kim's 1998 Renault Clio that surprised them both when it started this morning. It's been just over three weeks since Laura Aspinall's remains were found in Flat Three of Nelson Heights. The reports in the media have been that the cause is unexplained, and police are not looking for anyone in connection with her death.

'I can't stand this heat,' says Sarah, rolling down the window. 'It was freezing a few weeks ago. It's the middle of March, but I bet when summer comes it'll piss it down all the bloody time.'

Kim glances at her, her eyebrows raised.

'Sorry,' says Sarah. 'I'm a bit nervous. I've never been to one of these before. I feel as though we shouldn't be here.'

'I know what you mean,' says Kim, 'but how else are you going to get the information about how she died?

They might not report it all on the news. You can see the faces of the people who knew her.'

'It just feels a bit voyeuristic.'

They've been waiting for thirty minutes and no one has gone inside. They arrived far too early.

Kim opens the driver's door slightly.

'It feels wrong that it's so sunny today, doesn't it?'

'Yeah.'

Sarah dreamt of her last night, even though she doesn't know what Laura looks like. She found no photos of her online – Laura didn't appear to have a Facebook, Instagram or Twitter account – under her real name, at least. It was like she never existed.

Sarah's dressed in dark grey trousers and a patterned blue shirt. She straightened her hair and applied make-up using tutorials from *YouTube*. It feels as though she's going for an interview, but she didn't want to come here dressed in her scruffs.

'I still can't believe it's a young woman,' says Kim. 'Do you think she ever ate at the café?'

'We won't know until we see a photo,' says Sarah. 'And even then, who knows? We can't remember every single person who comes in, can we?'

'Wouldn't it be strange if she did?' says Kim. 'That the woman you've been researching for nearly a month had come into the café. You might have even talked to her.'

A black cab turns into the car park and stops outside the court.

A woman gets out. Mid-fifties, slim, dressed in black

trousers, a black blazer, and sunglasses. Her hair is auburn and runs down her back in thick curls.

Wordlessly, Sarah and Kim get out of the car. The inquest is due to start in seven minutes.

The woman lifts her sunglasses, slipping them onto her head. She catches Sarah's eye.

'Are you Amanda?' she says, walking towards them. She's clutching a scrunched-up letter. 'I've been talking with her about all of this. I only arrived from Newcastle this morning.'

'No, no,' says Sarah as Kim fiddles with the lock on the car. 'I'm ...'

Sarah doesn't know what to say. She can't tell the truth — the woman might be offended that Sarah isn't here in a professional capacity; she can't admit she's here to gather more information on the woman that she's been dreaming and obsessing about.

'I'm researching Laura's case,' says Sarah.

'Oh,' says the woman, pressing a button on the inter-com. 'I wondered when I'd hear from somebody. You're the first person I've met from the local newspaper. No one else has contacted me. Did you manage to get to the pre-inquest interview? Were you invited?'

She doesn't correct the assumption that Sarah's a journalist.

'I think that's just for those involved.'

'Hello there,' Kim says breezily, walking towards them. 'Lovely day, isn't it?'

Sarah cringes inside. As usual, Kim has misread the situation.

142

The woman doesn't seem to notice.

A blonde woman in a navy blue skirt suit opens the door and the other with the sunglasses goes straight into the ladies' toilets after briefly clutching the other woman's hands.

'Hello,' she says. 'I'm Amanda. Can I ask your names, please?'

'Oh,' says Kim. 'I'm Kim Stratton and this is Sarah Hayes. We're doing some research about Laura Aspinall. I thought anyone could come to an inquest.'

She smiles. 'Well, yes, but we don't normally get many people who just turn up. It's a very sad case.' She glances in the direction of the lavatory door. 'That's Laura's mother, Maria Aspinall. It's been very difficult for her. If it's OK with you, I'll ask her if she doesn't mind you sitting in.'

Sarah glances at Kim.

'It's so quiet in here,' hisses Kim in a stage whisper. 'I thought it would be as noisy as a Crown Court.'

'Shall we leave?' says Sarah. 'I feel really bad for Laura's mother.'

'We're here now,' says Kim. 'But, yeah. This feels really weird. It makes it all seem so human, so real.'

'Maria says it's fine,' says Amanda, walking back over.

Her voice is so quiet, it's as though they're in a funeral home, not a court.

Amanda guides Maria – who seems fragile, vulnerable – up the stairs and through a brown door into the court room.

It's not what Sarah anticipated. It's a small room filled with chairs. A witness box is on the left of the room and there's an elevated platform at the front. It's even quieter in here; the ticking of the clock on the back wall seems so loud.

Maria sits at the front, behind a long table that has a jug of water, plastic cups and boxes of tissues on it.

'So what's going to happen, Maria,' says Amanda, 'is that the coroner will enter the room at ten, then I will ask everyone to rise. He will then give an opening statement – a sort of agenda about what he will discuss and then he'll deliver his verdict. Do you have any questions?'

'Will the policeman I spoke to be here? He was very good – kept me informed of everything.'

'Yes,' says Amanda. 'He'll be reading out his statement and answer any questions the coroner has. We also have statements from the pathologist and the detective on Laura's case.'

The door opens and the coroner enters. Everyone stands until they're told to be seated again.

Sarah leans forward and takes out her notepad and pen. She should at least look the part.

She looks around the room; there aren't many people here. There's only one other person who was introduced as being from the *Lancashire Chronicle*, notepad in hand, bored look on his face.

'This is the inquest into the passing of Laura Aspinall, who was born 25th March 1987, and formerly of Flat Three, Nelson Heights, in Preston.' He seems to be writing down everything he says. 'We are here to examine who, how, when and where the deceased died, but we don't investigate the why. I will read out statements from the pathologist and from the lead detective who dealt with Laura's case. Then, PC Steve Wilson will read out his statement in the witness box.' He looks at Maria. 'Then, if you wish, you can read your statement about Laura. Firstly, however, may I say that I'm so sorry for your loss.'

Maria nods, dabbing a tissue to her face.

'Thank you.'

This is far more personal than Sarah was expecting. It feels so intimate and Maria's grief feels so raw. Laura Aspinall no longer feels like a stranger, whose mysterious death is sensationally intriguing. It's about a mother who has lost a daughter.

'Laura Aspinall was found deceased at her place of residence on 12th February 2019. A digital autopsy was performed on Laura. I will read out only part of the pathologist's statement to avoid any unnecessary upset to Laura's mother. It concludes, *There was no indication of a definitive cause of death due to deterioration post-mortem but there was no evidence of injury to Laura's remains.* A date of death was given as approximately 26th March 2017.

'Now we come to the statement of Detective Sergeant Julie Samuels of Preston Police. *On the morning of Tuesday 12th February 2019 at approximately six fifteen, the body of Laura Aspinall was found in Flat Three, Nelson Heights, Preston. Laura was identified using dental records due to the deterioration of her remains. Apart from the forced entry of bailiffs who attended the scene, there were no other signs of intruder entry, nor were there any signs of a struggle at the property. Neighbours reported nothing suspicious but due to the length of time between death and the discovery of Laura, it has been difficult to garner any pieces of useful information. Laura Aspinall worked briefly at the call centre, PeopleServe, but was only there a short time and her colleagues thought she had simply left the job. No one claimed to have known her well. Laura Aspinall's mother, Maria Aspinall, last saw her daughter on 26th March 2017, and she believed her daughter to be travelling. Laura had packed a rucksack which contained her passport, tickets, clothing, and an itinerary – all of which remained at the property. It was common for Maria Aspinall and her daughter to have long periods of time between contact. The first Ms Aspinall knew something was wrong was when police contacted her on 14th February 2019. We found nothing suspicious at the scene, nor after questioning people who came into contact with Laura, which would have contributed to Miss Aspinall's death.'*

Maria Aspinall's hands are shaking as she brings the handkerchief to her face.

'I can't believe she died alone,' she whispers.

Outside the court, Maria Aspinall stands in the road, mobile phone to her ear. As soon as she ends her call, Sarah walks towards her.

'Do you want to go for a coffee, or something stronger?' says Sarah. 'That must have been terrible for you.'

Maria lifts her sunglasses to reveal puffy red eyes. The make-up she had on earlier has worn off.

'I need to lie down,' she says. 'Do you have a card or something? It would be nice to talk to someone about her. Perhaps you could get her story out there? She was so young – she had her whole life to live.'

'I can put my number in your phone,' says Sarah, holding out her hand.

'OK.'

Maria drops her phone into Sarah's hands.

'I still don't understand all of this,' says Maria. 'Laura sent me postcards when she was travelling.'

Sarah looks up quickly.

'Have you given them to the police?'

'I can't find them. I put them somewhere safe. I've been looking for them for weeks. The police probably think I'm making it up – perhaps they didn't understand why I hadn't reported her missing after not hearing her voice for so long.'

Sarah narrows her eyes as she looks at Maria. She can't judge a woman she barely knows, but the whole situation is odd. What kind of mother didn't realise her daughter – her only child – was missing for nearly two years? Maybe she *is* making up the postcards to make herself feel better.

'Did you know any of her friends?' says Sarah, feeling terrible for asking another question when Laura's mother is so upset, but she might not get a chance to speak to Maria again. 'Or anyone that she worked with?'

'No,' says Maria. 'She had come off social media – said

she was having trouble with someone on there. I had assumed it was a boyfriend, but I've no idea. I should've asked her more questions.' She puts her phone into her handbag. 'What a waste. I ... I should've known, shouldn't I?'

Sarah opens her mouth to speak, but a mini cab turns into the car park and Maria has turned her back to her.

'Which hotel are you staying at?' asks Sarah quickly.

'Premier Inn, in town.'

She reaches for the handle of the cab.

'Maria!' says Sarah.

The woman turns around.

'Before you go,' Sarah says quickly. 'Do you have a photograph of Laura?'

Maria frowns. She hesitates a moment before reaching into the bag and takes out a small photo album.

'I have several,' she says, flipping through the sticky plastic pages. 'This is the last one I took of her. We didn't take many pictures of each other, that was always Robin's thing.'

Maria folds back the cover and passes the album to Sarah.

The photo is of a young woman, sitting at a table in a restaurant. Her hair is dark, like her mother's. It rests on the top of her arms; one side is pinned back with a flower tucked behind her ear. Her skin is pale, but she has rosy cheeks, and eyes that are dark brown – almost black.

'She was very pretty, wasn't she?' says Sarah.

'I suppose,' says Maria. 'We didn't really mention it.

She wasn't into buying clothes or getting her hair done. Probably 'cos I wasn't.'

Sarah wants to ask if she can capture the image on her phone. Would that be a strange request?

'I'll just take a pic,' says Kim, who's looking over Sarah's shoulder.

The click of her camera app sounds. Sarah wants to jump into the nearest drain.

Maria takes back the album and snaps it shut, dropping it into her bag. She inhales loudly.

'I suppose it wouldn't be a bad thing if you shared it online – with the right words, of course. It would be nice to have her picture out there.' She gets a tissue from her bag and catches the tears that fall. 'Especially after being forgotten for so long.'

The taxi driver beeps his horn.

'OK, OK!' says Maria. She reaches for the handle. 'I'll be in touch.'

Sarah watches as the car turns out of the car park. She has a feeling she might never see Maria Aspinall again.

Kim is staring at Laura's photograph on her mobile.

'I'm sure I've seen her before,' she says. 'I think I've spoken to her.'

'What about?' says Sarah, flicking through her notepad.

'I can't remember. It'll come to me.'

'PeopleServe,' says Sarah. 'The call centre that Laura worked at just before she died.'

'What about it?' says Kim. 'It's not far from here, is it?'

'Probably, but it's not that.'

PeopleServe. Why is the name familiar to her? Someone mentioned it not so long ago.

'Do you know someone who works there?' says Kim. 'Loads of people have — it's so easy to get a job there. My brother's friend was in telesales straight after he left school, and there's that girl from ...'

Sarah's thoughts drown out Kim's words.

It's Rob. Rob worked there. Two years ago.

15

Laura

It's Thursday and I've lasted three days longer than I thought I would. It seems I have a new friend in the shape of Suzanne, though she's not the type of person I thought I'd be friends with – the polar opposite of myself.

As the most (probably self-appointed) senior of the sales team, she asked the team leader if I could sit next to her permanently as I *have so much potential*. This is a lie. She said, 'I'd much rather you sit next to me than that twat Billy who thinks he's being filmed in a fly-on-the-wall documentary.'

I have learned that this company exists in its own little micro-bubble of society: one can say what one likes and it either goes over people's heads, or they laugh in fear of ridicule of not understanding something. Seems it doesn't matter what I say, so I've tried not to be so anxious about it on the bus journey to work.

It was a quick lesson – there are so many people

working here that I conclude I have seen everything. Treena (the crying woman) has broken down in tears three times. I'm surprised she keeps turning up. Gerard, who has been here fourteen months (time spent here seems to be a badge of honour as survival of the fittest), came back from lunch drunk on Tuesday and fell asleep on the toilet. He wasn't even reprimanded. His manager took a photo of him with his trousers around his ankles and put it on the noticeboard. I suspect that was punishment enough. As his genitals couldn't be seen in the picture, I think they avoided any sexual harassment issues. Had it been me instead of Gerard, however, I'd have been straight down to Citizens' Advice, and I'd never come here again.

But Gerard seems to love his new celebrity status.

It's all very odd.

If they don't care what they say and do, then why should I?

I have my (nearly the) end of week review with my team leader in a few minutes and I feel more nauseous than I did making my first call. His name is Ken, and he's not what you'd expect. He doesn't look like a Ken.

'Laura Aspinall?' he shouts from his office door.

He loves that he has an office, apparently. He's new to the role of team leader and has been abusing his position by *putting it about a bit* (Suzanne's words, not mine).

He keeps asking himself questions and answering them and I wish I hadn't noticed.

'Sit, sit,' he says, making his way to his chair. 'You've

settled in well then, Laura? Yes? I'm glad to hear it.'

I do as I'm told and sit, checking the seat is dry of other people's sweat. Treena was sitting here only a few moments ago.

'Unfortunately, I don't think Treena's going to make it,' he says, rather unprofessionally, while hammering his keyboard with two fingers. He might be one of those people who speak aloud what they're typing. I'm not sure he's bright enough to say one thing and type another. He presses enter with a flourish. 'I should've realised after they told me she cried during her interview. It takes a thick skin to get through this process.'

You'd have thought we were applying to be in the SAS the way he was talking. If there *was* such an application process. I've heard Ken's in the TA. Maybe this is as close to the front line as he's ever going to get.

'So, Laura, Laura,' he says as though imprinting my name to his memory. He searches for my file. 'How do *you* think you've done?'

Oh, it's one of *those* questions. I wait for him to answer himself.

He doesn't.

Fake it till you make it.

'I've managed to make a few sales,' I say, a little too quietly. 'I think I'm learning quickly.'

'Hmm.' He rubs his chin. He looks like someone who needs their face shaving twice a day. My dad was like that. 'You're by no means the worst, but we have a few other newbies who are exceeding expectations.'

I wasn't expecting such subtlety from him. What he's

trying to say is that I am average. Something I already knew.

When I was at school, my mum used to say that my teachers might have confused my quietness with stupidity. But my dad said, 'It's better to be a presumed idiot than a proven one.' It was his take on the proverb: *Even a fool is considered wise if he keeps silent*.

'Newbies?' I say.

'You've not heard that term before, then?' he says. 'Not much of a gamer, are you? No, I bet you're not.'

I try to stop my expression revealing my exasperation. Of course I've heard of the term *newbie* (which I'm sure is abbreviated even shorter to *newb* these days), but I was questioning his use of it in a professional environment.

I reason, at this point, that it's preferable to appear ignorant rather than petulant, so I say, 'No, I'm not familiar with the term.'

There's a tap on the window.

Tom Delaney opens the door to Ken's office and my heart gives a little flutter, though I wish it hadn't.

'Hey, Laura,' he says.

I blush.

Ken clears his throat, but Tom ignores it because Tom is Shift Manager, which trumps Ken by one. Things like that matter here at PeopleServe Northwest.

Tom glances at Ken, then at me.

'Are you going to Sally's leaving do tonight?'

'Naturally,' says Ken, even though Tom was looking

154

at me. 'Always good to show the newbies how we party here.'

'Hmm,' says Tom, wincing a little. 'Not sure if the term *newbies* is appropriate in a professional setting, are you?'

Ken shuffles in his chair.

'No,' says Tom, glancing at me. 'Didn't think so.'

Ken is silent until Tom has closed the door and disappeared from view – this office is made of glass walls.

'How do you know Tom?' he says.

'I can't really remember ...'

It seems silly to tell him I know Tom from primary school, but I should've just said it.

He tilts his head to the side.

'How odd,' he says. 'Tom mentioned that you two go way back. He speaks very highly of you.'

He's staring at me, but it seems as though his mind has veered somewhere else. He shakes his head as if bringing himself back into the present.

'Anyhow,' he says. 'I'm pleased to offer you a probationary period of one month.' He stands, pushing back his chair. 'How does that sound? Good, hey?'

I stand, too.

'That sounds excellent,' I say, hoping it hasn't come out as sarcastically as I intended.

He gestures to the door, and I take that as my exit cue.

A probationary period of one month.

If I last a whole month, I will deserve a medal.

If I'm fired before end of said month, I will probably kill myself.

'I *knew* you wouldn't've brought in a change of clothes,' says Suzanne, who has the ability to talk like a ventriloquist as she applies lipstick in the mirror of the ladies'. 'Which is why I brought a spare outfit.' She turns to face me, narrowing her eyes. 'And I'll do your make-up for you.' She unzips her vast cosmetics bag. 'Have you ever worn foundation?'

'No,' I say.

I was going to sit on the sink unit while I watch her do her make-up as I've seen people on the telly do that in the loos, but it just isn't me. I'm leaning against it instead.

'Do you really think it's necessary?' I say as she applies eyeliner with what looks like a felt tip. 'We're with these people all day – they know what I look like.'

She puts a hand on her hip.

'Well, yeah. Of course they do. But it's a night out.'

She rolls her eyes – I like to think it's in a good-natured way. She reaches into her tote bag and pulls out a belted black shirt dress.

'You're a twelve, right?' she says. 'This should fit you.'

It's not as bad as I expected. When I put it on in the cubical, I'm pleased it's not too tight.

Suzanne said there's a leaving do at least once a fortnight. Sally's the lucky escapee tonight. Whoever she is.

I guard the table while Suzanne gets the drinks because we are going to do rounds. I think it's actually because she wants to stand next to Tom at the bar, even though she already has a boyfriend. She's doing lots of hair flicking, but he has his back to her. I can see him in the mirror behind the optics.

He leaves the bar, carrying only one drink. His eyes are locked on mine as he walks towards me. He pulls out the small stool and sits.

'I've been trying to talk to you properly since you started,' he says. Or rather he shouts. For a pub so out of town, it has extremely loud music. 'How are you enjoying it so far?'

I must have pulled a face because he says, 'I guess *enjoying* is stretching it a bit.'

'I think I'm getting the hang of it,' I say.

Oh God, why do I come out with such boring rubbish?

He looks to the side, as though seeking someone out. He looks even better in the darkness (though, doesn't everyone?). The blue lights are reflecting in his eyes and I have to tear my gaze away in case he catches me staring at them.

Behind him, Suzanne has noticed that he's sitting at our table. Her eyes are wide; she's shaking her head about and I can't tell if she's pleased or annoyed. She still hasn't been served.

Tom's staring at me now; he's examining my face. It would be unnerving if it were someone else. 'How long has it been now?' he says. 'Must be nearly twenty

157

years.' He takes a sip of his drink. 'But I'd know you anywhere – you've hardly changed.'

'I've grown a few inches,' I say.

He raises his eyebrows. I hope he didn't take that the wrong way.

'I didn't know you still lived in Preston,' he says, his eyes glistening, his gaze unwavering. 'I thought you'd moved, then your friends explained that you were being home-schooled. Everyone was really jealous at first ... then I heard about your dad.'

'It was a build-up of things, really,' I say. 'I didn't have a good time at school.'

'Really?' He raises his eyebrows. 'I thought you were one of the popular ones.'

'People can be unkind,' I say.

I remember the note that was placed on my desk during the last year I was there. It had been snowing because my hands were freezing as I opened it.

'Who's it from?' said the girl from the other table: Tanya Greening. She wasn't a very nice person. Her mum was the head teacher and Tanya seemed to think *she* ruled the school, too. 'I think I saw Tom put it there before playtime.'

'Really?' I said, forgetting for a moment how much Tanya hated me.

I'd had a crush on Tom since we were in Year Four, which is pretty strange when you think we were only eight or nine.

I tore open the envelope. It had a simple red love

heart on the front and I nearly cried with happiness. Until I read the inside:

Dear Laura,
Your mum is a slag.
x

'Aren't you going to read it out?' said Tanya with a smirk on her face.

I recognised her stupid swirly handwriting – she hadn't tried to disguise it. I shoved the letter into my bag and threw it in the kitchen bin when I got home.

It's silly that I remember that from so long ago. We were all just children.

I shift in my seat opposite Tom, trying to think of a way to change the subject from school but I can't. I'll come up with loads of things when I get home.

'Hey,' he says, briefly touching my hand. 'Do you fancy going for a drink tomorrow night – sort of a catch up?'

'I ...' His eyes are so kind and his face is so familiar, I feel like I've always known him. 'Yes,' I say. 'I'd like that.'

'Great!' he says, standing. 'I'll text you tomorrow. See you later, Laura.'

Suzanne arrives at the table, clutching two giant glasses of white wine.

'Hey, Tom!' she says, beaming. 'Aren't you staying?'

'Better catch up with Ken,' he says. 'He's dying to tell me what mission he's going on this weekend.'

159

'That's a shame.' Suzanne's lips are ridiculously pouty. Maybe someone told her it was cute. 'Next time perhaps.'

He smiles, then wanders over to Ken, who's firing an invisible machine gun.

'What was he talking to you about?' she says.

'Just school stuff.'

She sighs and rests her chin on the heel of her hand.

'Imagine going to school with Tom,' she says. 'Wonder what he looked like as a little kid? Really cute, I bet.'

I stare at her, in her own little daydream. Why is she wasting so much thought on a bloke who mostly ignores her?

'You should come over to mine on Saturday,' she says. 'We can get some wine and a takeaway. You could stop over, if you like. Save you travelling home in the dark.'

I take a sip of the wine. It's quite tangy – not like the dry, sour red wine my dad used to order occasionally. It doesn't take much for it to go to my head, and I feel warm inside. I take another and lean back against the leather chair.

A Saturday night at someone else's house. Why would Suzanne be asking me to sleep over when we've only known each other for a week? I could be a murderer for all she knows. And she's probably got loads of friends that she could ask.

Perhaps she's as lonely as I am.

16

Sarah

Sarah was amazed and disappointed that there weren't more people at Laura's inquest. She shouldn't have been surprised, considering the length of time the woman's death went unnoticed.

The reporter with the notebook was scribbling all the way through it. Sarah had been looking out for the article, which had been posted online the day after. She clicks onto it and reads parts of it again.

… In a statement read out in court, Maria Aspinall described her daughter as caring, loyal and independent. 'From a young age, Laura helped care for her father, Robin Hartley, who was diagnosed with MS in 1997. She wanted to go travelling – in fact I thought that's where she was. The news of Laura's death has had a devastating effect on me. Time is so precious, and I have a lot of regrets. You should never take your loved ones for granted.'

Laura Aspinall attended St Xavier's Primary School

in Preston. A memorial page has been set up by former pupils.

'Such a sweet girl,' said one former pupil. 'It's so sad that she died alone.'

There are no listings of her at any of the senior schools in the region, which was confirmed by her mother. 'She was home-schooled by her father. He died in 2016, which I now know is only months before my Laura.' Maria Aspinall also added, 'Perhaps that, in the end, is why she died alone. She had no friends of her own age. I will carry the guilt with me forever.'

Laura Aspinall's funeral will be held 25th March on what would have been her thirty-second birthday. The family requests no flowers, but donations to Samaritans.

There are several things that stand out. Why would her mother think Laura had been travelling for two years without contacting her? If Maria *had* received postcards that she can't locate, Laura couldn't have written them. Wouldn't Maria have realised the handwriting was different?

And why request donations to the Samaritans? It hints that what happened to Laura might have been self-inflicted. A strange assumption to make with no evidence and no mention of it by the coroner. Had Laura a history of self-harm that wasn't documented? And how well could Laura's mother have known her if they had such limited contact – was not seeing her daughter for two years normal?

Maria Aspinall must have spoken to the newspaper after the inquest. The statement that was read out on her behalf at court didn't mention Laura being home-schooled or having no friends (though the latter Sarah had already assumed).

Now that the article has appeared in the press, Maria might think Sarah no longer wants to talk to her. She mentioned that she was staying at the Premier Inn. There is only one in the town centre.

Sarah brings up the hotel's website, writes down the telephone number, and dials.

'Would it be possible to leave a message for one of your guests? A Maria Aspinall?'

'I can't give out information on whether an individual is staying here,' says the receptionist, 'but I can take your details. Who's speaking, please?'

'Sarah Hayes, journalist,' says Sarah.

It's the only way Maria might remember her.

'And what is the message?'

Sarah hesitates. What can she say to make Maria call her?

'Can you tell her that I have information about her daughter?'

Sarah's stomach flutters. She's told so many untruths recently that they seem to just flow out of her mouth.

After giving her mobile number, Sarah hangs up. She clicks onto the school Facebook page that was mentioned in the newspaper report.

A link to the newspaper article has been posted and

underneath there are thirty-four comments (twenty-seven sad faces and two surprised faces).

Joanne Bett Is this the girl that left during the last year? She didn't come to St John's High – I thought she went to the grammar school??

Charlie Marsden I have no idea who this Laura is. Are you sure they've mentioned the right school?

Damian Lynn I think I remember her. She had a bad time of it, IIRC. Bullied? I heard that she was sent to an institution? Could be all BS though – 11 yos aren't the most reliable of sources LOL!

Joanne Bett Didn't she bring a knife into school? Threatened to kill herself or something?? Can't remember the details.

Damian Lynn I can't remember anything like that – but I didn't pay much attention most of the time. Didn't all the girls give her a hard time over something? Sure there was a fight.

Joanne Bett There was no fight! And there must've been a good reason if we all fell out with her.

Damian Lynn Can't of been that good a reason if you can't remember what it was.

Joanne Bett *have

Damian Lynn Lol. Thanks, Miss.

Justin Parkinson How disrespectful!! This woman is dead and you're saying you've never heard of her and spreading nasty rumours and 'LOL'ing. Shame on you!

Sally Chadwick Chill out, Justin! Actually, I've no idea who YOU are – did you even go to St Xavier's? RIP Laura. It's so very sad. Two years! Can you imagine?

Damian Lynn I wasn't being disrespectful, **Justin Parkinson**. Yes, **Sally Chadwick** it's terrible. Can't imagine what her mum is going through.

Charlie Marsden Fuck off **Justin Parkinson**

This is why Sarah avoids Facebook pages and groups. It doesn't take much for a thread to get out of hand and for people to throw insults at each other. Even when the post is in remembrance of a former pupil.

Laura must've had one or two friends, at least. If she had, none of them have posted on the school's page. She might not have had contact with them after she left.

It must have been hard for Laura – caring for her father without the relief of school to go to. And her mother leaving them both when they needed her most. There has to be more to this.

Sarah jumps as the letterbox flaps open and shut. It can't be the postman; he's already been.

She walks into the hall and picks up a brown envelope.

Sarah Joanne Hayes, mother of Alex.

How odd. If it were from the school, it would read *Parent or Guardian.*

The seal hasn't been stuck down. She slides out a white piece of paper. Only two words are printed:

Case closed.

What the hell is that supposed to mean? Is it something to do with Alex? Has someone reported Sarah to Social Services without her knowledge? Or is it something more sinister: the case of Laura Aspinall?

Her hands are shaking, but it's hardly a threatening letter. Perhaps the words were chosen carefully so it doesn't acknowledge anything about Laura.

It could mean anything. She should have looked out of the front door when she saw it lying on the mat.

She goes to the kitchen and wraps the letter and its envelope in cling film. Jesus, she's been watching too much *Silent Witness*. It's probably just some mix-up. She'll give Andy a call and see what he makes of it.

Back at her desk, she selects his number.

No reply. He must be working.

Sarah checks again to see if Maria Aspinall has left a message. Still no reply. But then, it was only ten minutes ago.

She needs to take her mind off the note.

Kim texted the photograph of Laura earlier. Sarah emails herself the photograph, transferring it to her laptop. She clicks on the file and Laura's face covers most of the screen. She does look familiar, but Sarah wouldn't have known her from living here at Nelson Heights. She's worked at the café for five years, though. It's close enough to the flats for Laura to have been a customer.

It's so unsettling to imagine what this vibrant young

woman – years younger than Sarah – would've looked like when she was found.

'What happened to you, Laura?'

There's no evidence of foul play, but there are suggestions of mental health issues. This is just speculation. Without talking to her mother or having access to Laura's medical records, conjecture is all Sarah has to work on. She needs to talk to people who actually knew Laura in the days and months before her death. Just because there's no evidence of foul play due to the time lapsed, it doesn't mean something untoward didn't happen to Laura.

Sarah opens the file with the announcement she drafted yesterday, and places Laura's picture underneath. If people don't remember her by name, they might remember her face.

DID YOU KNOW LAURA ASPINALL?
Born 25 March 1987, she went to
St Xavier's Primary School, Preston.
She lived at Nelson Heights,
also in Preston.
If you have any information, please contact Sarah on
07795182414 or SarahHayes@prestonmail.com

Sarah posts it on some of the many Preston Facebook pages and groups, and onto Twitter. She sends it to the local newspapers and the *Daily Telegraph*, which costs a small fortune.

The front door opens. Her heart pounds. She looks at the time on the bottom right of her screen. 11.42.

Has Alex been sent home from school?

'Hello?' she says.

There's no reply, just a heavy sigh and footsteps to the kitchen.

Sarah grabs her mobile and tiptoes to the hallway, looking right towards the kitchen.

It's Rob, downing a glass of water.

Sarah exhales, realising she'd been holding her breath.

'Jesus, Rob. What are you doing sneaking about? Didn't you hear me shout hello?'

He puts the glass down and wipes his mouth with the back of his hand.

'Sorry, no,' he says, walking towards her. 'I thought you'd be at the library or something.'

'So why are you here if you thought I wasn't in?'

She hadn't seen him for a few days, since before the inquest – he's been staying at his own place. There are shadows under his eyes, stubble on his face.

'Thought I might cook for us all,' he says.

Sarah looks behind him into the kitchen. He didn't bring any food.

'Have you been to work today?' she says.

'I phoned in sick. Haven't been feeling great.'

He walks past Sarah, into the living room, and flops onto the settee.

'Then why did you get out of bed? You should've stayed at home.'

He grabs the remote control and switches on the television, lowering the volume to zero. Rob always likes the television being on. He says it's company for him when he's on his own – a legacy of growing up in a household where the telly was always on.

'I didn't want to be alone when I'm poorly,' he says.

She stands at his feet. 'Did you see anyone on the stairs on your way here? I had a note posted through the door.'

'What kind of note?'

'It was addressed to me by my full name ... it said *mother of Alex*. Then all it said inside was: *Case closed.*'

'Let's have a look.'

She fetches it from the kitchen and places it on the arm of the chair.

'And it came sealed in cling film?' he says. 'How bloody weird.'

'No. I put it in that. In case there are fingerprints.'

'In case there are ...' He raises his eyebrows. 'Why would you do that?'

'In case someone's threatening me. Whoever it is, is hardly going to say they're going to murder me, are they? The police will look into it and wonder why.'

He shakes his head.

'Why would someone threaten you?'

'Because I'm looking into the Laura Aspinall case.'

'Sarah, love. The police have already looked into the case. They obviously think there's nothing suspicious about it.'

'It's not just the letter, though. I've been seeing a man loitering – dressed in black. And that strange woman was hanging around on the day the body was found.

Do you think these people know something about Laura Aspinall?'

He takes out a handkerchief – the only man under forty she's known to carry one – and dabs his forehead.

'I've no idea.'

'I'll ring Andy about it later,' she says, snatching the letter and returning it to the kitchen.

Just because Rob's feeling like shit, it doesn't mean she should, too.

'I've got a picture of Laura,' says Sarah, back in the living room. 'Do you want to see it?'

He stands and walks towards the window, pulling apart the blinds and looking outside.

'I heard a noise then,' he says. 'I think your mystery man might be outside.'

Sarah stands and joins him, looking outside. There is no one in the car park, and they can't see the balcony above or below from here.

'Are you taking the piss?' she says. 'It's not funny.'

He lets the blinds drop, inches from Sarah's nose.

'Sorry,' he says. 'I just wanted to lighten the mood. I came here to be cheered up.'

'You what?' Sarah sighs. Sometimes she'd rather be alone. 'And why did you say mystery man? It could be a woman who posted the note.'

She looks up at him. There's a sheen of sweat on his brow.

'Why don't you go and lie down?' she says. 'You look awful.'

He walks back to the settee and sits. 'I'm fine.'

Sarah grabs her phone off the desk, opening up the photo app. She hands the phone to Rob.

'This is Laura.'

He takes his glasses from his top pocket and puts them on, holding the phone closer to his face. He purses his lips and gives the phone back.

'Yeah, I think I knew her,' he says. 'Well, *know* is a strong word. I think she worked at PeopleServe Northwest when I was there.

'So you didn't recognise her name – just her face? I've been talking about her for weeks, Rob. And after the inquest, I told you she'd worked at PeopleServe.'

Sarah feels the skin on her arms prickle. He doesn't look at her.

'It's no big deal,' he says. 'I can't remember all the names of the people who worked there – it was massive. And to be honest, Sarah, you've been acting really weird about the whole thing. You didn't even know this woman.'

'Can you remember who her friends were? Who did she sit next to?'

He groans and pats his forehead again.

'I didn't work there for long. The place was full of idiots.' He takes the phone back for another look. 'I think she started just before I left, so about two years ago. Must be just before she died.'

'I didn't think you took any notice of the details when I spoke about her.'

'Of course I did,' he says, placing the mobile between them. 'I always listen to what you say. It's important to you, so it's important to me. Although I don't think I'd have the patience to do all the research you do.'

He keeps contradicting himself: first he can't recall her name, now he remembers when Laura started working there. Sarah keeps this observation to herself.

'You're patient enough to work out boring IT solutions, though,' she says.

'Ha!' he says, squeezing her knee. 'They're not boring to me. And they happen to make me quite a lot of money.'

Sarah picks up the phone and looks again at the picture.

'What was she like? I can't imagine her walking and talking – God, that's such a weird thing to say.'

'No, I know what you mean. I didn't see her much. We were in the IT department for the whole building. They had a techie on the call-centre floor, but they rotated us. I left just after a batch of new recruits came in. She was one of them, I'm sure she was. Thing is, everyone there was quite young, and she wasn't. You tend to notice people who aren't the same as the others.'

'And she was quite pretty.'

'I was far too busy to give any thought to that. I'm a professional.'

'Ha!'

Facebook Messenger pings an alert on Sarah's laptop.

'That was quick,' she says, getting up to sit at the desk in the corner of the room. 'It must be from the advert.'

'Did you post it?' he says. 'Have you set your privacy to open? Otherwise it wouldn't ping.'

'I posted it about twenty minutes ago. And yeah, I hardly ever use Facebook Messenger. I'm more of a WhatsApp woman.'

'Be careful, Sarah,' says Rob, serious for the first time since he arrived. 'You didn't post it that long ago. It's probably a scammer. People love being part of something bigger than themselves. They might have felt a connection to her after reading about her story. You won't be the only one who's interested in Laura.'

'I know,' says Sarah, clicking onto the message icon in Facebook. 'It's from a JP Veritas.'

'That's definitely not their real name,' says Rob. 'For sure.'

'I know, I know,' she says, exasperated with his narration. 'Veritas is Latin for truth. Which makes this more intriguing.'

She reads out the message.

Dear Sarah,

I was so pleased to see your request for information about Laura Aspinall. It seemed as though everyone else had forgotten her.

Laura was the love of my life. We were together for only a short time. Too short.

I still can't believe she has died. This whole thing has been such a shock, especially as I thought she was travelling the world. She had an Instagram account that documented these travels. How could this be possible? I find it very difficult to understand this

173

and hope that you can find more answers than I can find online. Help me make sense of this nightmare.

Kind regards.

'Jesus,' says Sarah. 'That's a bit intense, isn't it? So formal.'

'Hmm,' says Rob. 'Smells like bullshit to me. Sounds as though someone's trying to plug their Instagram account.'

'No one would do that for a few hits on a website.'

'Some people are ruthless. Especially online when they feel that no one can touch them. Did he or she mention the name of the Instagram account?'

'No,' says Sarah. 'Do you think I should reply and ask?'

'Don't reply yet. You might be on there all day. Think about what to say and then get back to them – if at all. Check out their profile, their friends, see if they have other social media profiles under the same name.'

'Wow, you've thought about this.'

'It's just common sense. Have you ever watched *Catfish*?'

'I might have watched a few,' she says. 'But this person wrote, *It seemed as though everyone else had forgotten her*. Past tense.'

'That's probably just a turn of phrase. It's been nearly a month since she was found.'

Sarah clicks onto JP Veritas' profile. The photo is of a man in his early thirties, dark hair and blue eyes. Quite good-looking, but she's not going to say that out loud.

'Bet you're more interested, now,' says Rob, peeking over her shoulder.

'It's probably not even his real picture.'

'Hang on,' says Rob. 'I know him, too.'

'From the same company you and Laura worked at?'

Rob leans over her shoulder, narrowing his eyes as he stares at the profile photo.

'Yeah. He was one of the managers. Tom Delaney. A quiet guy. He was the normal one – the others were a bit wankery. Tom went to the same school as I did. He was in a different year, though.'

'Really? That's a bit of a coincidence.'

'A few people from our old school worked at PeopleServe. To be honest, they let just about anyone work there and Preston's a pretty small place.'

Sarah looks at Rob as he concentrates on the photograph. Does she actually know him as well as she thought? But, then, he doesn't actually know the names of the schools Sarah went to, so it's not as if he's hiding anything. He's just volunteered the information. And this Tom person might not have even known Laura.

'Do you think this is his real profile but a different name, then?' she says.

'Who knows? Someone might've stolen his picture. It could be a woman behind it for all we know.'

Sarah clicks onto JP's friends list. There are only thirty-six, and no one by the name of Laura Aspinall, even though Sarah had already scoured Facebook for the right one.

His statuses are sparse, sharing various news stories and petitions against Brexit.

She clicks back onto his message where he says that someone has been posting on Instagram as Laura, documenting her travels. Sarah types in Laura's name and Instagram into Google – still she can't find any of the photos resembling her. She must have a different user name. That's if this JP or whoever he is, is telling the truth. And Sarah very much doubts that he is.

He's either someone who, like Rob said, wants a bit of attention – which is most likely. Or he's someone who knew her, and isn't at all shocked at the news of Laura Aspinall's death.

Today, she's had one message from someone who wants to talk about Laura. And another who, by the few words in the letter posted through Sarah's door, never wants to hear Laura's name again.

17

Laura

Friday, 17 March 2017

I woke this morning with a feeling of dread and regret alongside vague memories of the night before. I managed to get into work on time, though. I was probably still a bit pissed on the bus. Now, it's only ten thirty and already it feels like it should be home time. Going out on a work night should be illegal.

'Have you recovered from last night, then?' says Suzanne, dropping two Berocca into a glass of water.

Just the smell of it is making me nauseous. Suzanne has been on calls all morning and this is the first chance we've had to speak.

'I don't feel so bad,' I say, wishing I had sunglasses to dim the glare of my screen.

'What time did you get back?' she says.

'Er ... I ... I'm guessing about midnight.'

She raises her eyebrows.

'Really? I'm sure you left around one with the rest of us.'

She takes another sip of her strange effervescent drink.

'I'm sure I didn't.'

'Are you?'

I shift on the chair, wishing she'd change the subject. I was chatting to Tom online at some point, but I didn't have time to check what I wrote when I woke and I was too mortified to read them on the bus, but the time of the last message was 00.30. I could have typed those messages anywhere, though. Being unsure of what time I got home last night unnerves me. Is Suzanne winding me up by suggesting I left at 1 a.m. or is she telling the truth? Perhaps she remembers as much as I do: not a lot.

'Did you get the number from that bloke you were talking to?' I say.

'What bloke?' She sits up straighter.

'The one with the leather jacket, long red hair.'

'Really? I was talking to someone with long hair?'

'Definitely,' I say, nodding for emphasis.

'Oh, right.' She picks up her phone, checking her messages. Her shoulders relax. 'I didn't text anyone last night.' She puts it back on the table. 'Thank God. Anyway, enough about last night – I was so drunk I don't want to think about it. What was Tom talking to you about?' she says.

'I told you last night. And I thought you didn't want to think about it.'

She waves her hand.

'Oh, that doesn't count. This isn't about me, and it was early in the night.'

'He asked me to go for a drink to catch up.'

Her cheeks flush. I won't tell her that Tom and I were messaging last night. And for someone with a boyfriend, Suzanne seems to be taking a lot of interest in another man. I wouldn't be surprised if Jack was a figment of her imagination. We've all done that, haven't we? Well, maybe not all of us.

'And what did you say to him?' she says.

'I said yes. I'm curious as to what he's got to say.'

'What *could* there be to say? Weren't you just kids when you went to school? What could you have to talk about?'

She picks up her mobile phone again. I can see from the blue on her screen that she's opened up Facebook.

'I don't know,' I say. 'Should I not have said yes?'

She stands, leaving her desk without a word.

The skin around Suzanne's eyes looks slightly puffy when she comes back from the ladies'.

'I'll cancel it,' I say as she sits next to me. 'I don't like him that much anyway. I barely know him.'

She doesn't need to know how I really feel. I thought she and I were friends, but I have to keep a lot of things to myself when I'm talking with her. It's not like in school, where you're best friends with someone simply because you both like Britney Spears. I'm stupid for thinking it was.

She blots her nose with a tissue.

'No, no,' she says. 'I won't stand in your way. It's not as though we're in school.'

179

Perhaps she can read my mind.

'I've liked Tom for so long now,' she continues, 'and God, does he know it. I've missed my chance now – he doesn't even like me anyway.'

'Do you think Tom knows, though?' I don't wait for a reply. 'It doesn't seem like he does. We're only going for a drink as friends. Nothing will come of it.' I pause for a moment. 'I thought you had a boyfriend?'

'Not any more.'

She grabs the framed photograph of flash Jack and throws it into her desk drawer.

'He sent me a message before I went to the loos. Apparently it's over.' She puts her head in her hands. 'And *allegedly* I sent him a picture on Snapchat last night of me and some bloke. I was sitting on his lap.'

'Oh,' I say. 'Are you sure that's true? Did the man have long red hair and a leather jacket?'

I'm wicked, aren't I? I'm not sure if there was actually a bloke of that description there last night.

She glances at me with an evil look I deserve.

'I can't tell if it's bloody true, can I?' she says. 'Haven't you ever used Snapchat?'

She groans and puts her head back in her hands. So dramatic. And at work, too.

'No, I've never used it,' I say. 'I don't really text people that much.'

She waves a hand without looking at me.

'Yeah, course you don't,' she says. 'And the very nature of the bloody app is that the pictures sent are temporary – unless a screenshot is taken.'

'Did Jack send you the screenshot?'

'Obviously not!' She sits up, then flops backwards heavily in her chair. 'Oh God, this whole thing is a nightmare.'

I don't mention the fact that she's been saying that her and Jack the flash have nothing in common, and that all of last night she was trying to catch Tom's eye. 'Oh, Laura, Laura,' she'd said at about eleven fifteen last night, 'you've only been here a week and already everyone is after you. It's because you don't look your age, isn't it? I'm too old. I wear too much make-up. I should be more like you and not care — men seem to like that.'

I remember *that* conversation, unfortunately.

She picks up her glass of fizzy orange and downs it in one.

'Fuck it, eh?' she says, dabbing her lips with the back of her hand. 'Men are shits anyway. I'm sure you'll find that out for yourself very soon.'

She puts on her headphones and it seems our conversation is over.

18

The whole world knows it's you now, Laura. Did you ever want to be famous? I should know that, really, shouldn't I?

Someone else is looking for you. Sarah Hayes and I know where she lives. And you can't say I didn't warn her.

She wants to know all about you, but it's too late for that, isn't it?

I get the urge, sometimes, to tell everyone what happened that day. But if I did, my life as it is would be over. No one can ever find out.

You treated me like shit. No one should do that to me. I'm kind to everyone.

Almost everyone.

19

Laura

Friday, 17 March 2017

Every morning this week, I've been waking up feeling anxious at the thought of speaking to strangers on the telephone all day. I thought that it would get better, that my initial bravado would stick and I would get used to it all, but I can't see me staying at this call centre for the foreseeable.

Dad's pills are still in his bedside drawer. There are so many of them. I know their names, but I don't know what the combination of all of them would do to a person who didn't need them.

If everything gets too much, then at least—

No. I can't keep thinking like this.

It's Friday evening. Work is over, for now. I don't have to think about it until Sunday.

One day at a time. I just have to keep repeating that to myself.

I'm so relieved it's Saturday tomorrow. This must be a feeling shared by the majority of the working population. Looking after Dad was challenging, especially near the end, but at least I knew what to expect most days, and the people helping Dad would be there to listen if I had problems – most of the time, that is, when they weren't in a rush to get to the next patient.

Last night, when I got home, I saw that Tom had added me as a friend on Facebook. My profile must have come up as a suggestion after I'd been clicking on his so many times before.

He doesn't have many friends on his new one, even though he's friendly with everyone at work. Perhaps he wants to keep his private life separate. His other profile has 846 friends on it. On the account he added me from (Tom_Unofficial), he has thirty-six friends (which is still ten more than I have). I imagine he doesn't want his ex-wife checking up on his new life.

I couldn't find Suzanne on there. Perhaps she has a different Facebook name, too.

I only put a profile photo of me on when I started at PeopleServe (previously, it was of a tortoise – I've no idea why). It was a selfie, but I used the bathroom mirror as that was more flattering. I have a couple of comments under it from people I haven't seen since primary school. They added me when I joined the *For Those Who Went to St Xavier's Primary School* group.

Sarah Porthouse: You haven't changed one bit!

Grant Sullivan: Oh, I think I remember you.

I have no idea who these two people are.

I finally mustered the courage to read mine and Tom's exchange on Messenger last night. At least I know now what time I got home last night, though I must be mindful of drinking and typing in future. I could use the timestamps on the transcript as evidence to Suzanne that I arrived home earlier than she did. But obviously, I won't.

Tom: Hey, Laura! We're officially friends now! ☺ *00.05*

(I thought this was a bit of a trite thing to say, but I let it go.)

Laura: Hey, Tom! Did you get home OK? *00.06*

Tom: Yeah. Feeling lonely. You? *00.07*

Laura: Yeah, I got home OK. Just reading. *00.11*

(Oh God, it's even worse reading my replies back – I sound boring even after having four whole minutes to think of something to say.)

Tom: You alone? *00.11*

Laura: Yes, as always – haha! *00.15*

Tom: Me too. It's quiet here. *00.15*

Laura: Do you live on your own? *00.19*

Tom: I have housemates. Don't see much of them though.
00.27

Laura: I'd better go. Early start tomorrow ☺ *00.30*

Thirteen minutes after his last Facebook message, my phone bleeped with a text.

Hey, Laura, it's Tom. Are you still as drunk as I am? Still on for that drink tomorrow night? T

Hi, Tom. I'd love to. L

Great! Will text you in the morning xxx

I put the kisses on his text down to his alcohol intake. Shouldn't read too much into that.

But he must love me.

I'm just kidding.

In his texts today, he said he'd pick me up, and that he knows this area well as he still visits his grandad here.

I want to ask about his marriage, but I find it hard asking him things, and we didn't talk in person after our brief exchange in the pub last night. Perhaps with some Dutch courage this evening, I'll be more inquisitive, more confident.

He'll be here in ten minutes. I've cleaned everywhere in case he wants to pop in (do people still do that?), double-checked the window in Dad's room so there are no strange noises coming from his bedroom again. I keep contacting the landlord to fix it, but this place must be at the bottom of the list as I never hear back from her.

I'm wearing a dress from Top Shop (purchased from The Heart Foundation for £4.99) – the most up-to-date item of clothing I have. It's a denim shirt dress and ties in the middle and it's now my favourite. I've got black tights on as it's freezing out (typical North West in March – so unpredictable), and some black ankle boots that I've had for years. They still look OK. I bought a sparkly black dress, too, (£8.99 – went wild with that one, didn't I?), but it smells a bit musty. It's dry clean only so I've hung it on the curtain rail in my bedroom in the hope of getting some air into it. Not sure if that'll work. I'll give it a few days – there's always Febreze if that doesn't get rid of the smell.

Sitting next to Suzanne, I've started to take more of an interest in what I wear. She *loves a bargain*, but, like Mobile Mandy, said it was disgusting that I buy from charity shops. She said I could be wearing a dead person's clothes. Suzanne buys her *bargains* from eBay, but I doubt those clothes come with a certificate of provenance. When I said as much, she wrinkled her nose and said, 'No, but they have tags.'

I didn't take the discussion further. There's no arguing with her as she's always right. I used to think it could take years to get to know someone, but she's pretty transparent. She doesn't seek to impress me. Nor should she.

I wish I could be transparent with Tom. I am nervous and blush every time he talks to me. I have no idea why he takes such an interest in me – he must feel the connection between us, having known each other for so long. Suzanne says it's because I'm *quite attractive … in a classical sort of way*. I took it as a compliment, however backhanded it was batted towards me. It can't be because of my sparkling personality because I overthink *everything*.

The knock on the door makes me jump.

I go to the mirror in the bathroom and smooth down

my hair. I don't want to look too eager by rushing to the door. I managed a bit of tinted moisturiser. I haven't the confidence to fully contour my whole face like they do on *YouTube*. It'd look like I was wearing a mask, anyway.

When I open the door, he's standing a few feet away, looking up at the flats above. I'm so used to seeing him in smart clothing. He looks younger in jeans. He's wearing a white shirt with tiny black roses printed on it, and a navy blue overcoat that ends at his thighs. He looks as though he hasn't put gel in his hair like he normally does at work – he looks fresher, cleaner.

'Hey!' he says, stepping towards me. 'You look lovely!'

He sounds surprised. I don't know what to say in return.

He leans into the doorway.

'This place is so familiar,' he says, looking down the hallway. 'Do you mind if I have a look inside?'

'I ...'

It's such a strange request *before* the date, though it's not totally unexpected as I had cleaned the whole place.

'Sorry,' he says, standing straight back outside. 'That must sound odd. It's just that I feel as though I've been in this flat before.'

I frown.

'You probably *have* been here before,' I say. 'We played together nearly every summer from the age of seven until we were about ten.'

He places a hand on my arm.

188

'Sorry,' he says. 'I do remember. I just didn't want to freak you out by saying that I did.'

'Why would that freak me out?'

'I don't know.' He shrugs. 'It's like you didn't recognise me in the café the other week. I didn't want to be all weird and say I knew you from playing in the paddling pool when we were kids.' He smiles and nudges me with his shoulder. 'Come on. You'd have thought it was creepy if I'd have come out with that after not seeing you for decades.'

'I was surprised at seeing you that day. I had a bit of a crush on you at school.' Oh Jesus, what am I saying?

I close my front door.

'Anyway ...'

We walk along the path towards the main road.

'What made your family move here?' he says. 'It's not in the catchment area of our old primary, is it?' He winces. 'Sorry. Parent of a small child alert. It's all about the primary schools when you've a child about to enter the big bad world.'

'How old is your daughter?'

Shit. Woman stalking man online alert.

'Rosie's four.' He's walking so close that our arms are touching. 'She's already had a taster day at her new school and she loves it thank God. Sorry,' he says again. 'I didn't give you time to answer the question ... about you moving here.'

'Dad lost his job at the university. Mum and Dad had to sell the house near St Xavier's to help pay for his care.'

'Really? That's awful.'

I shrug. 'It's what happens.'

'When did your dad ...' He looks away as we turn the corner onto the high street. 'Doesn't matter.'

I know what he was going to ask. I wouldn't have minded if he did.

He's looking straight ahead.

He hasn't reached for my hand yet.

'I know this nice little pub just out of the centre,' he says.

Kim's Kaff still has its lights on and condensation on the glass.

'Oh,' I say. 'It's still open.'

He looks over, frowning.

'Ah.' He takes me by the hand to keep up with his increased pace. 'They don't even sell alcohol! And I don't really like going in there.'

'Why?' I say. 'It's not that bad. Cheap, too.' I should've brought a plaster to stick over my mouth. 'I wasn't suggesting we go there tonight.'

'My ex works there,' he says. 'It didn't end well.' He looks again at the café, then at his watch. 'They must be still cleaning. She doesn't usually open this late.'

'What's her name?' I say.

He looks at me, his eyes narrow.

'It doesn't matter. She was a bit cuckoo.'

He looks around. Is he afraid his ex is following us? My heart starts to pound a little as I imagine both of the women who work there chasing after us with knives ... or maybe machetes.

190

'It's fine,' I say, shivering and wishing I'd put my winter coat on. 'It's freezing tonight.'

He takes my hand in his.

'Come on, ' he says. 'Let's get you out of the cold.'

We're standing outside my door, and it's still freezing. It's 10.45 p.m., which is pretty early from what I've heard about Suzanne's nights out. I've had three vodka and Cokes that were upsold to doubles, and they have gone to my head. Or was it five? Time passed too quickly.

We talked only briefly about school because I said I didn't really want to, but what we did talk about were the nice times, before everything turned bad. He said he remembers that he liked me because I was so quiet. He mentioned the time I cried aged eight because I didn't understand a piece of comprehension that we had to do.

'It was so cute,' he said. 'I'd never seen someone cry in class like that before. It made me feel so sorry for you.'

'I actually remember that,' I said. 'Everyone else knew exactly what to do and I was so confused.'

'The teacher told me to sit next to you and talk you through it.'

'Was that you?' I leant back and looked at him again. 'But the boy who helped me had glasses on.'

'Ha!' he said. 'They've invented these things called contact lenses, you know.'

Maybe my childhood memories weren't as sharp as I thought they were. I'm sure he didn't wear glasses.

'Do you want to come in for a coffee?' I say now, using that age-old line.

'Yeah, sure,' he says.

Tom almost trips as he follows me inside. He had three (or five. It was definitely an odd number) pints of lager, paired with a shot of whisky for each round. I can smell the spirit on him.

He takes off his coat, hanging it on one of the hooks on the hallway wall and removes his shoes. He's certainly making himself at home.

'You didn't have to take your shoes off,' I say.

'It's a habit,' he says. 'We have cream carpets at home.'

I think our hall carpet used to be cream; now it's a strange grey colour. I'm pretty good at keeping on top of the cleaning, but it's had a lot of wear after so many people coming and going over the years.

Tom doesn't seem to notice, or care. He's looking at the photographs on the wall.

'This is how I remember you,' he says.

He's pointing a wobbly finger at the picture of Dad and me one Christmas. We're sitting at the kitchen table, wearing those cracker hats, our heads together. We had a paper tablecloth with gold reindeers printed on it, and our plates still had the Brussels sprouts on them. I cooked too many because Mum bought too many. She hated cooking. I only started doing it because I preferred home-cooked meals and she wasn't inclined. She preferred convenience over taste and we often had meals from tins. She tried to convince everyone that I cooked because I loved it. 'We can't keep her out of the kitchen,' she always said, eventually convincing herself of her own lie.

She must have taken the photo.

It was her last Christmas with us.

Tom shuffles down the hall. He puts his face close to the picture of Mum and Dad at the beach – my favourite one of them together.

He raises his finger again; the tip lands on my mother's face.

'Yes,' he says, almost whispering. 'I'd remember that face anywhere.'

'People say all the time that we look alike.'

All the time might be exaggerating a little – no one has said it for years.

He turns to face me, his eyes narrowed.

'You're nothing like her,' he says. 'What kind of mother does that? Especially when it caused so much pain.'

'I was fine, really,' I say. I hover at the kitchen door. 'Why don't you go and sit in the living room. I'll put the kettle on.'

He wrinkles his nose.

'Have you got something stronger?' he says. 'It's still early yet. And it's Friday night.'

'I think there's some brandy in the cupboard.'

He brings up his hand. I think he's trying to make the OK sign. If he isn't, he's signalling something entirely different and extremely inappropriate.

'Perfect,' he says.

I pour myself one, to be social, and carry the tumblers into the living room. He's sitting on the sofa, his legs crossed at the ankle. I'd half expected him to be sprawled across it, to be honest. I sit on the opposite end near Dad's side table.

'You don't have many pictures of your mum and dad in here,' he says.

'I don't like to look at them when I'm watching television. It's quite recent for Dad. He was in so much pain for a long time. All the pictures from the last five years or so, you can see it on his face. And the older pictures ... well, they were him in a previous life, really.'

'What did you used to do all day?' Tom takes a sip of the brandy, flinching slightly. 'I mean when you were home-schooled. I've never known anyone to be taught at home.'

'My mum was ... is ... a teacher. She used to post me a timetable every term that covered the whole day. I stuck to it ... most of the time.'

I roll my eyes and Tom laughs.

'You must have great self-motivation,' he says. 'I'd have been on my PlayStation all day.'

'Luckily I didn't have one. And my dad was pretty strict ... well, in the mornings he was ... at the beginning, when his illness wasn't so bad.'

'Can I ask ...' He leans forward, resting his elbows on his knees.

'He had MS.'

'Shit. I'm so sorry.'

'Me too,' I say. I take a sip, blinking to stop the tears

from falling. I gulp down too much. 'Bloody hell, that tastes awful.'

He laughs.

'I didn't like to say anything.' He takes another large sip, opening his mouth after swallowing to release the fumes. 'Hah!' He raises his glass. 'To shit brandy and getting pissed on a Friday night!'

'To shit and piss,' I say.

'Yes, and to that, too,' he says, his eyes glistening, probably from the strength of the drink.

I place my glass on the table next to me. Dad's table.

'I don't think I can drink any more of that,' I say.

The clock clunks and the cuckoo begins its song to welcome eleven o'clock.

'Jesus,' says Tom. 'That scared the shit out of me.' He places his empty glass on the floor. 'I haven't seen one of those since I was a kid.'

'I don't even register the sound of that clock any more,' I say.

He rubs his eyes.

'Yeah. I can see why. It just blends into the background – that loud, intrusive birdsong every hour, on the hour.' He stands, barely wobbling at all, this time. 'I'd better head off. Think I'm a bit pissed.'

I stand, too, and walk him to the front door.

He sticks his feet into his shoes and bends to tie up the laces. His hair is slightly thinning at the crown, in the way that my dad's did. He stands and grabs his coat, resting it in the crook of his arm.

'Aren't you going to put that on?' I say, opening the door.

'That brandy has set my stomach on fire,' he says.

He steps outside and turns to face me.

The alcohol has reached my cheeks – I'm sure my face is bright red. My stomach is churning. I've been imagining kissing him all night, yet now the time is here, I want to slam the door shut and run back inside.

He takes hold of my hand.

'I've had a lovely night, Laura.'

He pulls me gently towards him and kisses me softly on the lips.

An icy breeze comes between us as we part. I fold my arms, rubbing the tops of them.

'I've had a nice time, too,' I say.

He bows slightly.

'Hey,' he says. 'Do you want to go out on Sunday afternoon?'

'Are you not fed up of me already?' I say.

He laughs.

'Never!'

'OK then,' I say.

This is the busiest weekend I have ever had.

Tom turns and walks away.

I'm still watching him as he reaches the corner.

He stops, turns around, and smiles.

20

Sarah

The noise in Sarah's parents' house is always over-whelming. She has two brothers and three sisters, and between them all, they have nine children. After grow-ing up in such a large household, Sarah and her siblings made the decision, perhaps subliminally, to have only one or two children of their own.

The kids are sitting around the small table, some on camping chairs, others wobbling on little stools. Sarah's son is the oldest and has been promoted to the adult table. He's staring at his mobile phone.

'Alex,' hisses Sarah, sitting next to him. 'Put your phone away. It's your grandmother's birthday.'

He sighs loudly and shoves his mobile in his pocket.

'Grandma won't even notice,' he says. 'It's a mad house in here.'

'Shh,' says Sarah, trying not to smile. 'Try and look happy. Otherwise you're going back on the kids' table.'

He folds his arms and rolls his eyes. Sarah can't wait for this phase of mardiness to end.

'Any chance of a Smirnoff Ice?' he says, smirking.

'I seriously doubt it,' says Sarah. 'Grandma's given up alcohol for a month. And if *she* can't have any, no one else can.'

Sarah sips her fizzy water. Usually the wine flows freely at family gatherings, but today is going to be a long one. Sarah's sister, Amy, is sitting opposite. She's eight months pregnant and is definitely *not* blooming.

'I think I'm going to be sick,' says Amy. 'This heartburn is ridiculous. Why didn't anyone warn me about it? I've been living on milkshakes and even *they* don't keep the bloody indigestion away.'

'Less of the *bloody*,' says their mother, carrying a massive dish of roast potatoes to the table.

'But, Mum!' says Amy. 'I'm suffering here.'

'I can see that. But don't make the rest of us miserable, too.' She rubs Amy's hair. 'Anyway, I've bought you a treat.' She goes to one of the cupboards of their huge but dated kitchen, takes out a bottle and places it in front of Amy. 'There you go, my sweet.'

She kisses the top of her head.

'Gaviscon!' shouts Amy, over the noise. 'Worst present ever!'

Amy's always been like this. As the youngest (and a *surprise* when Mum was forty-six), she had all the attention of her brothers and sisters.

Mark, their brother, is sitting on Sarah's left. He leans towards her.

'I bet her husband can't wait for that baby to come out,' he whispers. 'In fact, none of us can wait.' He grabs his glass of water and takes a sip. 'Dad,' he hisses to their father sitting at the top of the table. He's always hiding behind a book or a giant newspaper – sometimes he can be fast asleep. 'Where have you stashed the secret wine? Or is there any chance of a whisky?'

Dad folds the newspaper slowly and flings it behind him so it lands on an already tall pile of papers.

'I've tried that,' he says. 'But your mother can smell alcohol from a hundred paces when she's on one of these sabbaticals. And let me tell you, it's not worth it.'

Mark slumps back in his chair. He always reverts to being a seventeen-year-old when he returns to the childhood home.

'So, Sarah,' says Dad, taking his glasses off. 'How's your latest project going?'

'Ooh, is this for the course you're doing at Preston Poly?' says Mum, stirring a pan of gravy.

How she can hear from over by the cooker, Sarah doesn't know.

'It's a university now, Mum,' she shouts. 'For the hundredth time. And it *has* been for over twenty years.'

'It'll always be Preston Poly to me,' she says, turning her attention back to the pot.

'It's going all right,' says Sarah. 'Actually, the woman I'm researching – Laura Aspinall – her father used to work at the university. Have you heard of him? His name was Robin Hartley.'

Dad puts an elbow on the table and rests his chin on his hand.

'Do you know when he worked there?' he says. 'I remember a Robin but we're going back a long time.'

'I'm not sure. Late Nineties, at a guess. From what I gather from the newspaper, Laura was home-schooled by him from 1997 after she finished primary school.'

'Well, if it's the same one – and there can't be many Robins about – then he lectured in English Literature. Though us engineers and those bookish types didn't mix much, as you can imagine. I don't think we said more than hello to each other. He retired young, though. He had some degenerative disease – it sticks in my mind because he was younger than me. He had this head of black curly hair. The ladies liked him. They tended to go for those brooding types.'

'Can you remember anything else about him?'

'Afraid not, love,' he says. 'And if he retired late Nineties, I bet there's not a lot on the internet about him either.'

'No,' says Sarah. 'There isn't. And even though Laura only died a couple of years ago, there's not a lot about her online either. She was young – just turned thirty.'

'That's unusual.' He sits straighter, clasping his hands on the table. 'Was that deliberate?'

'What do you mean?'

'Younger people tend to share everything these days. If she hasn't anything online, then perhaps it was on purpose. Has she any family you could talk to?'

'I left a message for her mother, but she hasn't got back to me yet. I don't think she will as it's been a few days now. Probably the last thing she wants to do is talk to me.'

Her mother brings a huge jug of gravy to the table.

'Everyone!' she shouts. 'Dinner's on the table.'

'Mum,' says Mark. 'We're all sitting here.'

She sits and looks around.

'Of course you are,' she says. 'Well, apart from the prodigal one.'

Charlotte is travelling again. This time she's in Australia.

'My child is approaching forty and she still has to prove there is more to life than having children,' says Mum. 'I suppose it's too much for her to imagine that I'd love another grandchild.'

'Mother!' says Amy, pointing to her belly. 'Hello?'

Their mother sighs. 'Yes, yes,' she says. 'I just want to see you *all* settled.' She looks pointedly at Sarah. 'And I still can't believe you left that darling Andy. What a lovely, handsome, responsible young man.'

'Sometimes things don't work out,' says Sarah. She's bored of saying it and wishes her mum would stop bringing it up. 'It's been years now,' she glances at Alex, 'and it's hardly appropriate dinner conversation.'

'Now, we're hardly the appropriate sort, are we, darling?'

The way she spoke, you'd think them posh, but they're not at all. Sarah's mother calls them all *darling* or *sweetie* because she can't remember their names fast enough.

'But, darling, you were so good together. You'd been through so much. Especially that time ...' She raises her eyebrows.

'I don't want to talk about it,' says Sarah.

201

Her mother is talking about the miscarriage only a year after Alex was born. The pregnancy wasn't planned, but it was welcome. Andy was as devastated as Sarah was. She thinks that's why he tried to take his mind off things by trying hobby after hobby. He didn't take to golf or cycling because he couldn't find what he was looking for. The answer is never as simple as that.

'If it's OK with everyone,' pipes up Amy, 'can I have the most stuffing?' She spoons half of it onto her plate. 'I've been craving it something stupid. I can eat it on its own, in a sandwich, on toast.'

'Be my guest, darling,' says Mum.

Sarah's phone pings with an email notification. She hopes it's not JP Veritas again, or whatever his name is. So far, she's had two other messages from him.

The first was a short one: **Do you have the contact details for Laura's mother? I would love to get in touch.** And the second: **I can see you're reading my messages, but you haven't replied. Is everything OK?**

She had to send him a quick reply, telling him she had many messages to go through and would get back to him shortly, obviously trying to sound as polite and as appreciative as she could. She didn't want him flouncing off if he did actually know Laura. Sarah would be grateful for any legitimate pieces of information.

She's had twelve emails and messages from people sending condolences. Kind gestures, but she wasn't the person who ought to be receiving them, and, when she had got back to them, none out of the twelve had actually known Laura.

Sarah opens the email app on her phone, under the table. After scolding Alex about it, she doesn't want to be caught doing the same thing.

Thankfully, it's not from JP. It's from a woman called Suzanne Anderson.

Dear Sarah,

I am writing in connection with Laura Aspinall after seeing your post on Facebook.

I worked with Laura, February – March 2017. I was surprised that she didn't get in touch after leaving PeopleServe so suddenly, but we only knew each other for a few weeks. If I can help at all, please let me know.

Regards,

Suzanne

Sarah fires off a quick reply, asking if it's possible to meet. She slides the phone back into her pocket.

'I saw that, Mum,' whispers Alex with a smirk on his face.

'Sorry, love,' she says quietly, though no one else is listening. 'But it was really important.'

Sarah asked Rob again about his time at PeopleServe. He said that he and another guy used to take it in turns to monitor the sales calls and help with any computer issues, but that he had barely spoken to Laura direct.

Barely spoken. That means he must have spoken to her at some point for him to say that. That Sarah has such a personal connection to Laura makes it all more intriguing. She lived in the same block of flats, she might have come into the café, and she might have talked to Rob. So close, yet so far.

She pushes the thought from her head. Sarah can't recall seeing Laura in the café, so if Rob can barely remember her in the workplace, then Sarah shouldn't be all that surprised. There will have been loads of people who worked at PeopleServe. And Preston is a small place. It's surprising how many people on Sarah's Facebook friends list know each other. There are random connections everywhere.

And now she has another contact from Laura's place of work. Suzanne Anderson.

Sarah rubs her hands together and picks up her knife and fork. The adrenaline makes her want to run around the room.

Finally, someone genuine who actually knew Laura just before she died.

21

Laura

Suzanne lives on the other side of town, near the football ground. Thankfully there isn't a match on today.

I took one bus to the station then walked the rest. According to the map on my phone it wasn't that far, but it's taken me nearly forty minutes. I don't know who they think is walking their calculated routes. I'm sweating by the time I'm at her door.

It's a three-bedroom semi; the garden is immaculate. I didn't have her down as a Charlie Dimmock. She ushers me inside and I hand her my carrier bag. Two bottles of wine that cost nearly fifteen pounds. Pinot Grigio. I remembered from the other night (at least I remembered something). I'm not sure I could drink any more after my date last night with Tom, though. I only got out of bed five hours ago and it's 7 p.m. now.

Her kitchen has pine cupboards, pine work surfaces, pine floors, and a pine table. If there were such a thing as pine taps, I think they'd be in this room.

205

'My mum and dad are away for the weekend,' she says.

'Oh, I see.'

That explains it. Though I'm hardly hot on interior design myself. Our – *my* kitchen is melamine, with a touch of Formica thrown in.

She gets out two glasses from the cupboard and another bottle of wine from the fridge.

I've realised that socialising with people from work means you have to drink an awful lot of alcohol. I don't think my body can take all that I've drunk this week. I'm trying not to think about it, but it's not sustainable. My anxiety is through the roof, hence my massive lie-in today. I almost had a tot of brandy so I could face the journey here, but that would have been a very slippery slide down the hill of gloom.

'Let's go through to the living room,' she says. 'Then I can hear all the gossip.'

Suzanne's house, it seems, is a shrine to all things wooden. The living-room walls are filled edge to edge with various items of varnished mahogany – even the TV cabinet, which has doors like a pair of wings, open to reveal a tiny flat-screen television.

'There's no telling them,' she says as she sits down on the smaller settee. 'If they ditched that monstrosity of a cupboard, then we could have a decent-sized telly.' She nods to the two armchairs. 'And they wouldn't have to sit so bloody close.'

She smiles at me, rolling her eyes, but her words are without a hint of malice.

'It must be nice to have both parents around,' I say.

'I guess.' She tucks her feet underneath her. 'But remind me of that at seven in the morning when my dad lingers in the bathroom.'

She wrinkles her nose, and I can't help but giggle.

'So how did it go with our lovely Tommy, then?'

'He's not really a Tommy, is he?'

'No, I suppose. He's quite serious ... when he chooses to be.'

I ignore the undertone.

'It was lovely,' I say, trying not to smile so much that I look like a fool. 'We went for drinks last night.'

'Drinks, eh? Things must be getting serious.'

'Are you being sarcastic?'

'Sorry.' She holds up a hand. 'I didn't mean it to sound like that. It's just that I've dated some arseholes in the past. Tom seems quite taken with you.' She smiles. 'I've never seen him loiter around the sales team so much. Where did you two go?'

'Hartley's,' I say. 'Weird, as that was my dad's surname.'

'Were your parents not married?'

'Yes, but Mum wanted me to have her name. She said she was the last of the Aspinalls. She thought she was kind of *out there*, doing that.'

Suzanne goes quiet.

I don't want to tell her that I'm going out with him on Sunday as well.

'You will be careful, won't you?' she says, finally. 'With Tom, I mean. I'm sure I saw him the other day.'

'What do you mean?' I try to keep my voice straight, even though my heart is hammering.

'There's something I can't put my finger on.'

She's not looking at me; she's reading the back cover of a DVD that she's just picked up. I don't know if I can trust her. There's a history with me and Tom, but I have nothing to connect myself with Suzanne, other than sitting next to her for a week. She has known Tom a lot longer than me in the present.

'Why haven't you mentioned this before?' I say. 'That you saw him.'

'I didn't know you were serious about him. You've only been on one date! I didn't think you would develop feelings for him so quickly – and I know that you have, even though you've not said as much. Before, I knew you had a crush on him, and that you were flattered because he knew you growing up and your situation. I thought he was kind to you because he felt sorry for you a bit.'

Tears rush to my eyes.

'Oh, Laura,' she says. 'I didn't mean for it to come out like that. I thought he was trying to be your friend. I don't want you to get hurt.'

I blink my tears away. I don't want to cry in front of her – I don't want her to think I'm crying over a man, when the truth is that I was stung by her words.

'I don't need anyone pitying me,' I say. 'I know I've had an unusual upbringing, but what's normal these days?'

She puts her glass on the mantelpiece, slides onto

the carpet, and crawls towards me. She must be pissed already.

'I don't pity you. I just thought ...' She rests a hand on my knee. 'You seem so innocent ... like you're alone in the world.'

I stare at the top of her head.

Do people think that about me? That I've no idea of what life is like and I've been isolated from the real world?

She looks up at me, and there are tears in *her* eyes now. She rests her chin on her hands that are still on my knees.

'I'm sorry.'

I take a sip of the now-warm wine. Her head feels heavy on my legs.

'Do you still like Tom?' I say. 'Is that why you're warning me off him?'

She sits up quickly.

'God, no!' Her head wobbles as she steadies herself. 'It's not that. I wouldn't do that to you. I like to think I'm more honest than that.' She picks at strands of the shag pile carpet. 'So, I should really tell you.'

'Tell me what?'

'I was in Asda the other day – last Sunday. I only went in for a few bits, but I ended up getting a trolley full ...'

'And?'

For God's sake, get on with it, Suzanne.

'Sorry ...' She stands, picks up her wine glass from the fireplace, and gulps the rest of it down. It almost makes me shudder. 'I saw Tom with his daughter. And his *ex*-wife.'

'So?' I say. 'There could be a reason for that. It's not like they're never going to spend time together, is it?'

'You're awfully trusting.' She flops onto the chair by the fire.

'Like you said – we've only been on one date. It's not like we're in a relationship. He can do what he wants.'

She laughs and stands, taking her empty wine glass into the kitchen.

'And that's why he likes you,' she says, returning with her glass topped up to the brim. She sits down more carefully this time. 'I bet you've not even asked if they're separated.'

'I haven't needed to,' I say. 'He said he lived with housemates.'

'Housemates?' she says quietly. 'Hmm.' She takes another sip. She's going to make herself ill if she carries on drinking so quickly. 'That's a classic. Just be careful, Laura.'

I place my drink on the table at the end of the sofa.

'I think I should go,' I say. 'I've obviously upset you in some way.'

Her eyes widen.

'No, don't go!' She stands, spilling wine all over her top. 'Oh God. I'm a mess, aren't I?' She plucks a tissue from a covered box on another wooden side table and dabs at her blouse. 'Won't be a second. I'll just go and change.'

I hear her rush up the stairs; the floorboards creak as

she walks to her room, and there's a bang of a wardrobe door as it's flung open. It sounds as though she's talking to herself.

This whole situation is bizarre. I only met Suzanne last week, and here we are pretending we're best friends. I hardly know anything about her. She lives with her parents; she's worked at the call centre for five years. She hasn't volunteered much information beyond that. I'm not even sure that her relationship with Jack the car salesman was real.

I stand and go to the mantelpiece; it's crammed with photographs. There's one of a couple dressed in Seventies clothes. Her parents, I imagine. The woman is in a yellow off-the-shoulder sundress with a wide-brimmed hat; the man in a beige print shirt and dark brown flared trousers. They must be older parents. Suzanne can't have been born in the Seventies.

The next picture is a school photo of what looks like Suzanne and her younger brother.

'That's better,' she says as she breezes back into the room.

She must've tiptoed down the stairs.

She's wearing a black vest top and indigo jeans that are turned up at the bottom. It might be two degrees outside, but inside we could be in Spain. The heating must be on full blast.

'I'm sorry about before,' she says. 'That wine went straight to my head. Shall we order some food in?'

'Yeah, sure.'

'Chinese food OK with you?' She already has the menu in her hand. 'I've been craving it all week.'

'That's fine.'

Her gaze moves to where I'm looking.

'Is that your brother?' I say.

'One second.' She raises her index finger as she presses the call button on her mobile phone. She walks into the kitchen as she talks. 'Chicken with cashew nuts, sweet and sour pork, and special fried rice. Can I have some vegetable spring rolls, and prawn crackers too, please?'

She didn't ask me what I wanted, but my mouth is watering at the mention of the food she's ordered.

I hear the beep of her hanging up, the fridge door opening, and the clinking of bottles being taken out. Then silence.

I walk into the kitchen.

'Can I help with ...'

She's standing in the middle of the room, holding two bottles of beer, just staring at the wall to the left.

'Suzanne?'

She turns on her heels.

'Sorry, I was miles away there.' She holds up the bottles. 'I thought we'd better give the wine a rest.'

I follow her back into the living room. It's only eight o'clock – it feels like it should be ten.

'I hope you don't mind that I ordered for both of us,' she says. 'We could make a buffet out of it.' She laughs. 'My parents make a buffet out of everything.'

She looks at the photograph that I noticed a few minutes ago.

'Yes,' she says. 'That's my brother.' She picks up the photograph and sits on the floor cross-legged. I kneel next to her. 'It seems such a long time ago when this was taken.' She lifts the picture so it's about ten inches from her face. 'I was ten and he was eight. It was our last school photo taken together. They didn't take sibling pictures in our high school.'

'Where does he live now?' I say.

She looks up from the photograph.

'He died in 2012. He was only twenty.'

'I'm so sorry, Suzanne,' I say. 'I'm sorry that I brought it up.'

'It's fine.' She sniffs. 'It's been years now.'

'You don't have to talk about it.'

I place a hand on hers, and she smiles at me.

'I like to talk about him,' she says. 'It makes me feel closer to him.'

'What was his name?'

'Jamie.' She touches his chin in the photograph. 'He was always getting into trouble. At the age of about two, he pulled out all of the next-door neighbour's plants.'

She laughs, kneels up, and places the frame back on the mantelpiece.

'Mum always said, "One day, he's going to get himself involved in something that he can't get himself out of."'

'Was she right?'

'Not really. It was a case of wrong place, wrong time. He'd just passed his driving test. He loved driving his

213

car – it was a Vauxhall Corsa – he used to give all his friends rides. He was never a big drinker – loved his freedom on the road too much. But one night, he'd just dropped his friend off home and was driving down the M55, and another driver was driving up the wrong side of the motorway. Three times over the limit, apparently.'

'Oh God, that's awful. Did they catch the driver?'

'Yes, they caught him. He got banned for two years and received a suspended sentence.'

'Oh.'

'Yes, nothing compared to what we lost that night. I've seen him around, you know. He still lives here. He looked a mess, though, I'll give him that. Still does.'

'Do you still see him?'

She looks up again at the photograph.

'I'll get the plates,' she says, getting up. 'Then we can sit around the table. Then how about a film?'

'Yes. That sounds great.'

She leaves the room and there's a car engine outside. The food can't be here already.

I look along the photographs. There's another of what looks to be Suzanne's brother but he looks a lot older than twenty. I stand to take a closer look.

'What are you looking at?'

She's standing at the doorway, her arms full of plates, cutlery, and a roll of kitchen towel.

I straighten quickly.

'Just looking at your parents in their Seventies out-fits.'

A cloud has shadowed her expression.

'I love your mum's hat,' I say quickly, grateful I remember the details in her parents' picture.

Suzanne smiles again. 'I think she still has that in the loft.'

The doorbell rings, and I'm thankful for it.

I don't know why Suzanne is acting so strangely. She's usually so straightforward.

It's probably the alcohol.

But, then, how would I know?

I barely know this woman at all.

22

Sarah

Sarah's sitting at a window seat in the pub that has views of the estuary at Preston Docks. She doesn't know what this Suzanne Anderson looks like, but the woman assured her that she would find Sarah. She sounded extremely confident on the phone; Sarah hopes she doesn't yell out her name in the middle of the pub.

A tall woman comes through the door. She has blonde hair, and is wearing a red raincoat, black capri pants and yellow pumps. She catches Sarah's eye; Sarah stands and walks towards her. God, she hopes this is the right person.

'Are you Sarah?' the woman says, her voice as loud as it was on the telephone.

'Suzanne?'

'That's right,' she says. 'Are you buying then? G&T for me, please. No work this afternoon. Hence the flat shoes.'

Suzanne winks at her. Her make-up is immaculate — it's like she spent hours getting ready and it's only a lunch-time meeting. Sarah thought she'd made an effort by putting a blazer over her jeans and T-shirt.

Sarah carries their drinks to the table.

'I *knew* something strange must have had happened to Laura,' Suzanne says, sitting down. She takes a long sip of her drink, sucking the straw. 'She left so suddenly.'

'How well did you know her?' says Sarah, glad that Suzanne got straight to the point without any annoying small talk.

'Pretty well,' says Suzanne. 'Well, as much as you can know a colleague after working with them for a few weeks. We sat next to each other at the call centre. And she stayed the night at mine once. Sort of a girlie night in type thing.'

Sarah takes her notepad and pen out of her handbag.

'She was quiet to start with,' Suzanne continues. 'It seemed odd that she applied for a job at the call centre – it's not a role for shy people. Though there were quite a few people who started at the same time who were just as bad.'

'Do you think she left because she was sacked?' says Sarah.

Sarah seriously doubts that Suzanne was Laura's true friend – she implied that Laura was bad at her job. From what Rob has said about the place, it was a horrible set-up. People being fired for not selling and colleagues pitted against each other.

'Sacked?' says Suzanne. 'No. Though, if she was, no one said anything about it.'

She sucks on the straw until there's no drink left.

'Another?' says Sarah.

'That'd be lovely.'

Sarah stands and goes to the bar. She doesn't know if it's ethical, but everyone knows that a person well-oiled is more forthcoming than a sober one.

'Cheers,' says Suzanne when Sarah places another in front of her. 'Anyway, she started seeing one of the managers at work. Laura said they'd been at the same primary school. He was really good-looking. Anyway ... she knew I had a thing for him, but I played it down a bit. She didn't owe me anything, I suppose, but it did piss me off a bit.'

'What was his name?'

'Tom,' she says. 'Tom Delaney.'

Sarah takes out her phone and brings up JP's Facebook profile.

'Is this him?' she says.

Suzanne grabs the phone to take a closer look.

'Yes, that's him.' She wrinkles her nose. 'Though I don't recognise the name he's given himself. He did have several profiles on there when I worked there, though.'

'You don't work there any more?'

'Nah,' she says. 'Left soon after Laura did. Tom left, too. I don't know where he went – he hasn't posted on his main profile for years.'

She's obviously been keeping tabs on this man.

'Is that unusual for Tom?'

Suzanne shrugs. 'I suppose. But how well do you know your colleagues, anyway?'

Sarah thinks of her relationship with Kim. They met

218

at work and have been best friends ever since. It's different for everyone, she supposes, and the type of work environment it is. She doubts she could ever be best friends with a go-getting booming salesperson.

'Did Laura reveal much to you about her background?' says Sarah.

'Yeah, bits. I don't think she got out much before she started at PeopleServe. It must have been a shock to the system when she realised how often we all went out.' She stirs her drink with the straw, the ice ringing like a bell. 'You know she cared for her father?'

Sarah nods.

'I think that affected her – it would affect anyone. She wasn't very confident – even though she was really pretty. I think that's why she was flattered when Tom took an interest in her. They moved quite fast, though I don't think they slept together.'

'What makes you say that?'

'She would've told me. We had almost a school friends kind of relationship. She always wanted advice about hair, make-up, clothes. She'd ask about Tom, about his situation. She was a bit too deep, though. When she came to stay at mine, she spent ages looking at the family photos. I lived with my mum and dad then. She asked about my brother and I told a bit of a lie. I don't know why I did it. I told her that he'd died – but he hadn't.' She leans forward, resting her palms on the table. 'Do you think that was weird of me?'

Yes, thinks Sarah.

'Why do you think you lied?' she says.

'Laura had so much sadness in her life. Her dad dying, limited contact with her mother who lived on the other side of the country. I guess I felt bad telling the truth. That my brother was successful and has four kids. It was like I was rubbing her face in my happy family.' She takes another long sip of her drink. 'And I was a bit pissed. I couldn't exactly own up to it the day after.'

'What was Laura like in the days before she left?'

'Hmm,' she says. 'I've been thinking about this. She kept getting presents from someone. I think it was one of the IT guys who took a shine to her. He was probably harmless enough, but it made Laura feel uncomfortable. Especially as it was such early days for her and Tom. Then I remember she was off sick for nearly a week, then she didn't come back. I spoke to her briefly, but I can't remember what she said. I feel terrible for not remembering.'

She rips the corner off a beer mat. 'I feel bad about the whole thing, really. If I wasn't so annoyed about the Tom thing, I would've been a better friend. To think of her dying alone is just so heart-breaking.' Tears well up in her eyes. 'She was a lovely person. She wasn't as naïve as you think she'd have been ... with not going to high school or mixing with kids her own age. It was like she was better than that, you know?'

'What do you mean?'

Sarah takes a tissue from her bag and passes it across the table.

'All I gabbed on about was trivial stuff with her. Make-up, men, stupid sales targets. When all of the time she had this past. She had seen her father die after caring for him. They got on really well, did you know that?'

'I don't know much about the relationship between her and her father.'

'She said they would listen to the radio together. She was waitress to his friends when they came around. She spoke once about seeing one of them in an old people's home, or sheltered accommodation or something. I can't remember his name.' She gazes out of the window. 'I wish I remembered every conversation we had. I've been looking online and she hasn't even a picture on the internet. *I* don't even have a picture of her on my phone.' She closes her eyes. 'But I can still see her in my mind. I can hear her voice and smell the Chanel No 5 she wore because her mother left it behind and that was the only nice perfume she had.' She opens her eyes again and a tear runs down her cheek. 'What a waste. I can't believe they don't know how she died. And I can't believe that she was alone.'

'But at least she made a friend in you towards the end.'

Suzanne dabs her eyes; there are no smudges in her make-up, it's still intact.

'Do you know where Tom is now?' says Sarah. 'Do you think he'll talk to me?'

'I've no idea,' says Suzanne, sniffing. 'He's probably still with his wife and daughter across town.'

'He was married?'

Suzanne nods.

'He told everyone – well, Laura and me at least – that

he was separated, but that was probably all bullshit.'

'Do you think Laura would have threatened to tell his wife about their affair?'

'No, no. She wasn't like that. She would've just finished with him if she knew.'

'Did she know?'

'I don't know. I only found out after Tom said Laura had left the job.'

'What did Tom say about Laura leaving? How would he have known?'

'I don't know if he knew why she left. No one could make contact with her. Every morning she wasn't there, he would look to the door at whoever came in. He seemed quite sad about her not coming back. He said to one of the managers that telesales mustn't have been for her, which was glaringly obvious to everyone working there. There was one woman called Treena who cried literally every time she spoke to one of the managers. Telesales is awful, really. I was surprised Laura hadn't told me herself that she was leaving, but maybe I wasn't her cup of tea. We were total opposites, but I thought we clicked.' Another tear falls down her face. 'God, I shouldn't be drinking gin. I thought I'd be OK.'

'She didn't leave on purpose though, did she?' says Sarah.

'What do you mean?'

'You shouldn't take it personally that she didn't contact you about leaving. From what I gather, she died before anyone at work knew her intentions. Only her mother seemed to know that Laura planned to travel.'

'I didn't think of it like that.'

Obviously.

Sarah tries not to sigh. This woman is more bothered about herself than Laura.

'So she might not have chosen to have left,' says Suzanne.

'That's what I meant, yes.'

Suzanne looks at the ceiling.

'It makes sense now,' she says. 'I knew it can't have been anything I said.'

Jesus. How did Laura stand sitting next to this self-centred woman?

'Thanks so much for talking to me,' says Sarah.

'It's a relief, to be honest. No one around me knew her. It's nice to remember her. Do you know when her funeral is?'

'In a few days, I think.'

Suzanne finishes the rest of her drink quickly, despite her misgivings about the demon gin. Sarah calls her a taxi from her app and waits with her to make sure Suzanne gets in safely.

There's a bleep from her phone. A message from Suzanne.

Hi again, Sarah. I've just remembered something else. About Laura getting cards, flowers delivered to her desk and at home. Tom had to transfer one of the IT guys to a different department – Justin Parkinson or Rob Roscoe – they kinda blurred into one. He was besotted with Laura. Hope this helps. Suzanne xx

A cold shiver runs down the back of Sarah's neck.

23

Sarah

Sarah barely registered the short journey home after Suzanne mentioned Rob's name in connection with Laura. And there was the school connection, too. Rob had mentioned that he went to the same school as Tom. She now knows that Tom went to the same school as Laura.

Why would Rob keep that from her? Has he been acting differently? He didn't reply to her calls and text messages when she first found out about Laura Aspinall's body downstairs. He actively ignored her. In the evening, he didn't come home as planned. Instead, he said he got drunk with customers. Was he *really* with potential clients?

Sarah pays the driver and looks up at Nelson Heights.

She used to feel safe here. Now, the block of flats seems to loom over her: grey, miserable, sinister.

When she reaches her door, she hesitates.

She turns around and looks over the balcony.

A man — the man with the same silhouette she saw weeks ago in the darkness of the flats, the man she's sure was the one who waved at her at the university — is standing on the grass verge on the edge of the car park. The hood of his jacket is pulled over his head; his hands are in his pockets. He takes one out; it looks like he's holding a mobile phone.

Sarah's heart is hammering in her chest. She should run inside, call the police.

But she can't take her eyes off him.

As he puts a phone back in his pocket, her mobile makes a sound.

She takes it out of her bag.

A Twitter notification.

It quotes a tweet she sent last week:

@Anon1mouse Hello. I'm a journalist based in Preston and am looking for information on the body found in Nelson Heights. I would be grateful if you could contact me. Thanks, Sarah.

She opens Twitter and reads the reply.

@SarahHayesP175 So now you know who I am. Or do you? How about we meet? I can tell you all about what happened to Laura.

She looks up. The man has gone. Is he already in the block?

Sarah's knees almost buckle. She scrambles through her bag and grabs her keys; her hands shaking as she reaches for the lock.

The foyer door downstairs slams shut.

Oh God, he's coming.

She pushes open her front door and slams it behind her. She double locks it and pushes across the bolts, top and bottom.

'Hello!' she shouts. Her voice sounds as though it's in a vacuum. 'Is anyone in? Alex?'

The silence seems to pulsate in her ears.

She's still leaning against the front door.

Footsteps are coming towards her.

A key slides into the lock.

She can't control her breathing; it feels as though she's choking.

Who lived here before? Had she made sure the locks were changed?

He's turning the key back and forth.

He can't get in; she double locked it.

She drags the strap of her handbag towards her, taking out her phone.

Thud, thud. Fists pound against the front door.

The vibrations bang her head.

The letterbox opens.

'What are you doing on the floor?'

She crawls away towards the door of the living room.

'It's me,' he says. 'Rob.'

'I know it's you,' she says, her voice almost breaking.

'What are you talking about?'

'You're anonymous, aren't you?'

She types 999 into her phone.

'What are you talking about?' he repeats, shouting.

'You've been sending me messages about Laura.'

'What?' His voice is high-pitched. 'Why would I do that when I can just talk to you?'

'Throw me your phone,' she shouts. The adrenaline makes her feel braver than her common sense usually allows. 'If it's not you, then give me your phone. Put your hand through the letterbox and show me you're unlocking it.'

'This is ridiculous, Sarah.' He sighs, but seconds later he shoves his hands through the letterbox. He's holding his mobile phone and using the index finger from his other hand to unlock the screen. 'There you go,' he says, throwing the phone onto the carpet.

She reaches over for it.

She clicks on his Twitter account. He's signed in with his own name.

There are no tweets to Sarah's account.

She could search through the whole of his phone and she would find nothing. Rob might be too clever for that.

No, no. It's Rob.

She's known him for over two years – he's always been transparent, honest with her. They met at the university – it was nothing to do with the flats. He couldn't have known she lived here when they met. He had an IT contract – helping to set up a new system in the library.

It can't be Rob who was sending Laura gifts and cards. He had never sent Sarah anything like that.

Was that because he didn't love Sarah enough?

Did he love Laura because she was beautiful, vulnerable?

'Tell me the truth, Rob,' she says. 'How well did you know Laura Aspinall?'

'What the—' A thud sounds, as though he has slumped against the front door. 'I only knew of her. When I did my rotation on the sales floor, she was only there for a few days. I've already told you all of this. The most I would have said to her is hello.'

'Who did she sit next to?'

'Eh?' he says, high-pitched again. 'How am I supposed to remember that? They were all bloody loud and full of themselves. Apart from one woman who cried most of the time.'

'What was that woman's name?'

'Treena or Tina or something. I don't know. Can you remember everyone who comes into the café?'

So he doesn't just remember Laura from working there. That's a good sign, right?

Sarah stands and walks to the door. She unbolts and unlocks it and takes a deep breath when she flicks off the lock and opens the door.

Rob is standing a few feet away from the door. His hair is sticking up in places; his face flushed.

'What the hell was all that about?' he says.

Sarah looks outside, left and right.

'There was a man over there. He was about your height – the same sort of jacket that you had the other day. The navy blue one. He was just standing there, staring at me. He asked me to meet him – said he knew what happened to Laura.'

228

'Wait – what?' Rob looks over the balcony, across the car park. 'Navy blue? I haven't got a navy blue jacket.'

'You haven't?'

Sarah's sure she's seen a man wearing one recently. He was in her flat – sitting at her kitchen table.

'Oh,' she says. 'It was Andy.'

'Your ex?'

Sarah nods, grabs Rob's arm and pulls him inside, locking the door.

He stands with his hands on his hips. His brow is furrowed; she can hardly see his eyes.

'So you think it's Andy, now?' he says, slowly, calmly. 'This person who's been following you?'

Sarah walks through to the living room and sits at her desk.

'No. I don't know.'

Andy might be trying to frame Rob. But how could he have done that? Andy hinted that he knew nearly everyone in Preston. Did he know Laura?

Shit. Sarah's thoughts aren't rational any more.

But someone has made contact with her. Someone wants her to stop digging. All she wanted to do was find out more about the person behind the story. Not the reason she died. This is getting too much.

Rob sits on the settee, close to her. His knees almost touch the back of her chair.

'But you were quick to assume it was me.'

'It's because of what Laura's colleague said – that Laura was being hounded by one of the tech guys at PeopleServe.'

Sarah doesn't want to give away the name of the other person Suzanne mentioned. Justin Parkinson.

'What was her colleague's name?'

'It doesn't matter,' says Sarah. 'But it's a coincidence, don't you think? That you worked with Laura and now you're seeing me and I live in the flat right above where she died? Plus those tweets – the man's handle was Techie Dude.'

Sarah takes a screenshot of the tweet she received from Anon1mouse and sends it to Andy.

'So you've put two and two together and made a million,' says Rob. 'And you think I could kill someone and then start seeing someone above where the dead body is? That's insane.'

He would say that, wouldn't he? Because that's what might have happened.

'I didn't say I thought she was murdered.'

'That's what you insinuated.' He flops back against the settee. 'And you thought it was me because I worked at PeopleServe and I'm the only technical person you know. Brilliant, Sarah. Where does this leave us now? You think I'm a fucking murderer!'

'I don't,' she says, turning her chair to face him, still clinging onto her mobile phone. 'It was terrifying seeing that man, then getting a message from him.'

'OK,' he says, rubbing his forehead. 'I get that. But if he wanted to hurt you, he wouldn't mess around with Twitter – he'd have done something by now. Maybe tell Andy what's going on.'

'I've just sent him a picture of the tweet,' says Sarah.

230

She pauses for a moment. 'Suzanne mentioned that Tom went to the same school as Laura.'

'What? I can barely keep up with all of this. Laura went to St John's, too?'

'No.'

Sarah takes a deep breath. She should write all of this down, send it to her tutor so she can get an objective opinion. Are the people closest to her lying? The thoughts in her head don't make sense. She gets up and sits on the edge of the settee next to Rob.

'I'm exhausted.' Her mobile phone beeps with a message. 'I want to throw that bloody phone away!'

'I'll have a look,' says Rob, leaning forward and reaching for it. He glances at the message preview. 'It's OK. It's from Kim.'

Sarah takes the phone and opens the message.

Hey Sarah. Feels like I haven't seen you for ages! Hope you're having a nice few days off. Btw – I've finally remembered about Laura. She came into the café. Give us a ring when you're free. Kim x

It's not unsurprising that Laura visited the café. It's only up the road.

Sarah places her phone on her lap as a thought runs through her mind. One she's had before.

An anonymous person messaged her wanting to talk about Laura; another sent a hand-delivered note hinting they didn't want Sarah digging any further.

What if it's not one, but two people who know what happened to Laura?

24

Laura

Sunday, 19 March 2017

I've tried not to think about the strange way Suzanne acted last night. After the food, she seemed to go back to her normal, chatty self. I've also tried not to think about Suzanne saying she saw Tom in the supermarket playing happy families. I was so desperate to get home after staying somewhere unfamiliar overnight that I didn't stay for breakfast. I didn't want to chat, I just wanted to get under my quilt and into my own bed. Especially after I received a text message from Tom.

Hey Laura.

Think it's best if we keep things between ourselves at work for the time being.

Look forward to seeing you this afternoon.

T xx

I hung my outfit on the curtain rail yesterday: jeans, a bird-print shirt, and white Converse pumps. Perfect for a casual Sunday afternoon lunch date. The whole outfit cost £11.50. I googled the items and it would have cost over a hundred pounds new, so really I'm at least £88.50 better off.

My phone beeps again. I grab the phone from my bedside table. The message preview on my screen saver doesn't sound good. It's another message from Tom.

Hi Laura, I'm really sorry but ...

I flop back onto the pillow, knowing what is about to follow.

I tap in my pin code and open the message.

Hi Laura, I'm really sorry but I'm going to be late this afternoon. My ex isn't collecting Rosie until twelve, so it's going to be about one-ish.

Hope that's ok.

T xx

I was wrong. I was expecting him to cancel.

I tap a quick reply, saying that it's fine, and almost leap out of bed.

He still hasn't told me the name of his ex-wife, but I suppose it shouldn't matter to me right now – this is only our second date. It's probably for the best as I'd only try to stalk her on Facebook, and we all know that never leads to anything good.

I'm showered, dressed and ready, and it's only ten thirty. I've had two cups of coffee, had a quick look at the telly, but nothing holds my attention for more than five minutes.

It'll only take me ten minutes to walk to where we're meeting. I could do a little detour. Perhaps have a quick coffee in the café. Maybe even a little breakfast. That'll pass the time.

233

It's not busy at this time on a Sunday (it's a recent thing, this Sunday opening; don't know how long that'll last). The early breakfast rush has finished and it's a good hour till lunch time. Still, there are a couple of the older faces I recognise. A man that I'm sure lives in Nelson Heights, but I haven't seen him in a long time.

I sit at mine and Mum's favourite table near the window.

One of the ladies comes to my table. I think it's the owner as I'm sure I've heard other customers call her Kim. She's got wavy, chin-length hair and always has rosy cheeks. I imagine it gets a little hot standing next to a stove all day. Maybe *she's* Tom's ex.

'Hi, love,' she says, barely glancing at me. 'What'll it be today?'

'A tea, please. And a slice of flapjack, please.'

Please, please, please. I can't help it, ignore me.

'Right you are.'

She saunters back to the counter. The other woman has her back to the seating area. She has her hair in a bun today. In her left hand is a scrunched-up tissue (which can't be very hygienic) and she seems to be dabbing it on her eyes.

I wish I wasn't sitting near the window now.

The sun's shining in my face, though. It's an excuse to move.

Should I? It'll look weird, won't it?

Sod it.

I grab my bag and coat and move to the table near the right wall.

'The sun's in my eyes,' I say to who I think is Kim. 'Is that OK?'

I've always been overly polite. My dad said I shouldn't do it because it was like I was apologising for simply being alive.

Kim looks up and wrinkles her nose. Her eyes meet mine in a way I know she's not really registering me.

'Course, love,' she says.

It's now ten past eleven. In around half an hour, one of them will leave because Tom's ex is picking up Rosie soon.

The woman with the tissue is sobbing now. I chance a glance to my right. Kim has her arm around her.

'It might be something innocent,' Kim says, rubbing her back.

I go back to reading, well pretending, to read the newspaper that was left on the table. It's a local paper, dated last week, and the headline reads: *Body Found Identified as Missing Student.*

I'd forgotten about the dead body they found a few weeks ago. I'm usually good at following-up things like that. Relationships are so distracting.

'But I found the messages on his phone,' says the woman behind the counter.

My shoulders tense.

'Oh, Sarah,' says Kim. 'You've got to have it out with him. Tell him what you've found.'

Sarah. Her name is Sarah.

I wish I knew more about her. She's been working here for at least three years. I bet she doesn't even know *my* name.

'I didn't mean to snoop,' she says to Kim. 'They were on his lock screen.'

'Who were they from?'

I hold my breath. The newspaper is shaking with my hands.

'Work,' she says. 'It just said work. It could've been anyone.'

I curse the toaster as it pops. They are no longer huddled together but busying themselves. The one time that I want them to stand around and chat.

'Here you go, love.' Sarah places the flapjack and tea on my table. 'Hope you enjoy.'

I look up to her as she reaches over me and places one of the serviettes next to the plate. Her eyes are red. Some of the mascara that was once on her lashes is splattered in tiny flecks around her eyes. She looks as though she applies make-up as well as I do.

'Thank you,' I say.

She gives me a small smile and retreats back behind the counter.

A plate smashes. Even the radio in the background seems to pause.

'Do you want to go home?' Kim says. 'This is the third item you've broken today.' She doesn't say it unkindly. 'And I can come round to yours later ... we can have wine ... get pissed ... talk shit about everyone.'

'I guess,' says Sarah. 'I have to go now anyway.'

She disappears into the back and comes out wearing a coat, scarf, and a dark grey beret. She looks effortlessly stylish even though I bet she just threw it on, and I feel a pang of jealousy. Must be because she's so slim.

I look at the clock. It's a quarter to twelve.

I didn't think his ex would still be so upset about everything – if Sarah *is* the one he was married to. I haven't actually asked Tom outright what happened in his marriage. All he's said is that he had to drop his daughter off with his ex. How much do you ask after two dates?

You see, this is why snooping never comes to any good.

Sarah and I both know that now. It's strange to think that I know a little about her life and she barely knows me at all. I'm almost invisible to her.

I can't mention to Tom that I've been in the café. He might think I'm prying (which I am) – it probably wasn't Sarah he was married to. It's too much of a coincidence that his ex-wife would work in the café up the road from where I live.

The beginnings of a crush always take over me. I should learn to rein it in a bit – it's doing me no good at all. I think about him all the time and I replay our conversations constantly. But it seems to be reciprocal. I've never had that before.

He's waiting at the corner of the high street. He's wearing black jeans, his blue overcoat and a bright red scarf.

'Hey, Laura!' he says, as always.

'Hi.' I go to kiss his cheek, but he turns his head so I catch his lips. My cheeks flush. 'Did Rosie get off OK?'

'Yes, yes.'

'You don't have any pictures of her on Facebook,' I say as we continue through the park. 'Though I don't blame you.'

'No,' he says. 'I don't understand how people can put pictures of their kids online. It's not like they can give their permission, is it? You never know what's going to happen with the internet in a few years' time.'

'I guess. I don't really put anything of my life on there.'

He takes hold of my hand.

'You do right,' he says. 'Sorry. I can be a bit of a bore on data protection and all of that. It's part of my job knowing what personal details we can use and all that.' He laughs. 'Sorry, I'm doing it again. I can't help being a bit of a nerd. Tech is all I've known, really. In the workplace, that is. I try to keep off computers at home. A Kindle is all I manage.'

'You read?'

'Of course!'

'It's just that some people don't bother with books.'

'You can't trust a person who doesn't read. What else have they to fill their minds with?'

'What's your favourite book?' I ask.

'Now, that's a question. I am quite partial to *A Game of Thrones*. Though some people just watch the TV adaptations these days.'

'Oh,' I say. 'I've not read that one.'

'One? One? It's not one! It's a whole universe.'

'I guess you really like it, then?'

'Sorry, yes. I do.'

238

He's apologising in the same way I do. It makes me feel warm inside even though it's freezing cold. He looks across at me and now I wish I'd read every book in the series. I'm going to order them all when I get home.

'How come you have two different Facebook profiles?' I say.

'Been stalking me online, have you?'

'Hardly ...'

'I'm just kidding. I don't really use Facebook. One of the profiles must've been an old one and I forgot my password.'

'But what about the messages you sent me?'

He frowns. 'On Facebook?' he says. 'I don't really use that. Must've been a bit pissed.' He grimaces then smiles. 'I'll have to have a read through and learn what shit things I've said to you.'

'They weren't shit,' I say.

He must've been really drunk when he sent them for him not to remember using it. I try not to dwell on the fact that he might be a binge drinker. Everyone I have encountered at PeopleServe seems to be a binge drinker.

'I want to show you somewhere before we head to lunch,' he says.

He tugs my hand gently and leads me down a ginnel. It looks like it should be the side of someone's garden. Either side are dilapidated wooden fences and overgrown weeds. The grassy path underfoot is soggy and slippery.

'It's better in the summer,' he says over his shoulder.

The bottoms of my pumps are now covered in a layer

of mud. This had better be worth it. I've never been much of an off-road person, as you can imagine.

'Not long now,' he says.

He's wearing boots that are much more suited to this weather. He must have planned this.

Finally, we come to a small clearing, with a semi-circle of trees. A bench faces the Ribble Estuary; it's gently babbling along. Even in the foggy drizzle, it looks beautiful.

'There's no one else around here,' I say. 'How did you find this?'

He smiles, takes out a wad of tissues from his pocket and wipes the bench. He gestures for me to sit.

'I used to do a lot of walking when Mum was really bad. It's great for thinking. I don't get out now as much as I used to.'

'What happened to your mum?'

'She had an accident. It was a few years ago, now. My dad married someone else.'

'I'm so sorry.'

'It's OK,' he says. 'It's not your ...' He sighs as he sits. 'It's lovely here, isn't it?'

The water laps against the bank below. A single magpie lands on a collection of twigs. I salute it, and say, 'Good afternoon, Mr Magpie.'

Tom almost snorts with laughter.

'I've never heard that bit before,' he says. 'Saluting, yes, but not that little greeting.' He closes his eyes for a moment; the breeze glides across his lashes. 'It's just superstition, anyway,' he says. 'If something bad is

240

going to happen, it's going to happen. Saluting a bird isn't going to change anything.'

I shrug, even though he's not looking.

'There's no harm in it, though.'

I pull my coat tighter around me and fold my arms around my middle.

Tom sits up straight.

'Yes, it's bloody cold, isn't it?' He puts his arm around my shoulders and rubs the top of my right arm. 'I just wanted to show you this place.'

I lean my head on his shoulder.

'I love it,' I say. 'We should come again when it's sunny.'

'Yes!' He almost jumps up. 'I knew you'd like it.'

He holds out his hand, and I take it – letting him pull me up from the bench.

He links his arm through mine and we huddle together as we walk side-by-side back to the main road.

We're almost at the restaurant on the edge of town.

'And after lunch,' he says, giving my arm a gentle squeeze, 'I thought we could go to the cinema. There's this old film they're re-running … it's an absolute classic.'

I smile, and imagine us holding hands, popcorn between us in a near-empty theatre, an old black and white film casting flattering shadows on our faces like candlelight.

'That sounds lovely,' I say. 'I love those black and white films. Dad and I used to watch them on Friday afternoons.'

We reach the restaurant and he holds the door open for me.

If that had happened with Mum, she'd have said, 'Do I look decrepit? I'm perfectly capable of opening a door myself.' She could be offended by the kindest of gestures: a good deed never goes unpunished.

I follow him to the table and sit on the chair the waiter pulled out for me.

'Black and white?' says Tom, sitting opposite me. 'God, no. I can't stand monochrome. It's *Ferris Bueller's Day Off*. An absolute classic. You have seen it, right?'

He rubs his hands together and takes off his gloves.

'Yeah,' I say, laughing. 'An absolute classic.'

He raises his eyebrows.

'Are you taking the piss?' he says, leaning forward, his mouth in a half smile. 'I actually know all the dialogue.' He hides his face briefly behind the menu. 'Yeah, I know, it's sad. But I can't help what I like.'

'It'll be nice,' I say. 'I haven't been to the cinema in a long time.'

He looks at me. 'I bet you haven't. What was the last film you saw at the pictures?'

'Oh God. I think it was *Pretty Woman* in the final year of primary school.'

'Bloody hell. That's years ago. And isn't that a 15?'

'Yeah, but Mum wasn't really paying much attention to what I was up to then.'

The waiter comes to take our order. Tom asks for a bottle of wine to share. I'm going to be asleep if I drink that in the afternoon. My liver is going to hate me.

'Where did your mum go when she left?'

'What?'

I drop the menu onto the table.

'Sorry – was that too invasive?'

'No, no. It's fine.' I take a sip of the wine, feeling the effects of it go straight to my head. This weekend I have drunk more wine than I have in my whole life. My head feels twice as light. 'I'm not sure. One morning she was there, and when I got home from school she was gone.'

'And she didn't tell you she was going?' His eyes are wide. 'That's shocking.'

'I suppose she'd made up her mind and didn't want anyone to change it. It was difficult with my dad. She had seen him become dependent on others. Before, he was such a strong, tall man. I know that sounds strange – how does someone stop being tall? But it was like he got smaller and smaller every year. I suppose she wanted to be a wife and not a carer. It's not for everyone.'

'Did she meet anyone else?'

The waiter places our starters in front of us. I pick up the fork and push a bit of salad around.

'Not until a few years after. It didn't last. He was a teacher as well.'

'A few years after, eh? Are you sure about that?'

I put a forkful of fishcake in my mouth at the wrong time.

'Hmm.'

I nod and chew; the food is so hot, it's making my eyes water.

Why is he asking so many strange questions?

'When did you last see her?'

I take a sip of water, feeling its delicious coldness soothe my scalded throat.

'Erm.'

'Sorry. I know I'm asking a lot of questions about your mum. It's just that mine isn't with me any more. It must be so hard for you not having yours in your life – and she's out there somewhere. It seems such a waste.'

'I can't change who she is,' I say. 'It hurt for a long time, but I knew it was because of Dad and not because of me. She was very open about that. And she did used to ring me a lot.'

'Well, that's good then.' He purses his lips. 'Even though you didn't know where she lived.'

'Only at first.'

'So when was the last time you saw her?'

'About two years ago.'

His eyes widen briefly, he shakes his head gently.

He places a hand over mine.

'Now I know you,' he says, 'I could never leave it that long to see you. I could barely go a week.'

'Oh.'

I think the wine has gone to his head, too.

'You're frowning,' he says. 'Was that too forward?' He dabs his mouth with the cotton napkin. 'I'm sorry. I always give away my feelings too quickly. My mum used to say I'd get hurt if I kept doing that.' He takes a sip of the wine. 'I've been hurt in the past.'

'I'm sorry.'

'The woman who owns the café up the road from you – she was my first girlfriend ... until she started playing mind games with me ... gaslighting they call it these days. It took me a long time to recover from that - I thought I was going mad.'

'Really? That's awful! What sort of things did she do?'

'She used to flirt with others, then say I was making it up ... imagining things. She'd arrange to meet me, not turn up ... said I had the wrong time, the wrong place. I started to question my sanity, if I'm honest.'

'I'm sorry you went through that,' I say. I want to get up and hug him. 'You weren't married to her, then?'

He waves a hand.

'Kim? God no. We were teenagers.'

Kim.

I totally misread what he told me. I feel like an idiot. Thank God I didn't tell him I'd been into the café, putting two and two together to make a hundred.

'I'm too trusting,' he continues, his cheeks flushing lightly in the middle of his cheeks. 'But I shouldn't admit to that. Anyway, enough depressing conversation.'

I close my knife and fork on the plate.

'That was one of the best fish cakes I've ever had,' I say, copying him and dabbing my mouth.

His smile is wide.

'Good,' he says. 'Though you must be easily pleased.'

I tap his foot gently under the table with mine. He tops up my wine.

'I like it when you're a little bit liberated with your words,' he says.

'Yeah, you're just trying to get me drunk.'

'Maybe. Listen, I was thinking – I've made some arrangements for this evening with Rosie and her mum. I thought it would be nice if I could come round to yours – or vice versa of course – and I could cook you a meal. What do you think?'

'Come round to yours?' I say. 'That would be really nice.'

It seems alcohol doesn't facilitate me with sparkling conversation. I think I might have been drunk for days now.

Suzanne was wrong. It's not happy families. He has his own place.

'Though,' he says, raising his glass to me, 'it might be a takeaway as I've not had time to plan.'

He's slurring his words a bit.

'It's OK,' I say. 'As long as it's not Chinese food.' God, I'm slurring, too. 'I had it at Suzanne's when I stayed over.'

He bends over.

Is he choking?

His shoulders are shaking; he sits up straight, taking a deep breath.

'You went to Suzanne's?'

'What's wrong with that?'

'Nothing, nothing.' He places his glass on the table and leans towards me. 'Did you lock the bedroom door before you went to sleep?'

I fold my arms, smirking slightly.

'No. I put the bedside cabinet behind the door.'

'Ha! I knew there was something weird about her.'

We were a bit too drunk to go to the cinema. I went home to change and sober up a bit while Tom 'prepared' his flat.

It's such a lovely evening I decided to walk over there. I'm useless with directions, even though I've lived in Preston all my life, but I recognise this road. And there's no avoiding it unless I make myself fifteen minutes late, according to Google Maps.

St Xavier's is on the right in about two hundred yards. I feel the dread I've always felt coming down this road.

I walk faster. It's only a building.

Nothing can harm me now.

On the gates are murals of the smiling faces of children. They look so harmless like that, don't they?

There are new climbing frames in the infants' playground; new doors, new windows.

I bet there are a lot of things new about it.

I look down at my phone. I should arrive any minute now. I'm tempted to run there but I don't want to arrive flustered.

He opens the door as I'm still halfway down the street.

'Hurry up, then!' he shouts.

'What are you doing, you nutter? Can't you just wait at the window like everyone else?'

'Ha!' He has a glass of wine in his hand. He must've

had a few while he waited. He stands aside to let me in. 'And welcome to my very humble, very tiny abode.'

'Thanks,' I say. 'Shall I take my shoes off?'

The carpet in the hallway is cream.

'I thought everyone laminated floors these days?' I say.

'That's so Nineties, Laura.' He closes the front door. 'And don't worry about the shoes.'

I follow him through to a kitchen-diner. It has high ceilings and shiny kitchen cabinets. I feel underdressed.

'Wine?' he says, placing a glass in my hands anyway.

'It's strange that you live so close to St Xavier's, isn't it?' I say.

'Not that strange,' he says, sitting at the kitchen table. 'It was a bargain, though.'

'I don't think I could stand being so close to the place.'

'Surely it wasn't that bad?'

'Oh it was.' I take a massive gulp of wine. Too much. I feel slightly nauseous. 'I had an awful time there. The teachers did what they could, but I couldn't follow them about everywhere.'

'The teachers were involved?' He looks genuinely surprised. 'I didn't know it had got to that stage. What happened?'

'Lots of things,' I say. 'I got called names, I was sent a horrible letter. There was one time in the girls' toilets. Tanya Greening came in when I was washing my hands. She didn't say anything, just walked straight up to me. She grabbed me by the hair and shoved me into a cubicle. She held a pair of scissors to my neck ... those round-ended school ones but she still managed to cut a chunk of my hair off with them. I can still see it as it landed in the toilet bowl. I don't know what else she would've done if a teacher hadn't come in.'

'Jesus, Laura,' he says. 'That's bloody scary.'

'I know. And she wasn't excluded – her mother was the head teacher.' I swirl the wine in my glass. I don't think I can drink any more. 'I bet you had a fantastic experience at school.'

'It was OK. I had all the shit afterwards, though. Like what happened with my mum.'

'What did happen?'

'She was killed.'

'What? How?'

He's looking at the table; his eyes are glazed.

'She found out something my dad didn't want her to know.'

'Did he hurt her?'

'She died in a car accident. Though, there was no evidence of another vehicle being involved. Her car crashed into a wall.'

'Oh God, Tom.' I reach over and place my hand over his. 'I'm so sorry.'

He looks up, his eyes glistening.

'So am I.'

He stands and swipes his hand from under mine.

'Let's order some takeaway, shall we?' he says. 'And let's stop being so bloody miserable. If we carry on like this, we'll be killing ourselves by the end of the night.'

25

Laura

Friday, 24 March 2017

It's now Friday, and Tom has been messaging me every morning, throughout the day and every evening to say goodnight. He phoned me last night and we talked for nearly two hours. Afterwards, my phone nearly burned my hands.

I've been trying to play it down to Suzanne. She's always asking about him and I know that she used to like him. She constantly hints that he's still married. And now I've seen his flat; I'm the one he says goodnight to – the one who talks to him before he goes to sleep.

'So have you heard from Tom today?' she says.

She waited until eleven this morning to ask.

'No,' I say. It seems disloyal to talk about him to her. 'But I'm not reading too much into it. I'm keeping my options open.'

I've always been quite good at lying because no one expects it from me.

'I'm so sorry, Laura,' she says in that disingenuous way of hers and I want to kick her chair across the room. With her still in it. 'It sounds as though he's ghosting you,' she says. 'Maybe even gaslighting you. I've read all about it.'

If she felt any glee in pointing it out, she didn't let it show. But I didn't care anyway because she had no idea of what was really going on.

'Delivery for Laura!'

The voice next to me makes me jump. A man wearing brown trousers and a brown shirt is standing in front of me holding a bunch of flowers.

'Someone's got an admirer,' he says.

He places them on my desk and walks away.

'Bloody hell,' says Suzanne. 'They must've cost a small fortune. Is there a card?'

I peer into the bouquet and reach for the little white envelope.

'It just says, *To Laura, with love x*.'

'Do you think they're from Tom?' she says.

I can see him out of the corner of my eye in his glass-walled office. He looks over, smiling, but when he sees the flowers, he turns his back to me. They mustn't be from him.

'Do you like them?'

I turn my chair; Justin's standing right behind me.

'I told him you were a yellow rose kind of person. Friendly, beautiful.'

Oh my God.

'These are from you?'

251

I'm trying not to sound ungrateful.

'I thought you needed cheering up. Especially after what happened with your dad last year. And with Tom and his ... er ... situation.'

I glance at Suzanne.

She shrugs. 'I didn't say anything to anyone.'

But I don't believe her. She's been telling everyone that Tom is still married, hasn't she? Jesus, this woman is something else.

'So you ordered these, Justin?'

What made him think this was appropriate?

He looks at the carpet and pushes his glasses up to the top of his nose.

'He wanted it to be a secret,' he says, and walks slowly back to his desk. 'I'll tell him he made a mistake.'

'What the fuck?' whispers Suzanne. 'Is he talking about himself in the third person? Or do you think they're from his geeky friend, Rob?'

'I've no idea,' I hiss. 'What am I supposed to do with them? I can't leave them on my desk. I'm meant to be seeing Tom.'

'Yeah, but *he's* not sending you flowers, is he?'

Suzanne leans over, grabs the bouquet, and plonks them next to her pencil pot.

'I'll look after them while you think about it. I love yellow. It really brightens up the place.'

The clock is moving so slowly this morning. Is this what it's going to be like for the rest of my working life? Watching time pass me by whilst in the company of

252

people I don't really like. Especially as I've felt Justin's gaze on me. He seems harmless enough, but it's freaking me out a bit. Even when he's on the telephone it feels as though he's talking about me.

He was huddled together with Rob ten minutes after the flowers were delivered. Are they playing some sort of prank on me? It's like being back at school.

I've been working here for three weeks now but it feels like forever. I can't see me lasting much longer. Plus, I'm really shit at telesales, but at least I'm not the worst. That's why I've not been 'let go' yet. I don't think anyone actually likes working here. It's only the competitive professional bullshitters who tend to have a knack for it – those who have a skin as thick as a rhino. Which accurately describes Suzanne. She talks to everyone on the telephone as if they're her life-long friends; face to face, too.

I have no desire to do well in this job because it feels as though I'm taking advantage of people. Because we call them during the day, it's either the elderly, un-employed or the long-term sick who we are getting to sign up. It's making me anxious. The people around me make me feel anxious. It's like they're all pretending, all fake.

I hesitate before making my first call of the afternoon.

'Just think of it as us *helping* them,' says Suzanne, chewing gum loudly. 'Loft insulation will save them a fortune in heating bills.'

Yes, it's loft insulation this week.

I see Tom from the corner of my eye. He's standing

up from his chair, leaving his office. I can't help but stare at him as he walks out.

He's coming towards me.

'Hey, Laura,' he says. 'Can I have a quick word?'

I stand and follow him to his office. He leans on the edge of his desk, gesturing for me to sit in the chair opposite his.

'I've noticed that you're way behind with your targets.' He gets out a file and flicks through the list of names. 'You're third from the bottom, which is not *so* bad, considering you've only been here a few weeks, but I would like to see an improvement in the next few days.'

'I didn't encourage Justin or Rob or whoever it was,' I say. 'I didn't want the flowers.'

He walks round to his chair and sits. He leans towards his monitor.

'Did you go on the training session last week?'

'No,' I say. 'I didn't know there was one.'

'Really? There were three sessions last week.' He types and my heart begins to pound. I feel like I'm being judged for something out of my control. 'No, your name isn't listed. Must've been an oversight. OK. I've signed you up for the one on Monday. That should help with your technique.'

Tears are welling in my eyes.

'Thank you,' I say.

He puts his hands on the desk and inhales loudly.

'Sorry,' he says. 'I shouldn't have let it bother me. But Justin!' He leans back in his leather chair and swivels to the side so he can see the other man. 'Is he being a bit weird with you? I suppose he doesn't get out much. I can get the other guy, Rob, to replace him. In fact, me and Rob go way back. Went to the same high school. Good guy. Bit nerdy. Not Justin nerdy, though.'

'I don't want to get Justin into trouble,' I say. 'They might not even be from him. I saw him talking to Rob.'

'Rob wouldn't do something like that.'

'How do you know? This whole thing is ridiculous. I hate the attention. I'm not used to it at all.'

'Really?' says Tom. 'After the way it was at school? You must know that most of the boys liked you.'

'What? No, not at all. I felt the exact opposite. I thought everyone hated me. Towards the end, anyway. Except Chloe. Do you remember Chloe?'

'Yes,' he says. 'You two were so close. She turned out to be a rather nasty person, didn't she?'

My ears prick at this information.

'Did she? I always thought it was Tanya who was the bully. I told you the other night what she did to me.'

'Ah, yes. Tanya.'

'What did you hear about Chloe?'

He shakes his head and waves his left hand.

'Nothing, it was nothing. Just stupid playground stuff. School was shit and we have to move on from that time.'

'OK,' I say.

But this doesn't feel right. He's always talked about how great school was, how lovely everything and everyone was.

255

Tom looks through the glass across to my desk just as Justin seems to drop something onto it.

Tom frowns.

'Yes,' he says. 'Maybe it's time we rotated Justin anyway. He's getting too familiar around people and I don't think he's doing his job with full concentration.'

He stands. I do, too.

'Hey,' he says. 'Come here.'

His back faces the window. I walk to him and face him.

His kisses me on the lips for longer than he should with the risk of us being spotted. I want to take him home – I want us to be away from here.

'Are you doing anything tomorrow night?' he says. 'Shall I come to yours?'

I was about to say yes please, but stopped myself.

'That would be lovely,' I say.

I leave his office and float back to my desk. There is nothing untoward on it after seeing Justin putting something on there. But Suzanne might have claimed it as her own by now.

'What's wrong?' says Suzanne.

'I think I've just been told off,' I say, trying to bluff my way out of receiving the Spanish Inquisition. 'I've been put on a training session.' I fold my arms in an attempt to look annoyed. 'I'm too old for this.'

'That's sales for you,' she says. 'It's bloody brutal and they treat us like second-class citizens.' She nods towards Tom. 'I thought he might go a bit softly, softly on you.'

'No.'

I smell a whiff of David Beckham aftershave, and I know before I look up that it's Ken.

'I don't see any headsets on, ladies,' he says. He puts his hands on his waist; his crotch is just inches from my face. 'Tick, tock, tick, tock.'

I'm the man with a tiny cock. Suzanne whispers it every time. Funnily enough, not now he's two feet away from us.

'We were just discussing strategy,' pipes up Suzanne.

'It's all written there in black and white,' says Ken, picking up my folder of *things to say*.

'But *some* things aren't,' says Suzanne, tapping the side of her nose, then pointing to the sellers' league.

'Gotcha!' says Ken, winking.

He strides off, still with hands on his hips like he's in the Wild West.

Good God, I need to leave this place.

'Jesus,' says Suzanne. 'I hate being micro-managed. Especially by such a dick like that.' She puts on her headset. 'Come on, Laura,' she says, 'tick, tock.' She gives me a lascivious wink.

I put on my headset. I hate it. It's like hearing voices in my head.

I hesitate before dialling the next number on my list. Tom opens his office door.

'Justin!' He almost barks the man's name. 'Can I see you for a minute?'

It's more of a command than a question.

Justin's eyes narrow at me as he stands and walks

wordlessly to Tom's office. He stares at me until he reaches Tom, who stands aside to let him in.

Suzanne nudges my arm.

'What's going on in there?' she says. 'Is Justin going to get told off, too?'

'I think Tom is going to relocate Justin. He mentioned getting someone else in.'

'What the ...?' She removes her headphones. 'Just for sending you flowers? That's not on – he can't get personal in the workplace.'

'Which one are you talking about?' I say. 'Tom or Justin?'

'Fair point,' she says. She stands and crouches, peeking over the monitors. 'I would love to be a fly on that wall.'

I slide down in my chair. It feels as though the whole room is talking about me.

Tom's door slams open – the glass walls wobble from the force. Justin storms out, heading straight to his desk. He opens his drawers, taking out his belongings and putting them in a carrier bag.

'Didn't have him down as a Waitrose kinda guy, did you?'

'Suzanne!' I hiss. 'He's upset and he probably heard that.'

'It's not my fault,' she says. 'If anything, it's your fault.'

'No, it's not!' I say. 'Typical victim blaming.'

'How are you the victim?' she says. 'You got flowers, and you're going out with Tom. It's not like Justin tapped your phone and was stalking you, was it?'

A shiver runs through me. 'Very funny,' I say.

She wrinkles her nose. 'Have you had any strange notifications on your mobile?'

'Stop it, Suzanne. You're starting to make me paranoid.'

Suzanne shrugs and puts her headphones back on.

It seems her interest in the drama is over.

The whole office quietens as Justin walks over to me. Tom stands behind his glass wall, folding his arms.

'I've been told to apologise to you, Laura,' he says quietly. His eyes appear to be filled with hate. 'Though I haven't done anything wrong. Apparently, you're dating someone who wants to control whoever speaks to you. It's surprising the lengths someone will go to to keep a beautiful woman to themselves. Take care of yourself.'

His eyes fall to the floor as he walks away, his head bowed.

'Jesus,' whispers Suzanne, who was obviously just pretending to work. 'What a bloody weird thing to say ... *to keep a beautiful woman to themselves*? Who says things like that? Maybe Tom was right letting him go – that was really odd.'

'I suppose.'

It can't be just about the flowers, can it? Perhaps there's more to this than Tom is letting on.

26

Laura

Saturday, 25 March 2017

I didn't tell anyone – even Tom – that it's my birthday today. I wasn't quite sure if I had wanted him to tell everyone at work yesterday after all the drama. Did whoever sent the flowers know it was my birthday? It would've been a more valid reason. And if it wasn't Justin, why didn't he just say? It wouldn't have looked so strange.

Though, for all I know, he might have done.

His replacement, Rob, arrived just half an hour after Justin left. There was no big fanfare to mark his entrance; he just quietly sat in Justin's seat that was probably still warm. He didn't look at me or Suzanne, but chatted quietly with some of the other blokes that he seemed familiar with. He probably *daren't* look at me after what happened with Justin.

I put the birthday card I got from Mum on the mantelpiece. It looks so sad on its own. It's my fault – I should've told people. I can be a right martyr sometimes.

It's the first birthday without Dad. He's not here to arrange for a surprise like he used to. Even when he was at his weakest, he'd get one of his friends to get a load of cream cakes from Greggs.

I bought myself a few things the other day from TK Maxx with my first wages. Would it be too sad to wrap them?

I have seven hours until Tom gets here. He's been inside, but only as far as the living room, which is still as tidy as it was the other day. I don't make much mess on my own. The kitchen is straightforward, but the room I'm most dreading is my father's.

I stand outside his door. There's still a draught underneath it, cold wind at my ankles. All of his things are still in there. It's been almost six months since he died, and I've not wanted to look at them, let alone clear them out.

I could start slowly; just go in there. Sit down on the bed.

I hardly ever look at the bed. His ashes are still on it. I haven't moved them yet. I need to do that. Give him a final resting place, so he's not confined to this room like he was before he died.

It's like he's still in it.

I push open the door. The window is open again – even though I locked it last time I was in here. The breeze is gently blowing the closed curtains. I pull them back and a gust blows over me. The smell from the collection of bins around the corner wafts into the bedroom, almost making me retch. I'm surprised it hasn't been stinking out the whole flat, with a window that keeps opening.

We're on the ground floor; the patch of grass outside is bare and unloved. An old sofa is nestled in the hedge about thirty feet away. I remember when we had a paddling pool out the back here; a few of the kids from the other flats would come together. I don't think the paddling pool was ours – it's not something my mother would buy.

On the left in his room are fitted wardrobes – white MDF. They look like they were built in the Seventies. I open the wardrobe. Some of Mum's clothes are still hanging to the left. She travelled lightly when she left.

I start with her things. If she wanted them, she's had over twenty years to get them. I fold them carefully and lay them in a black bin liner. These dresses haven't aged well, and they haven't come back into fashion yet, except for one. It's black and it's sparkly. I keep it on the hanger to put in my room.

The rest of her clothes fill two bin liners. It's like she's dead, too.

I open the door on Dad's side. Five pairs of identical trousers, five of the same shirts and five of the same jumpers. One winter coat and one lightweight summer jacket. He didn't like to think about what he wore – life was complicated enough without having to make another choice.

But in the end, our life became quite simple.

His clothes take up only one bin liner. I emptied

his underwear drawer without looking too closely. He wouldn't have liked me looking at his pants.

I sit cross-legged on the floor and open one of the drawers in the middle.

It is crammed full of paper and exercise books: my old school work.

I flick through one of my English books. A comprehension task on *Watership Down*; a pretend news article on why seat belts are compulsory; a short story about the fairies who visited while we slept. There are love hearts drawn on the inside covers. The names Robbie Williams and Mark Owen scrawled everywhere, which is strange as I can't remember liking Take That for long.

It must've been hard for Dad, bringing up a teenage girl. I started my periods at the age of thirteen – two years after Mum had left. I had tried to get hold of Mum – though she wouldn't have been much help from all that way.

I started crying when she didn't answer.

'What's the matter?' Dad asked. Well, he shouted it from his chair in the living room.

My face burned. I'd rather have gone into a shop on my own or even made do with using toilet roll for the rest of my life rather than tell him.

'Nothing,' I shouted, rushing to my room and slamming the door behind me.

If I'd been at school, I'd have been able to confide in one of my friends. I hadn't seen Chloe for a fortnight as her mum was making her revise for mocks or something.

She was coming round the following weekend, but that would be too late.

At least I was at home.

Dad knocked on my bedroom door.

'Lola?' he said. It's what he called me when he was trying to be nice. 'Everything all right in there?'

'It's fine, Dad.'

'Can I come in?'

'No, Dad!'

'So this is going to be one of our divided by the door chats, then?'

'Hmm,' I said.

'You were crying on the phone. Did someone upset you?'

'I hardly speak to *anyone*. I'm hardly going to be upset by anyone, am I?'

I folded my arms huffily, which was pointless with no one watching.

'Eric was saying the other day – I don't know if he mentioned it to you – but there's a youth club starting next to the Catholic church. There's a get-together tomorrow night if you fancy it?'

Tomorrow night. I couldn't go out for another week!

'I'm poorly,' I said. 'I've got strange pains in my tummy.'

'Have you eaten something dodgy?'

'We eat the same things, Dad!' I said. 'Are *you* feeling poorly?'

'I've got a strong constitution,' he said. 'I could eat raw chicken and not feel a thing.'

'You'd get salmonella.'

'I didn't say I was going to try it,' he said. 'Wait there a sec, Lola.'

As if I was going anywhere.

I heard the floorboard squeak outside my door when he came back.

'I've left some things outside for you. I'm going back to the living room now. I'll shut the door and leave you to it.'

When I heard the living-room door click shut, I crawled to my door and opened it.

On the floor was a brown paper bag. Inside was a packet of sanitary towels. I grabbed it and raced to the bathroom. Only when I opened the bag did I see what he'd written on it.

I'll make sure there's a packet of these every month
in the medicine cabinet. If you need anything else,
just write it on the bag. Love Dad

Tears land on the roll of bin liners on the floor. I tear another one off and shake it out. There's no point in keeping all of these papers and exercise books out of sentimentality. They're just taking up space, holding me back.

As I'm placing the books in the bag, the cobalt blue cardboard and metal clasp catch my eye. My diary.

Laura Aspinall

Age 9

I click the lock, which is just a buckle, and flick through the pages.

Mummy said she just had some bad news and that she doesn't feel very well ...

Daddy has been good today. He said he's going to take me to the park in half an hour ...

There are pages and pages of things that I can't remember writing about, but I recognise my childish handwriting. I always used to doodle a flower in the bottom-right corner of every page. I thought I had put this diary in the bin after Mum left. Dad must have found it and rescued it.

It's so strange what the memory erases.

I scan the next couple of pages to see if I managed to find anything out about my mother.

18 July 1995

I was listening to Mummy and Tommy's mum talking the other day. Tommy's mummy said she thought Brian (who is Tommy's daddy) was having a fair, but she didn't seem too happy about it. I was going to say that everyone loves fairs, but Mummy's already told me off twice in two days for being a nosy parker and listening in to grown-ups.

Mummy didn't say anything back to Tommy's mummy. It's probably because she's going to sneak into his daddy's fair anyway. I hope she takes me, too.

I have to go now as Mummy has just told Daddy she's going to check on me. I can hear everything in this flat.

I let the diary slip through my fingers and drop to the floor.

I pull open the bottom drawer; I know there's a photo album in there.

I flick through the sticky pages, scanning each of them.

Mum, Dad, Christmas, Grandma. A summer in the back garden.

A bright orange inflatable paddling pool. Me sitting next to Tommy. He's trying to dunk my head under the water, but the grown-ups aren't trying to stop him. Mum isn't even looking in our direction.

And it's not Dad that she's sitting next to. It's Tommy's father. Their heads are so close together and she's looking right into his eyes.

Was my mother having an affair?

27

Sarah

The Premier Inn stands in Preston city centre – one of the only hotels off the main shopping area. Sarah's waiting in the small reception area for Maria Aspinall.

'I'm going home after Laura's funeral on Friday,' Maria said on the phone this morning. 'Would you be able to meet me for a chat?'

'Yes, of course.'

Sarah had wanted to jump up and down after hearing from Laura's mother. It had taken her mind off the man who had tweeted her while standing outside the flats yesterday. Sarah's had no message from him since, but her stomach still flipped whenever her phone tweeted. So much so that she deleted Twitter from her mobile.

She checks her phone again. She wished she'd taken a photograph of the man loitering around the flats. She finds herself constantly hyperaware of her surroundings. Sarah saw Mr Bennett as she was on her way out. He seemed agitated, nervous. After what he was saying about his daughter the other day, Sarah has been worried about him.

He was standing next to the bench outside the foyer.

'Why aren't you sitting down, Silver?' she said. 'Are you waiting for someone?'

'It's my grandson,' he said. 'He's coming over. I don't think he's well. He was nearly in tears.'

'Is he Catherine's son?'

He nodded quickly.

'I think he wants to talk about it all, but he knows everything there is to know.'

'Do you want me to wait with you?' said Sarah.

'No, no, love,' he said. 'I don't need looking after at my age. I'm just worried about him, that's all. My family's small enough as it is. I always feel it when there's something wrong.'

'I'll catch up with you another time then, Silver,' she said, walking slowly away.

She felt a little better when she saw him sit down and take out his mobile phone. Sarah had never met Mr Bennett's grandson. It seemed a shame that Silver didn't get many visitors. Sarah promised herself that she'd spend more time with him – check in on him more regularly.

The lift in the hotel reception pings. Now, ten minutes later than arranged, Maria walks out as the doors swish open. She's wearing jeans, but they look expensive. Even though it's cloudy and dull outside, she has sunglasses on the top of her head. Her coat is bright yellow, tied around the waist.

'I only got your message from reception last night, I'm so sorry,' she says, reaching out to shake Sarah's hand. 'I've not known what to do with myself since the inquest. It's the limbo before saying a proper goodbye – it's been horrendous.'

'Do you want a coffee here? Or somewhere outside?'

'I've found a nice coffee shop,' she says. 'Although it's been here for years.' She laughs lightly as they leave the hotel. 'I haven't stayed in Preston for more than a night for decades.'

'Have you someone waiting for you in Newcastle?' says Sarah.

'Only a cat,' says Maria. 'My neighbour's feeding him for me.'

It's not far to the café, which Sarah knows *has* been here for decades. The counter is next to the entrance, with a display of beautiful-looking cakes and sandwiches.

Once ordered, they take a seat at the back – away from the bustle of the front.

'I've been here every day for lunch since I got here,' says Maria. 'I'm a creature of habit.'

Sarah smiles at her. She must be going through hell, though it's well hidden by make-up. But the make-up can't hide that the white of her eyes are tinged with red veins.

'Did you see the article about Laura in the *Chronicle*?' says Sarah.

'I did, though I could only glance at the words. I've packed a copy, though. I'll read it again when everything isn't so raw. I expected to hear from you sooner – and then the article was written by someone else.'

270

'I don't actually work for the *Chronicle*,' says Sarah. It's so hot in here. 'I'm freelance – well, I'm doing a journalism degree.'

'Oh right,' says Maria. 'I see.'

'I hope you don't mind. I wanted to do more of an in-depth piece about your daughter.'

'I suppose that would be nice. Especially as I haven't managed to trace any friends she might have had – though she didn't mention anyone the last time I saw her.'

'When did you last see Laura?'

Maria takes off her coat, revealing a black polo jumper with a beige scarf tied around the neck.

'It's going to sound terrible,' she says, 'but it was on her birthday two years ago. I surprised her with a visit.'

The waiter places the hot drinks on the table.

'Thank you,' says Maria. 'She had packed a rucksack, ready to go. She said she was going to Cornwall first. She sent me postcards. I got the first one a few weeks later from Paris, saying that she was just about to head to Madrid, then Berlin.'

Paris, Madrid, Berlin. Sarah's sure that was the route Rob said he travelled.

'The coroner said that Laura most likely died on or around her birthday,' says Sarah, trying to rid the image of Rob writing the postcards from her mind. 'There were no transactions on her bank account – she didn't turn up for work.'

Maria looks briefly at the ceiling.

'I'm sure the postcards were in her photograph album.

The police said that her travel documents and passport were packed in her rucksack. How could that be? I'm sure they thought I was batty saying I had heard from her after she ... I'm going to search the whole damn house for them when I get home. There's no way I'd have thrown them away.'

Maria grabs a teaspoon and scoops up the fluffy cream from the top of her hot chocolate, popping it into her mouth. She makes it look so delicious.

'What made you and Laura's dad decide to home-school her? Was she being bullied at school?'

'What makes you say that?'

'There were a few comments on her primary school Facebook page.'

'Ah. Good old Facebook.' She grimaces. 'Without the correct information people just make stuff up to enter-tain themselves, don't they?' She places the spoon on the saucer. 'Robin had the diagnosis about a year before Laura finished primary school. Soon after, he was given the option of early retirement from the university. His memory wasn't as good, and sometimes he had difficulty getting out of bed – he was so tired all the time.

'Laura had some difficulties at school. People weren't very nice to her – kids don't like people who are differ-ent. Laura is – *was* – so intense, deep, but she's – she *was* – so caring, loving. She got this poison pen letter from one of the children at school. She didn't under-stand the meaning behind it – but it hurt. I think it was from one of her best friends as well, which makes it even more heart-breaking. Poor Laura. She always

272

trusted the wrong people. I think her friend's name was Chloe, but Laura wouldn't hear a bad word against her. The letter said: "Your mum is a slag".'

'Really?'

Sarah's mouth drops open.

Maria nods.

'Yeah, I know. Charming, huh? It all coincided with Robin being at home, and he wasn't so bad then. The spasms didn't happen often – yes, he was still tired a lot of the time, but he was perfectly capable of helping her with her studies. She got really good GCSEs, you know.' She takes a small sip of hot chocolate. 'Laura was so good with her dad. She used to help him dress, make his lunch – she was such a good little cook. She used to make Christmas dinner. I'd buy the food and she'd cook it. I wasn't so great in the kitchen. I'm not much of a foodie, but those two were. They got along so well – both loved reading and watching Eighties sitcoms.' She smiles as she picks up the spoon and stirs what's left of the drink. A single tear drops down her cheek. 'I ruined everything.' She looks up at Sarah. 'But you must understand I wanted to stay with them both. I never wanted to leave.'

'What happened?'

'Robin couldn't look at me any more – said I wasn't the person he married. He didn't want Laura to know what happened between us – to find out what I did. He didn't want her to know that he was the one making me leave. He said if I stayed then he'd tell her everything.' She picks up a serviette and wipes the tear away. 'But I shouldn't have listened to him. Everything was so raw, then. You do what you think is best at the time.'

'But what did you do?'

'I had an affair. It was with one of the fathers of a child at Laura's school. Which explains the letter that Laura was given.'

'Oh.'

'It was different, then. There was a close community around the school and around the flats. Brian his name was. His wife's parents lived at Nelson Heights. They probably still do. Catherine her name is. She was a really nice person, too. She didn't deserve it. I don't know why I did it. And Robin couldn't bear the humiliation of it all, but I don't know if anyone else found out.'

'Who are Catherine's parents?' asks Sarah, but she already knows the answer.

'Angela and Sylvester,' she said. 'Mr and Mrs Bennett.'

28

Laura

25 March 2017

Tom's grandparents must live in the same flat as before. Will they remember me? I don't know what I'm going to say to them, but I find myself outside, climbing the stairs to their front door. At least, I think it's theirs.

I tap gently at first.

The sound from the radio comes from the open window. It's the smaller bedroom that faces the balcony, like mine.

'Hello?' I say.

I think I can make out a person sitting in a chair – a man.

Since Mum left, we haven't really mixed with the neighbours. Dad was never a big fan of the people on this block. He said they reminded him of Mum too much. He'd have moved if he were able to. But we were stuck here – stuck here with the memories of her.

And now, Tom is part of my past that has come into my present.

Is it fate that we've come back together?

He says he remembers everything.

Does he remember the details of my mum leaving?

I tap louder this time.

The figure through the window is sitting so still.

I go to the other window: the living room. It's quiet. I don't think there's anyone in there.

I jump when the front door opens.

A woman dressed in navy blue closes the door behind her.

'Excuse me,' I say.

She puts a hand on her chest.

'Oh! You gave me a fright,' she says. 'I didn't see you standing there.'

'I don't suppose you know if Tom's granddad's in?' I say. I wish I remembered his name. 'His surname is Delaney.'

'I'm sorry, love,' she says. 'It's only Mr Bennett at home.' She leans towards me, resting a hand on the top of my arm. 'I'm afraid he's just lost his wife.'

'Was that Tom's mum?' I say.

She must think I'm insane.

'No, dear. I believe they have a daughter.' She hoists the strap of her handbag onto her shoulder. 'I'd best be getting on,' she says. 'Tick, tock, the clock never stops.'

She rushes off down the outside balcony. It's so windy up here.

I take a step back. Have I made the whole scenario up? Did I fabricate the whole conversation between my mum and Tom's mum when I was a child?

No, no. I can't have.

And there's a photograph of Tom and me in the paddling pool.

I walk slowly back down the stairs, down the path towards my flat.

If Tom's dad was having an affair, I have a terrible feeling about who it was with.

I've taken the bin bags full of clothes to The Heart Foundation, but I've kept the diaries and the photo album. I've still to go through Dad's bedside cabinets, but I can't go back into his room. It's like he's trying to tell me something – it's like he's still there. Well, he is, in a way, isn't he?

The photograph could mean nothing – the words in my diary could mean nothing. I was only nine; I could have misheard, made things up. I'll ask Tom tonight if he remembers playing together outside.

My mobile bleeps with a message.

Hey Laura,

I thought instead we could have a picnic at our spot near the estuary – seems a shame to be inside on such a lovely day. Meet you there in an hour?

Tom

Is it sunny outside?

I go to the window. There are a few clouds. I suppose in between the gaps the sun's rays are trying to escape. At least I hadn't got round to cleaning the kitchen – there's nothing more hideous than wasting time on cleaning.

I've packed a blanket (one of Dad's) and have put on my ankle boots in case it's as muddy as last time we went.

I'm nearly at the spot. Are you there yet? Laura x
Yes, I'm nearly there.

I put my phone into my bag as I turn into the ginnel. I look up and the clouds are beginning to fill the sky.

The route seems narrower than it did the other day; the fences appear taller. Tall weeds cross my path; stinging nettles threaten to graze my bare legs. Where's the clearing? I might have got the wrong path. Something doesn't feel right.

There are footsteps behind me. The rustle of a decaying hedge next to me.

I turn, but there's nothing, no one there.

I'm being ridiculous.

I turn right into the clearing. I have the right place.

Tom isn't here yet. I sit on the bench. *Our bench*, he called it.

The river is flowing quickly today, after so much rain these past few days. Restless, I get up and stand at the edge of the bank. If I were to be pushed in, I'd be dragged away by the strong current. Would I survive? I haven't been swimming since primary school, but I was a pretty good swimmer. I imagine it to be freezing cold. The sun that was peeking through before is now totally hidden behind thick grey cloud. A shiver runs down my arms.

I sit back down on the bench, pulling the blanket out of my bag and draping it round me.

278

The trees rustle above me. Birds flap about, scrapping.

I hear the crunch of footsteps behind me, coming from the path.

At last.

It seems like twilight has come in minutes; the wind is picking up leaves, swirling around near my feet. Like someone invisible is stirring them with a stick.

Footsteps are getting closer.

I get up, preparing myself to say that a picnic's not a good idea after all. Tom will probably agree.

I step out towards the path.

But it's not Tom walking towards me. It's a woman. Her brown curly hair bounces on her shoulders. It's shiny, healthy. She looks like she's in a shampoo advert.

Her face is unsmiling; her eyes fixed on mine. I recognise her face from somewhere – from a photograph.

She brings a hand from one of her pockets. She's holding something. She holds it up towards me. A mobile phone. She takes my picture.

'What are you doing?' I say.

'You don't get to ask *me* questions,' she says.

'What? Who are you?'

She's still walking towards me.

'Were you expecting someone else?' she says.

She stops just a couple of feet away from me.

'I don't know what you mean,' I say.

'You were here to meet my husband, weren't you?'

Instinctively, I shake my head.

'No,' I say. 'I think you have the wrong person.'

'Really. This is my husband's mobile. I've seen the

texts he's been sending.' She swipes the phone, and presses *call* on the open contact. I can hear the ring tone. 'Now we'll see if I've got the wrong person.'

Silence.

My phone doesn't ring.

'Oh,' she says, her face pale. 'I'm really sorry. I thought ...'

'I don't know who you are,' I say.

She takes a few steps backwards.

'I'm so sorry.' There are tears in her eyes. 'Really sorry.'

'Can I help at all?' I reach an arm out to her; I don't know why. What was I going to do – hold her hand? 'You look so upset.'

'No.'

She spins around and starts running towards the main road.

My legs are shaking, weak. I grab hold of a nearby branch to steady myself.

I take my phone from my bag.

I must've put it on silent by mistake.

Phone   1m ago

Tom Delaney

Missed Call

Oh God.

She didn't have the wrong person.

I can't stop the tears falling as I run down the ginnel, across the street. I slow to a walk when I reach the high street, conscious of the stares I'm getting. I dab my face with the stray glove I have in my pocket.

I take my phone out, too, and bring up Tom's Facebook profile. I scroll his pictures from only a few months ago. It's the woman with the curly hair who's sitting next to him, cuddling their child, who has her little back to the camera. She has the same hair as her mother. They must be still married. Why else would she – Nicole Delaney – come searching, expecting Tom to be with me?

I'm almost at Kim's café but the shutters are down.

A woman comes out and locks the door.

It's Kim, I think. Curly, frizzy hair that's been freed from its ponytail surrounds her face. It hasn't the healthy bounce that the other woman's had.

Kim's gaze meets mine.

'Are you all right, love?' she says.

'I ...'

She steps towards me, placing a hand on my arm.

'I know you,' she says. 'You come in here a lot.'

Tears fall from my eyes. I wipe them away with my sleeve.

'I'm OK.'

She purses her lips and tilts her head to the side.

'You're obviously not.'

She glances at her watch.

'Come in for a cuppa,' she says. 'I've turned the urn off, but I can put the kettle on.'

She doesn't wait for a reply but unlocks the door and ushers me inside.

She takes hold of my hand and guides me through to the back room where there's a small table and two wooden chairs either side.

'If people see us in the café, they'll bang on the door to get in.'

She takes off her coat and hangs it on the chair nearest the sink. The room has a tiny kitchenette, which feels strange behind a café.

'Sit, sit.'

I pull out the chair and she flicks on the kettle, grabbing two mugs from a shelf above the counter.

'I'm Kim,' she says, placing two coffees on the table.

It wobbles as she leans on it to sit.

'I know,' I say. 'I come here a lot. It's like you're famous – a lot of people know your name, but you won't know theirs.'

Oh, shut up, Laura.

She smiles as she cradles the hot drink in her hands.

'I'm Laura,' I say.

'What's the matter, Laura? Your eyes are still red.'

'I think the man I've been seeing has been lying to me.'

She takes a deep breath in and breathes out loudly.

'In what way?'

She says it kindly, even though I know what she's thinking. That she's probably heard it all before. After all, she was talking about Sarah's husband only the other day. I bet she hears things like that all the time, working here.

'I think he's still married. At least, his wife thinks so.'

She places the mug down and rests her palm on the table. She leans towards me.

282

'What's his name?'

'Tom Delaney.'

She leans back in her chair.

'Oh,' she says. 'I wasn't expecting that.'

'You went out with him, didn't you?'

'Yes,' she says. 'A long time ago.'

She's frowning at me. I sound like a proper stalker now. My cheeks burn; fresh tears come to my eyes.

'I'm sorry,' I say. 'You must think I'm strange, knowing that.'

She picks up her cup and pours what coffee is left down the sink.

'Tom told me his ex worked here,' I say. 'I wasn't spying on anyone.'

My heart is pounding. I'm making it worse and she's going to throw me out in a minute.

She puts on her coat and sits back down.

'I feel the cold,' she says. She folds her arms. 'I was with him when I was eighteen. I thought I'd heard the last of him – thought he'd moved away after what happened between us.'

'What happened?' I say. 'You don't have to tell me if you don't want to.'

'It got physical during one of our arguments.'

'Really?' I say. 'That's awful! He has a different version of what happened between you.'

'I bet he does,' she says. 'He told a different version to the police, too. The marks had gone by the time I worked up the courage to report him. He talked himself out of trouble.'

I don't know what or who to believe – both of them blame each other. But then, Kim has no reason to lie to me – she has nothing to gain.

I take the photograph out of my pocket.

'We used to go to school together – we played in the summer holidays.'

I slide the photograph of Tom and me in the paddling pool. She brings it up for a closer look.

'Oh yeah,' she says. 'That's him.'

She puts the photo back on the table.

'If I were you, I'd just forget about him.'

'I suppose,' I say. 'I just felt sorry for him – what with his mother dying. It was like we had that in common, that both our mothers weren't around.'

'People like him don't change, love.' Kim stands and zips up her coat. 'He's already lied to you about that.'

'About what?'

'Tom's mother isn't dead.'

29

Sarah

Sarah has been trying to put together the last few days of Laura's life. It seems as though just days before she died, her mother had confessed to her the affair that led to her leaving the marital home when Laura was a child. Would this be a reason for her to end her own life?

Sarah scrolls through Laura's primary school Facebook page. There are several new comments on the post about her. Sarah pulls her chair in closer.

Tanya Mason was Greening Such terrible news about Laura. RIP

Chloe Walsh RIP? You're a bloody hypocrite, Tanya! You made Laura's life hell!

Tanya Mason was Greening I think you must be confusing me with someone else.

Chloe Walsh I don't think so. You sent her that terrible letter, didn't you? You and that little boyfriend of yours, thinking of ways to torment her.

Joanne Bett Actually, I think I remember that!

The last comment was only twenty minutes ago. Sarah clicks the refresh button several times. There's a knock at the door.

'It's me, Sarah!' shouts Kim.

Sarah smiles as she goes to answer it. Her friend knows that she's been a little afraid of opening the front door recently.

'You've caught me lurking on Facebook,' says Sarah. 'There's a bit of drama going down on Laura's school page.'

'You really need to get out more,' says Kim. 'I haven't seen you for ages! Have you become a bit of a recluse, too?'

'Hey, that's not funny,' says Sarah, leading them through to the living room. 'And from the sound of it, Laura wasn't as reclusive as we thought. I spoke to one of her colleagues, Suzanne Anderson, and it seems Laura had a few admirers.'

'That's what I was coming to tell you about – well, sort of.'

Kim takes out a photograph and hands it to Sarah.

'She left this at the café.'

'Who did?' says Sarah, sitting at her desk.

'Laura. I wasn't sure if I was right, but I found the photograph she left. It was her who came in – she was that woman I told you about who was crying outside the café, two years ago. She said she was seeing Tom Delaney – who I went out with years ago.'

'*You* went out with this mysterious Tom Delaney?' Sarah says, almost shrieking.

Kim shrugs. 'It was years ago. I've tried to forget that chapter in my life. We had a very fiery relationship. I suppose Tom and I were as bad as each other, but I was hardly going to tell a stranger that, was I? I didn't know who this Laura was – even though she seemed to know a lot about me.'

'Did she? I've been looking for Tom. I thought at first that he was the one who's been sending me messages.' Sarah leans back in her chair. 'Why was Laura crying?'

Kim sighs. 'From what I remember, she said that Tom lied about being separated. He was still married while he was seeing her.'

'Oh no.'

'And in that photograph, Tom and Laura are kids playing in a paddling pool. She left it behind – she almost ran out.'

'No way!'

Sarah looks down at the photograph. The poor girl looks terrified as the little boy holds her head close to the water in the paddling pool.

'It looks like the grass behind these flats,' she says. 'Do you still have the number for Tom?'

Kim shakes her head.

'God no.'

'I don't suppose you know a Justin Parkinson, too? I had a message from him a couple of hours ago. And he's been posting on Laura's primary school page.'

'Let's have a look at him,' says Kim, sitting on the arm of the settee.

Sarah brings up the message from Justin.

Dear Sarah Hayes,

I knew Laura Aspinall very well. I have information in connection with her.

Please contact me.

Justin

'Well, that's brief and to the point,' says Kim.

Sarah goes to St Xavier's Primary School Facebook page and clicks on the article about Laura. 'There he is.' She points to the screen. 'He commented: How disrespectful!! This woman is dead and you're saying you've never heard of her and spreading nasty rumours and "LOL"ing. Shame on you!' Sarah goes back to her Messenger inbox. 'And there.' She points to another message. 'It's from JP Veritas. I thought it was one of Tom's other Facebook accounts, but JP could be Justin Parkinson.'

'Or someone trying to frame Justin Parkinson. Do you think he'd put his own initials on these messages? It doesn't take a mastermind to figure it out. Do one of those photo searches on Google with Tom's picture,' says Kim. 'See if he has any other profiles.'

Tom Delaney's profile photograph has three different website results. The first is what looks like Tom's real profile – with links to his workplace, references to his wife and university and schools he attended. The second site is a Facebook profile for *JP_Veritas*; the third, is one for *Tom_Unofficial*.

'Do you think that the second two are this Justin Parkinson?' says Kim.

'I don't know,' says Sarah. 'I'll check out his *LinkedIn* page.'

A picture of Justin Parkinson from Preston has a profile photo of the same guy that's on his Facebook profile. He's wearing a T-shirt with a fleece over the top; there's a lanyard around his neck. His hair looks to be thinning at the front, but it's long and wispy at the back.

'I knew it,' says Sarah. 'He's listed as working at PeopleServe the time Laura was working there. I'm going to message him back.'

30

Laura

I'm back at home, standing in a lukewarm shower, trying to block out the events of today. I can't believe what has happened. It's officially the worst birthday I've ever had. It makes me wish for simpler times when it was just me and Dad. But I can't travel back in time. I have to make something of this mess.

By the time I arrived back here, I had three missed calls from Tom and three texts:

Hey Laura,

Sorry I lost my phone. Then my contacts were wiped so I didn't know who was texting me. You weren't there when I got to the bench. Everything OK? T x

Laura – I've left you a message. I hope everything is all right. I'll come to your flat if you don't answer. T x

My ex told me what happened today. Let me come round to explain. It's not what you think.

I didn't even know which ex he's talking about. It's all ridiculous. Why is he so bothered by what I think? We've only known each other for a few weeks – knowing each other as children doesn't count when we haven't seen one another in nearly twenty years. That's plenty of time for a person to change.

And he's lied to me about his mother. How can someone lie about something so important? Especially after what happened with my mum.

I don't want to hear what he has to say. I just want to forget about him. I'll hand my notice in on Monday and delete all my social media so he can't find me.

I've been paid my month's wages; that should get me through a few weeks until I find something else – maybe some agency work; maybe I could go travelling. There's still a lot of money left in Dad's savings. There's also some Premium Bonds that I've been keeping for emergencies.

I can't stay around here any longer.

There's nothing for me here.

I get out of the shower and wrap myself in my old dressing gown that's been warmed by the radiator. I wipe the condensation from the mirror. My cheeks are rosy, and my hair is in rats' tails. I look about thirteen years old.

What happened with Tom is so humiliating. People will think that I knew he was married. I should go back, tell everyone that I didn't know, but I don't care enough about them to bother. They don't mean anything to me.

When I open the bathroom door, the cold air hits me, but it's refreshing. The heating is too old in this place. I need to leave here. There are memories in each of the rooms, in every inch of the walls.

I can travel light. Dad still has a rucksack under his

bed from the times we used to go on family camping trips.

I go into his room.

The window has come open again, but I leave it.

I kneel on the floor and drag the bag from under the bed. It's caked in dust.

I take it to the window and slap my hands against the fabric. Clouds of particles float onto the pavement outside.

I place the rucksack onto the bed.

I can't leave Dad's ashes here while I go off gallivanting. He can't be abandoned a second time. I move to his side of the bed and pull back the covers.

His box is beautiful. Carved mahogany with a bird painted in gold. I chose it.

Robin J Hartley.
4 July 1956 to 18 November 2016

I close the box, running my fingers over the beautiful wood.

I know exactly where he wants to be because he told me. He had everything arranged so I wouldn't have to worry about anything. I think his letter is still in this room somewhere.

I open the drawer of his bedside cabinet. It's still in its yellow envelope. It's dated May 2014, two years before he died.

My dearest Laura,

*Thank you for everything you have done for me.
I couldn't have asked for a more loving, caring and
loyal daughter. I wish I could have given you a
better life. You deserve the best that it can give you.*

*I know you haven't wanted to talk about what
happens when I've gone, so I've put everything in
a folder. I have made all the arrangements. Eric
should help (if he hasn't carked it first – sorry that's
a terrible joke, but we've kept our sense of humour,
haven't we, love?).*

*But here is something you can do for me. You can
do it months after, or years after – it's totally up to
you – in your own time.*

*There's a place in Cornwall that your mother
and I took you to. I'll write the details down with
all the other official stuff. There's a cottage where
we stayed for a week – it overlooks the beach. We
usually went camping in Cornwall, but this time
your mother wanted somewhere with a proper,
private bath for a change, so we splashed out a bit.
As soon as we arrived at that cottage, I knew she
had chosen perfectly.*

*It didn't have a television – well, it did, but it
only played VHS, and there wasn't a big selection.
We played a different board game every night.
Do you remember? You would have been about
eight years old. We went to the beach every day,
and every evening we would sit outside, having
a barbeque, then talking and playing Monopoly,*

293

*Scrabble, cards, until we started shivering at
nightfall.*

Perfect days.

*I would love it if you could scatter my ashes
there. I want to be part of that beach. It would be a
lovely place for you to visit and think of me. I've set
up a savings account for you – a separate one that
I put some of my pension in. I hope that one day,
you will use it to travel – to see the world that you
missed out on when you were looking after me.*

*Before you were born, your mother and I went
to some amazing places: Thailand, Canada, and
southern Ireland was amazing, and not too far away
if you need to work up to travelling further afield.*

I will stop going on now.

*You always said I used to go on and on about
things, didn't you? I can't rabbit on as much these
days, though.*

*I can hear you in the living room. Eric is trying
to teach you Texas Hold 'Em, even though I taught
you it years ago. I think you might be hustling him.
That's my girl.*

With all my love,

Dad xxx

I have to move the letter quickly away when the tears
fall onto my lap.

Oh, Dad.

It's too hard to be here in this flat without you.

The silence of your bedroom feels like it's suffocating me.

I fold the letter and put it back in the envelope. I open one of the rucksack pockets and place it inside. I can take his words with me, even though I know I'll never forget them.

There is another letter inside his bedside drawer. A white envelope.

The name and address are written in small capitals: Mum.

The postmark is dated October 1997. Just a few months after she left.

I've never seen this letter before. It feels an invasion to open it, but I can't help myself.

There are only a few lines.

Dear Robin,

I'm so very sorry.

Please stop hanging up on me. I've tried to explain everything to you.

Please let me come home. You and Laura are my whole world. I'm nothing without you both.

He didn't mean anything to me, and I regret it every single day.

Please, Robin. I love you.

Maria x

He.

It's what I had feared when I was reading my childhood diary. It was Mum who had an affair with her

295

friend's husband. Did she regret it – or was she just saying that? Was it just a one-time thing?

There's no point in me speculating.

I grab my mobile phone and try Mum's number again. No reply.

What did you do, Mum?

I go into my room and lie down on my bed. I'm still a little cold from my shower so I get under the covers.

There's banging on my front door.

I've closed my bedroom curtains; whoever it is can't see that I'm here.

'Laura. I'm sorry to bother you at home.'

A voice through the letterbox: it sounds like Justin Parkinson from work. Or is it Rob? They both sound the same.

Oh God. How does he know where I live? Is it the first time he's been here? What if he's been coming through Dad's bedroom window?

My imagination is getting the better of me.

'Come on, Laura,' he says, after banging three times on the door again. 'I know you're in there. I've something important to tell you. I need to warn you about something.'

I'm going to be far away from here soon enough. Away from this mess.

I won't tell anyone that I'm going.

'Laura!' He's shouting through the letterbox now. 'It's about Tom ....'

I reach over for my headphones and connect them to my phone.

Mr Blue Sky by ELO.

It was one of Dad's favourites.

I picture the beach in Cornwall, even though I can't specifically remember the cottage we stayed in.

I picture the sand and the sound of the sea.

Cornwall will be my first destination. I can say a proper farewell to Dad. And then I can fly.

31

Laura

The day after a birthday is a good day for decisions and making plans. I have packed all of my favourite clothes and every pair of knickers I have.

I didn't want to waste most of the money on train fares, so I've booked a coach to Cornwall. It will take nearly two days, after changing at London, but I always liked road trips as a child. I'll pack as many books as I can fit in.

I don't know how long Justin stayed outside my door last night. It was one of the times I've been most grateful that I live in the ground-floor flat. People would have seen him loitering outside.

I deleted the two voicemails and the twelve texts that Tom sent me without listening or reading them. I've blocked him because nothing he can say will have an effect on me. Now I've made the decision to leave, I am finally excited about something.

There's a sound from the front door.

God, please don't let it be Justin or Rob again.

I tiptoe into the hall.

It sounds as though a key's going into the lock.

I walk quietly into the kitchen, opening the junk drawer. The spare key – Dad's key should be inside, on his keyring. I can't see it. It's always in here.

I lift out the tea towels and Dad's old apron.

Still, someone fiddles with the lock.

Whoever it is might be trying to pick it.

My heart is racing as I empty the drawer.

It's there. Dad's keyring is there.

The letterbox opens. I can't move from the kitchen.

If it opens any further, they'll be able to see me.

It closes again and I run into Dad's bedroom. No one at the front can see me from there.

But *I* can't see who it is either.

I check my phone. Would it be silly to dial 999? No one has broken in yet.

There's a tap on the window in the living room. The curtains are open, but I haven't left the television on. The screen can't be seen from there anyway.

The flap of the letterbox sounds again.

'Laura?'

It's a woman's voice. A voice I'd know anywhere.

I stride towards the front door and open it.

She's holding a key; it would have worked years ago.

'Mum!' I say. 'What the hell are you doing here?'

'Well, that's a lovely greeting, I am sure,' she says, walking into the hall, pushing me slightly aside. 'I thought I'd surprise my lovely daughter on her birthday.'

'Why haven't you been answering your phone?' I say. 'And my birthday was yesterday.'

'That's what I meant,' she says.

I close the door and follow her into the living room. She stands in the centre. Her dyed brown long hair has been straightened so much it looks as though it might snap if bent. She's wearing a tan leather jacket that skims her hips, belted in the middle, a long denim skirt, with long burgundy leather boots. She's walked in straight from the Seventies.

'You didn't come to Dad's funeral,' I say.

She takes a deep breath, looks around and sits on the settee.

'He asked me not to,' she says. She looks around the place. 'It's hardly changed at all.'

I look around it, too.

'It's different carpet, wallpaper. New telly, new sideboard.'

'It must be just the settee that's the same, then.'

'Have you travelled far?' I say.

A peculiar question to ask my own mother.

'Newcastle,' she says. She hands me a card. She's already written her details on it. 'Address is the same, but here's my new mobile number. I lost the last phone. I got rid of the landline. I never answered it – I only used it for the Wi-Fi. What does Wi-Fi stand for, anyway?'

I sigh. 'It doesn't stand for anything.' I sit in Dad's chair; our knees almost touch. 'Why didn't he want you to come to the funeral? *I* would've liked you there.'

'He didn't want me having too much to drink and

start saying things I shouldn't. He wanted me to wait a few months, at least. Not that I've had a drink or anything.'

'I haven't seen you since before he died, Mum.'

'It's been hard for me, too, love.' She takes off her jacket. 'He didn't want you even more upset after he died.'

'More upset about what?' I stand, leaving to go to Dad's room. I come back and hand the letter to her. 'Is it about this?'

She looks at the envelope in my hand. Her eyes flash with what looks like horror.

She doesn't take it from me.

'You know what it is, don't you?' I say. 'What did you mean when you wrote, *He didn't mean anything to me*?'

She slumps back into the settee. She rubs her face with her left hand.

'How long have you known?'

'I only found this letter yesterday.'

'Oh, Laura. I didn't want to do this today – not around your birthday.'

'When were you saving it for? Christmas? Or maybe on your deathbed when you wouldn't have to deal with the consequences?'

'It was a long time ago. It wasn't a full-on affair.'

'Did Dad know him?'

She looks at the carpet.

'He'd met him once. He was always working, then. Remember the summer holidays that you and I used to

301

spend together alone? He didn't *have* to work. He chose to tutor – to spend time away from us.'

'So you didn't have an affair because he was ill?'

She makes a sound; it's as though I've winded her.

'No.' She's breathing heavily, as though she's just run up two flights of stairs. 'It happened long before your dad started showing signs of his illness.'

'Why did you tell him? You could've kept quiet for *his* sake.'

She looks at me, shaking her head, her lips pursed.

'I didn't tell him. It was bad enough that it happened in the first place. I didn't want to admit what I'd done. Your dad had just been forced to take early retirement at the university – he was more vulnerable than ever.'

'Don't call him vulnerable!' I'm almost shouting. 'He had this horrific disease, but even when he was at his worst, he was the strongest person I've ever known.'

'I'm sorry. Bad choice of words.'

'So who was it?'

'No one you know.'

'Which won't be hard. I barely know anyone. Remember? I was home-schooled because you made me.'

'Laura.' There are tears rolling down her face. 'I didn't want that for you. Do you remember how miserable you were at school? The bullying, the headaches, the illnesses you used to fake to stay at home with me and Dad?' She takes a tissue from her handbag and dabs her face. 'Why haven't you asked about this before?'

I collapse onto the chair.

'I didn't want to sound as though I was complaining

about being home with Dad. Because I didn't mind, you know. It was bad, sometimes. Really, really bad. But I got to spend all that time with him. Time I won't ever have again. And he kept his sense of humour, you know.'

'I bet he did.'

'What did you talk about, that last time you saw him – it was the last time I saw you, too. Two years ago, last November?'

'I wanted to tell him that I was sorry. I asked him, one last time, if I could come back ... I wanted to help him ... to help you. I know that if you knew I was going to ask him that, then you'd blame *him* if he said no.'

'And he said no, didn't he?'

She nods; her tears are still flowing.

I get up and sit next to her, taking her hands in mine.

'This is why he didn't want me coming to the funeral,' she says. 'He knows I would have just blurted this all out – like I'm doing right now. I'm so sorry, love. It must be really shit to hear all of this.'

I look down at our hands.

'Not really. In fact, it couldn't have come at a better time. To learn that you both cared so much about me that you each had your own pain at being apart.'

'You idolised your father,' she says, stroking my hand. 'I didn't want you hating him because I did something wrong.'

'Did you see this man again? Was it him who told Dad?'

'I saw him around,' she says, 'but we were never in

303

a relationship. And yes. It was him who told Dad. He told his wife, too – though not for many years after, I believe. I had gone away and he thought that if it was all out in the open then we could be together, but it was never like that for me.'

'But it was like that for him?'

She nods, brushing strands of hair away that had fallen on her face.

'So he told dad out of spite?'

She shrugs. 'It doesn't matter now, does it? It's all in the past.'

I take the tissue from her hands and wipe the mascara streaks from her face.

'How about we go out for some lunch?' I say. 'I know a lovely little place.'

'That café we used to go to?'

'I've kind of gone off there,' I say. 'But there is a restaurant that specialises in chicken – I love chicken.'

She wrinkles her nose.

'Are you talking about Nando's?'

Her eyes are glistening and there's a faint smile on her lips.

'What's wrong with that?' I stand and pull her up. 'I've never been to Nando's.'

'You poor neglected child.'

I elbow her arm gently.

'You really shouldn't joke about that, Mother,' I say.

I go to the kitchen and take Dad's key from the drawer. I take it off the keyring.

'Here,' I say, handing it to her. 'Don't be a stranger any more.'

'Promise you'll write to me? I want to hear about all the lovely places you go to.'

'Yes,' I say. 'And if you're lucky, you might get a postcard.'

32
Sarah

It's nine o'clock on a Sunday morning, the only time Kim could get away with closing the café, and the only time Justin was free, apparently. He's very keen to talk about Laura, and Sarah wants to know if he's been travelling in the past two years.

Last night, Maria messaged Sarah to say that she had found the postcards she thought had been sent from Laura and had handed them into her local police station.

I thought I was going crazy, she said. *At least the police know I'm not making it up now.*

She sent Sarah photographs of the postcards.

I took pictures of them, Maria said, *in case I didn't get them back from the police. I realise this is silly as they weren't even written by Laura.*

The postcards were from Paris, Madrid, Berlin, and the words were the same in all of them, written in small capitals.

WISH YOU WERE HERE.
LAURA

It must be near impossible for the police to discover who wrote them, but surely this was proof that someone knew Laura was dead.

Andy is waiting in the car outside with his mobile phone in his hands. When Sarah told him about the messages she'd been getting and the man who'd been prowling the flats, he was annoyed that she hadn't told him before.

He has the car window open and he hasn't taken his eyes from Sarah and Kim as they wait outside the front door of Justin Parkinson's house. Kim peers through the living-room window.

'Who has net curtains these days?' she says.

'Be bloody quiet,' Sarah hisses, trying to keep her voice quiet and her lips still. 'He's a bloody IT guy. He's probably watching *and* listening.'

'Shit, I never thought of that,' says Kim, doing her best impression of the worst ventriloquist ever. 'And I suppose you should know – you're dating one.'

The front garden could do with some attention and the paint on the front door is flaking.

It sounds as though chains are being pulled across the front door.

Sarah can pinpoint each of the latches as they're being pulled across: top, middle, bottom.

The door opens slightly. When she messaged him online, Sarah had pictured an overweight bloke with shoulder-length straggly hair, but this man is clean-shaven.

'Sarah Hayes, I presume,' he says.

307

The place doesn't smell of sweaty socks like her son Alex's room does. Though she shouldn't compare them.

He beckons them in and leads them to a living room with oak laminate flooring. She curses herself, again, on her prejudgement.

There's a plush white velvet sofa with a matching round chair, straight out of DFS. At least seven purple cushions are scattered across them. Sarah doesn't trust people who like purple. They're either spiritual or have bad taste; people who call themselves 'crazy', 'wacky' or even worse, 'zany'.

'Would you like a drink?' says Justin, standing in the middle of the room.

His hands are on his hips, but Sarah can tell he's not comfortable with the pose.

Trying to appear cockier than he actually is? He's hiding something.

But then, Sarah's thought that about everyone she's talked to. Even Laura's mother.

He's probably just nervous. That's all.

'What have you got?' says Kim.

Sarah wants to grab her friend's hand and bring her closer. Thank God she's here. Sarah would probably have fled by now had she been alone.

Justin wrinkles his nose and looks out of the window.

'Are you meaning alcohol or soft drinks?' he says.

What is he looking at? Is he avoiding eye contact?

'What are you having?' says Kim.

'It's nine in the morning,' says Sarah. 'And I'm OK for drinks, thank you, Justin.'

308

'I'll get us a coffee,' he says to Kim.

He claps his hands and rubs them together. He's older than Sarah thought he would be. His trousers seem too big for him, though. He keeps pulling them up at the waist.

'Thank you, Justin,' says Kim, flopping down onto the sofa, which looks almost *too* comfortable.

'Why are you being like that?' says Sarah, perching on the sofa next to her.

'Like what?' She's struggling to sit up properly.

'So blasé,' says Sarah. 'Like you've known him for years.'

'Well, if he *is* some kind of weirdo – maybe even the man who was outside your house the other day – then we don't want to get his back up by being so uptight. We don't want him to think that we're on to him.'

Sarah gets out her mobile phone, switches the voice recorder on, and puts it on the seat next to her.

'There we go,' says Justin, carrying through two mugs of coffee. 'Now what is it you're trying to find out about Laura? It's a terrible shame, isn't it?'

Sarah hesitates. In one of his messages, he called Laura the love of his life. Now he's talking as though she were a mere acquaintance. Perhaps he doesn't know that they've figured out that one of his pseudonyms is JP Veritas.

'You worked with Laura,' says Sarah. 'Would you say you were close?'

He nods while holding his coffee, almost spilling it on the carpet.

'I knew almost everything about her,' he says, smiling. 'She was such a sweet girl. And I have to say, very beautiful. Have you seen a picture?' He stands up and grabs a mobile phone from a sideboard.

He scrolls through, then holds up a picture. He hands his phone to Sarah.

The picture is of Laura Aspinall sitting at her desk, seemingly lost in thought. It looks as though it's zoomed in on her; Sarah can see the blur of two computer monitors either side.

'Did she know you took this picture?' says Sarah.

Kim snatches the phone from Sarah's hands.

'Oh, that *is* a lovely photo, Justin,' she says. 'You've caught her brooding side perfectly.'

Sarah frowns at Kim. Where is she getting all of this from?

'Do you think?' he says. 'Did you know her as well?'

'I knew her for a short time,' says Kim.

One brief incident in the bloody café, thinks Sarah. She has never seen Kim wing it so effectively.

'Sometimes it doesn't matter how long you've known someone,' says Justin. 'It's about what impact you've had on their lives. And I like to think I had an impact on Laura's.'

'What sort of impact?' says Sarah.

'Oh, you know. I cheered her up when Tom Delaney messed her about. He was married, you know. But he was a bad one, that Tom. He asked me to do something I wasn't comfortable with.'

'Really?' says Sarah. 'What did he make you do?'

'He made me put a tracker on her phone,' he says. 'Do you know if the police found it?'

Sarah narrows her eyes at the man. He talks so sincerely, as if he really believes what he's saying.

'I don't know. Have the police contacted you about it?'

He shakes his head.

'I tried to tell them about how much I loved her, but they didn't come back to me.'

'Ah, I see,' says Sarah.

She seriously doubts that this man is telling her the truth.

'You know he made me leave the department,' he says. 'After I sent Laura some yellow roses. Yellow is for friendship, you see. I didn't want to come on too strong and overwhelm her. And then he went ballistic. Got me in his office and made me leave.'

'Are you talking about Tom Delaney?' says Sarah.

'Yeah,' he says. 'Total prick. Absolutely deluded. Thought he owned the place and he thought he owned Laura. She trusted the wrong people, though. Even her friend Suzanne was odd. She used to make up stories. She told everyone that she had a boyfriend called Jack who worked in sales, but I recognised the picture she had on her desk from one of my motoring magazine covers. She even told a few other people that her brother was dead. What kind of person does that?'

'Do you have any other pictures of Laura?' says Kim, smiling, swiping the photos.

'No, no,' he says. 'Just that one.'

'Did you see her before she died?' says Sarah.

'I tried to warn her about Tom. I went round to her house,' he says. 'But there was no answer.'

He downs his coffee, gets up and takes the empty cup to the kitchen.

'We have to go now, Kim,' says Sarah. 'Do you realise what he just said?'

Kim has already placed her cup on the coffee table.

'I do,' she says. 'But I think he has, too.'

Sarah switches off the voice recorder and selects Andy's contact details. He answers after just one ring.

'You have to come here,' she says. 'I think he knows he's slipped up. It seems like he knows which day Laura died.'

Sarah and Kim stand up. Sarah expects Justin to race back into the living room brandishing a knife or machete, but there's no sound coming from the kitchen.

'We have to be going now, Justin,' Sarah shouts. 'My husband is waiting in the car outside and he's a police officer. He's coming to collect us.'

There's no answer.

'Has he gone?' says Kim. 'Is this even his house?'

'I'm not waiting any longer to find out,' says Sarah, walking to the front door.

Thank God it's unlocked.

They run to the car, parked at the end of Justin's drive. There are people outside; it's still early in the morning. His neighbours don't realise they've been living on the same street as someone dangerous.

'Did you see him leave?' Sarah says to Rob.

'I haven't seen anyone,' he says. 'I've been staring at that door. I should've come in with you. He could have done anything to you.'

Sarah looks up at the house as she gets in the car and puts on the seatbelt.

He must be still in there.

'Do you think that's enough to give to the police?' says Kim from the back.

'What did he say?' asks Andy, driving them back to the flats.

'When I asked if he'd seen her before she died, he said that he'd knocked on her door but there was no reply.'

'That's not exactly incriminating, Sarah,' he says. 'It's been nearly a month since her body was found – it's given him plenty of time to think about things. He's probably thought back to when he was last there and has now assumed – in hindsight – that she was dead when he went round.'

'Damn,' says Sarah. 'But there was something really odd about the way he talked about her. He said that he knew everything about her.'

'Sometimes people are just weird,' says Andy. 'It doesn't make them killers.'

Sarah gets out her phone and opens the Facebook app. She's been checking several times a day for Chloe Walsh to respond to the comment about Laura, and the name of the boy who tormented her.

'Finally!' she says aloud.

They turn into Nelson Heights' car park.

'Look up there,' says Kim, leaning between the front seats and pointing to the second floor. 'There's a man in a hoodie outside one of the flats. Whose is it?'

Sarah follows Kim's gaze.

Standing outside Flat Eleven is a man with a navy blue top – its hood pulled over his head. The door opens and the man simply walks inside.

'It can't be Justin,' she says. 'He can't have got here so quickly. Whoever it is, he went inside Mr Bennett's flat.'

33

Laura

I've booked all of my tickets and printed them out using the old black and white printer that I thought would never work again. I took that as Dad fixing the gremlins – he always loved a bit of tech.

I've put the print-outs and my passport in my rucksack, along with the Cornwall guidebook that Dad left me. It's filled with his jottings in pencil, which totally goes against his theory that *one should never write in books*.

I told Mum what Dad requested me to do with his ashes. Before I had a chance to ask if she wanted to come (out of politeness, mainly), she said,

'This is something you have to do. He wouldn't have wanted me there. I've always tried to follow his wishes. God knows he had such a shit time of it at the end.'

You could say that we *all* had a shit time of it in the end.

But I had so many wonderful times with Dad. He

always said it would be horrendous at the end, but he tried to protect me from it as much as he could. Twenty-four-hour care that he had to pay for; his friends who were also there, taking it in turns so I was never alone – even if they were sitting in the living room and I was in the bedroom, wanting to be alone, wanting to pretend that it wasn't happening.

He had MS for so many years, I had prayed, hoped, that a medical miracle would happen before it took him, or that science would come up with a way to manage the symptoms so he could live a life.

But it never happened.

Near the end, every day with him had been a gift.

That sounds so trite, so Hallmark. But it was true.

I didn't want my dad to leave me, but he was suffering too much to hang on for me. And that's what he had been doing, near the end.

I had read one of the booklets, a few days before, that said that sometimes the dying need our permission in order to slip away – that sometimes they hold on until we say something, or they wait for someone who is trying to get to them from miles away.

Sometimes that happens. Other times, it just happens.

When you lose someone, you have to believe there is more to death than just the body shutting down. Sometimes, there's more.

I went to him, two days before he died.

He was asleep; I didn't think he would hear me.

'I'll be all right, Dad,' I said. 'You can let go if you need to.' I put my hand on his. They were cold. I was worried that he was cold all over, but the nurse said, 'Don't worry, love. You will feel his hands colder than he does.'

I still wanted to get him a hot-water bottle, an extra blanket.

'Can you leave me alone with him?' I said. 'Just for a minute.'

She didn't say anything. Just smiled and left the room.

'They're right bossy, these nurses,' I said. The tears dribbled over my lips as I smiled. 'I'll be fine, Dad,' I said. 'Eric will be here for me.'

I rubbed his hands.

I looked up to the ceiling. Then to the window, which was open.

'Sorry, Dad,' I said. 'No wonder your hands are bloody cold.'

I went over and closed it.

'Don't forget,' I said, 'to come and get me when it's my time.'

I leant down and kissed him on the cheek. A pool of my tears landed on his temple. I didn't wipe them off.

'I love you, Dad.'

Now, I wipe the tears from my eyes, check for the hundredth time that I have my passport and debit card ('You can buy a toothbrush wherever you go,' Dad said).

My phone rings.

I don't recognise the number – it's probably someone from work.

Jesus, I'd forgotten about work.

'Hello?' I say.

'Hey, Laura, it's me.'

'Tom?' I say. 'I wouldn't have answered if I'd known it was you.'

'I borrowed someone else's phone. I'm outside, and I've brought you a few birthday presents. I know you're inside, Laura.'

'You're outside my flat?'

Why is he behaving as though everything is normal, and that nothing has happened?

Three knocks on the door.

I press *end call* and open the door.

It's him.

'I'm going out in a minute,' I say. 'Actually, I'm going travelling. I need to get away from here.'

'You can't leave, Laura,' he says, smiling.

Did I hear what he said correctly? He follows me through to the living room, taking several presents out of his carrier bag.

'These are for you,' he says, placing them on the settee. 'I hope you like them.'

'How did you know it was my birthday?' I say.

'I know when everyone's birthday is,' he says. 'It's my job as manager to make sure that everyone is remembered.'

'OK,' I say. 'But I have to leave soon.'

I go into the kitchen and fill a glass of water.

Has he always been this intense? Have I been so pre-occupied that I hadn't noticed?

I take the drink through to the living room. He's sitting on our— *my* settee.

'Here you go,' I say, handing him the glass. 'I don't think we've got anything else to say to each other, Tom. I met your wife.' My voice is shaking but I have to be strong. 'You made her think she was crazy. And I spoke to Kim, your ex-girlfriend. She said I shouldn't have anything more to do with you.'

He looks at the floor and shakes his head.

'You're just the same as your mother, aren't you? You think it's OK to make someone fall in love with you and then just break their heart.'

'This has nothing to do with my mother.'

He stands and steps towards me. I look around the room, but I can't see my mobile phone. I'm sure I put it on the mantelpiece.

'Do you know what she did to *my* mother?' his voice is eerily quiet.

My heart is pounding. I don't like where this is going. I walk towards the living-room door, but he gets up and blocks my way.

'My mother, Catherine, was lovely. So caring, gentle. Then she found out about my dad's affair with your bitch of a mother. And after so many years. She found one of the letters your mother sent to my dad. It broke her. She got in her car and crashed it into a wall at sixty miles an hour. She's never been the same since. She can't talk, can't wash herself. It's like she's just a shell of a person. Do you know what that's like? No, you wouldn't because your mum is walking around, in her own little bubble, not giving a shit about the people she comes into contact with. And now I can see so clearly. You are just the same, aren't you?'

'I ... I'm really sorry about your mum, Tom,' I say. I need to calm him down; he needs to snap out of whatever trance he seems to be in. 'We can talk about it some more if you like? Maybe we can go for a walk. I can cancel my bus for now. We can go to our special place – on the bench near the estuary.'

He tilts his head to the side.

'You're bullshitting me now, aren't you, Laura?'

'No, I'm honestly not.'

'But when I arrived, you were clearly not interested in what I had to say.'

'Why would I lie to you?' I say. I try to push past him, but he doesn't move. 'I just have to make a phone call. My friend is on his way round. I'm expecting him any minute.'

He puts a hand on my shoulder.

'Another *friend*, hey? You seem to be picking up admirers and then dropping them in your wake. You don't care who you hurt, do you?'

'No, no,' I say quickly. 'I was talking about one of my dad's friends. Eric. He's taking me to the bus station.'

He takes hold of my other shoulder, pushes me towards the settee. He forces me to sit.

'I thought we were soul mates, Laura. I thought it was fate that you came to work at the same place as I worked. I tried to see past what your mother did to mine – do you know how hard that was? It was like your mum had killed mine. At first, I felt sorry for you – she abandoned you, so you were a victim, too. But you're not a victim, are you, Laura? You've been playing quite the martyr, haven't you? Had everyone fooled.'

I feel too stunned to stand – too weak in the legs, but I have to get up.

'No, Tom,' I say, shouting louder, sounding braver, than I feel. 'You've got me all wrong. I'm nothing like my mother. I stayed!' I don't know what else to say to him. I try to slip through his arms to get to the floor. I could crawl to the landline in the hallway. 'Please let me get up, Tom. You're hurting me.'

'You don't plan on staying though, do you, Laura?'

My back is halfway down the settee, but he drags me up under my arms.

He lays me down, sitting next to me, but he's almost crushing me with his weight.

'Please,' I say, my voice barely a whisper. 'I can't breathe.'

He puts his hands around my neck.

'I loved you, Laura.'

He's squeezing too hard, right in the middle of my throat. My arms thrash at him – I'm not even controlling them.

They're useless against him.

There's buzzing in my ears.

He's not letting go.

The swirling plaster of the ceiling seems to move like drops of rain in water. I seem to be floating up towards it.

The blackness starts and I hear no more.

34

I left you lying there, Laura. You looked so peaceful, so beautiful. You don't know how much you meant to me because you ruined it all.

You didn't even open your presents, but it would have been wrong to take them from you after I spent so much time choosing them for you.

I left the television on; I didn't want you to lay there in silence.

I didn't leave you alone, though, did I?

I left your father with you, Laura.

My wife, Nicole, said the police had been round today. They've taken my computer. How would they know to look for me?

It's probably that journalist woman. I shouldn't have sent her that message on Twitter – it was too cocky.

Perhaps I wanted to get caught.

'The police asked if we'd been on holiday in the past two years,' Nicole said on the phone to me.

I haven't been home for days. Too afraid that she'll be able to tell what I've done just by looking at me.

'Did you tell them?' I asked her.

'Of course,' she said. 'Why wouldn't I?'

I think Nicole knows. Maybe she always knew.

She went to meet you the day before you died, didn't she?

And I saw her, my wife, from a distance on the day they finally found your body, Laura. She tried to disguise her curly hair with a hat. She went into the café – she must have talked to Kim. Or the other one. The one who has caused all of this: Sarah Hayes.

I suppose it was going to all come out in the end.

The door to Flat Eleven opens.

'Hi, Grandad,' I say. 'I need to talk to someone.'

'I've been so worried about you,' he says as he closes the door behind me.

I take the hood off my head.

'Can I sit down?' I say. 'I feel as though I've been wandering for weeks.'

There's a knock at the door.

'Mr Bennett!' It's a male voice through the letterbox. 'We know he's in there! I'm a police officer. Please answer the door.'

'What are they talking about, lad?'

My poor grandad. After what happened to my mum – his lovely daughter – he doesn't deserve all of this.

'It's a long story, Grandad,' I say. 'I'll write to you, though. If you'll let me.'

There are police sirens in the distance. They're probably not even for me.

I could run. Or I could just get this nightmare over with.

Then maybe, Laura, you will stop haunting me in my dreams.

35
Sarah

Kim pulls the car onto the driveway. It's one of the most stunning cottages Sarah has ever seen. Small, but made of beige stone and a dark grey slate roof. There are roses, daisies and marigolds in the front garden.

Maria gets out of the back seat and pushes her sunglasses to the top of her head.

'It's more beautiful than I remember,' she says. 'Thanks so much for coming all this way with me.'

'I feel like I know Laura,' says Sarah. 'I'm honoured that you asked me.'

'Bloody long drive, though,' says Kim. 'Good job we set off at three in the morning.'

Sarah can always rely on Kim to kill a mood.

Laura's funeral was held on 25 March 2019 on what would have been her thirty-second birthday. Maria had worried that there would be no one there, but the church was packed. There were fellow pupils from St Xavier's, Laura's former colleagues from PeopleServe, and most of the residents from Nelson Heights. It probably helped that her death was widely reported in the news.

Tom Delaney wasn't there.

Sarah can hardly bear to say his name, not even in her head.

She had suspected Justin Parkinson, though that had been no accident. Tom had set up accounts using Justin's initials. It was true what Justin said about Tom instructing him to put a tracking app on Laura's phone.

Sarah had even suspected Rob.

The mind games that Tom played without Sarah even meeting him.

Poor Mr Bennett has been through enough without having a grandson as a murderer.

'It's just a short walk down this little lane,' says Maria, carrying the box containing her daughter's ashes.

Sarah goes to the boot and takes out the mahogany box with the name *Robin Hartley* engraved on it.

They follow Maria Aspinall down a short, sloping lane, allowing Laura's mother to walk alone, cradling her daughter's ashes.

The beach is secluded. Light grey rocks, and a smattering of sand dunes, shelter it from the few houses and the road close by.

There are tears in Sarah's eyes as she opens Robin's box. She had never met him, but she can't help but feel the emotion of the situation.

His ashes float on the wind.

Maria walks towards the sea. She opens the lid and scatters Laura's ashes. They swirl in the air before making their way onto the water.

'Be free, my little one.'

Acknowledgements

A huge thank you to my editor Francesca Pathak whose insight has been invaluable. Thank you to Harriet Bourton, Lucy Frederick, Alex Layt, and Brittany Sankey.

A big thank you to my agent, Caroline Hardman, and to Jo Swainson, Therese Coen, and Nicole Etherington at Hardman & Swainson.

Thank you to Jenny Ashton for sharing your son Alex Rogahn's story.

To the bloggers who have taken part in my blog tours — I really appreciate you taking the time to read and review. The generous way in which you champion books is fantastic.

To Alison Stokes, for spreading the word in Warrington! To Claire and Lou for your friendship and support. To the lovely ladies at Random Makes — thank you for the friendship and the laughs; without our Tuesday mornings, I'd be a full-time hermit!

To Mum, Nick, James, Conor and Sam — thank you. A shout-out to Chris (who I know won't read this!), Loretta, Emma, Oliver, and Janny and Graham Probert.

To my Psych Thriller Killers: Sam Carrington, Caroline

England, Carolyn Gillis, thank you for your friendship, the laughs, and for always being there. It would be a lot lonelier without you.

To my readers – thank you. It's wonderful to receive messages to say you've enjoyed reading my books. I hope you enjoy this one, too.

Credits

Elisabeth Carpenter and Orion Fiction would like to thank everyone at Orion who worked on the publication of *The Woman Downstairs* in the UK.

Editorial
Harriet Bourton
Francesca Pathak
Lucy Frederick

Copy editor
Clare Wallis

Proof reader
Linda Joyce

Audio
Paul Stark
Amber Bates

Contracts
Anne Goddard
Paul Bulos
Jake Alderson

Design
Debbie Holmes
Joanna Ridley
Nick May

Editorial Management
Charlie Panayiotou
Jane Hughes
Alice Davis

Finance
Jasdip Nandra
Afeera Ahmed
Elizabeth Beaumont
Sue Baker

Marketing
Brittany Sankey

Production
Hannah Cox

Publicity
Alex Layt

Sales
Jen Wilson
Esther Waters
Victoria Laws
Rachael Hum
Ellie Kyrke-Smith
Frances Doyle
Georgina Cutler

Operations
Jo Jacobs
Sharon Willis
Lisa Pryde
Lucy Brem

If you loved *The Woman Downstairs*, don't miss *Only A Mother* ...

ONLY A MOTHER ...

Erica Wright hasn't needed to scrub 'MURDERER'
off her house in over a year.
Then her son, Craig, is released from prison.

COULD BELIEVE HIM

Erica has always believed Craig was innocent,
but when he arrives home, she doesn't recognise
her son anymore.

COULD LIE FOR HIM

So, when another girl goes missing, she questions
everything. But how can a mother turn her back on
her son? And how far will she go to protect him?

COULD BURY THE TRUTH